MYSTERY

RUNNING FROM THE LAW

Lisa Scottoline

RUNNING FROM
THE LAW

WHEELER
PUBLISHING, INC.
ROCKLAND, MA

★ AN AMERICAN COMPANY ★

Published in Large Print by arrangement with
HarperCollins Publishers in the
United States and Canada.

Wheeler Large Print Book Series.

Set in 16 pt. Plantin.

Library of Congress Cataloging-in-Publication Data

Scottoline, Lisa.
    Running from the law / Lisa Scottoline.
      p.   cm.
    ISBN 1-56895-319-4 (hardcover)
    1. Women lawyers—United States—Fiction. 2. Large type
books. I. Title.
    [PS3569.C725R86   1996]
    813'.54—dc20   96-11052
                                                         CIP

For Kiki and Peter
with love

Acknowledgments

Rita Morrone was harder to contain then most Italian girls, so I needed a great deal of advice in writing this book. I relied heavily and shamelessly on Lieutenant Jerry Gregory of the Radnor Police Department, who gave me so much of his time and expertise. I can't thank him enough, and hope he'll forgive the liberties I've taken here with his lovely police station, which is cleaner than my house. Special thanks, too, to Detective John Moroney (no relation, merely excellent karma) and Detective Lennie Azzaroni of the Philadelphia police, who answered all of my questions with patience and humor. Thanks to Maureen Rowley, Esq., of the superb federal public defenders office in Philadelphia. Any errors or omissions are on me.

This is the first time you're reading me between hardcovers, and for that I want to thank Geoff Hannell, my wonderful publisher. Thanks to Gene Mydlowski, associate publisher and art director, for the best covers on legal thrillers anywhere and for his improvements to this manuscript. Special thanks to Carolyn Marino, my editor, who has been so supportive of me and my career from the outset. Carolyn is solely responsible for my content (when it's good, that is), and her suggestions for improving this manuscript were, as always, right on the money. She is, quite simply, invaluable.

Permit me a kind word to the staff at HarperCollins, who have worked so hard on my behalf, including Laura Baker, publicist extraordinaire, her assistant, Marshall Trow, and the sales representatives. No author ever acknowledges the sales reps, but they should, because their efforts, though unseen, are the reason this book gets from me to you. Thank you, all of you. And for the Krispy Kremes, Bruce Unck.

Heartfelt thanks to my agent, Linda Hayes of Columbia Literary Associates, who made it all happen and who looks out for me and my work every day, and to Maggie Field of the Maggie Field Agency.

Thank you to the Giuntas in the Italian Market, and to Gene and Arlene Grossblatt, who taught me about gambling chip collecting. Many thanks to author, nurse, and friend Eileen Dreyer, as well as Pat Isenberg and Helene Tulsky, all for medical advice given at a most inconvenient time. Judge Hamilton's favorite chess book, and mine, too, is *Chess in Literature* (Avon, 1974), edited by Marcello Truzzi.

All my love to my father and Fayne, and to my mother. To Rachel Kull, Franca Palumbo, and Sandy Steingard. To Kiki, a gem. And to Peter Tobey, who changed everything.

Finally, to the memory of Uncle Mikey, Uncle Domenic, and Uncle Rocky. All of them are very much with me, and each deserves a book to himself. Someday they'll get it.

1

Any good poker player will tell you the secret to a winning bluff is believing it yourself. I know this, so by the time I cross-examined the last witness, I believed. I was in deep, albeit fraudulent, mourning. Now all I had to do was convince the jury.

"Would you examine this document for me, sir?" I said, my voice hoarse with fake grief. I did the bereavement shuffle to the witness stand and handed an exhibit to Frankie Costello, a lump of a plant manager with a pencil-thin mustache.

"You want I should read it?" Costello asked.

No, I want you should make a paper airplane. "Yes, read it, please."

Costello bent over the document, and I snuck a glance at the jury through my imaginary black veil. A few returned my gaze with mounting sympathy. The trial had been postponed last week because of the death of counsel's mother, but the jury wasn't told which lawyer's mother had died. It was defense counsel's mother who'd just passed on, not mine, but don't split hairs, okay? You hand me an ace, I'm gonna use it.

"I'm done," Costello said, after the first page.

"Please examine the attachments, sir."

"Attachments?" he asked, cranky as a student on the vocational track.

"Yes, sir." I leaned heavily on the burled edge of the witness stand and looked down with a mournful sigh. I was wearing black all over: black suit, black pumps, black hair pulled back with a black grosgrain ribbon. My eyes were raccoony, too, but from weeks of lost sleep over this trial, which had been slipping through my manicured fingers until somebody choked on her last chicken bone.

"Give me a minute," Costello said, tracing a graph with a stubby finger.

"Take all the time you need, sir."

He labored over the chart as the courtroom fell silent. The only sound was the death rattle of an ancient air conditioner that proved no match for a Philadelphia summer. It strained to cool the large Victorian courtroom, one of the most ornate in City Hall. The courtroom was surrounded by rose marble wainscotting and its high ceiling was painted robin's-egg blue with gold crown molding. A mahogany rail contained the jury, and I stole another glance at them. The old woman and the pregnant mother in the front row were with me all the way. But I couldn't read the grim-faced engineer who'd been peering at me all morning. Was he sympathetic or suspicious?

"I'm done," Costello said, and thrust the exhibit at me in a Speedy Gonzales fit of pique. *We don't need no steenking badges.*

"Thank you," I said, meaning it. It was a

mistake not to keep the exhibit. You'll see why. "Mr. Costello, have you had an adequate opportunity to read Joint Exhibit 121?"

"Yeh."

"This isn't the first time you've seen these documents, is it, sir?" My voice echoed in the empty courtroom. There were no spectators in the pews, not even the homeless. The Free Library was cooler, and this trial was boring even me until today.

"Nah," Costello said. "I seen it before."

"You prepared the memorandum yourself, didn't you?"

"Yeh." Costello shifted in the direction of his lawyer, George W. Vandivoort IV, the stiff-necked fellow at the defense table. Vandivoort wore a pin-striped suit, horn-rimmed glasses, and a bright-eyed expression. He manifested none of the grief of a man who had buried his own mother only days ago, which was fine with me. I had rehearsed enough grief for both of us.

"Mr. Costello, did you send Exhibit 121 to Bob Brown, director of operations at Northfolk Paper, with a copy to Mr. Saltzman?"

Costello paused, at a loss without the memo in front of him. Who can remember what they just read? Nobody. Who would ask for the memo back? Everybody except an Italian male. "I think so," he said slowly.

"And you sent Mr. Rizzo a blind copy, isn't that correct, sir?"

He tried to remember. "Yeh."

3

"Just so I'm clear on this, a blind copy is when you send a memo or letter to someone, but the memo doesn't show that you did, isn't that right?" A point with no legal significance, but juries hate blind copies.

"Yeh. It's standard procedure to Mr. Rizzo, Mr. Dell'Orefice, and Mr. Facelli."

Even better, it sounded like the Mafia. I glanced at one of the black jurors, who was frowning deeply. He lived in Southeast Philly on the ragged fringe of the Italian neighborhood, and had undoubtedly taken his share of abuse. His frown meant I had collected six jurors so far. But what about the engineer? I tried to look sadder.

Suddenly an authoritative cough issued from the direction of the judge's paneled dais. "Ms. Morrone, I don't appreciate what you're doing," snapped the Honorable Gordon H. Kroungold, a sharp Democrat who was elevated to the bench from an estates practice, where nobody would ever dream of exploiting someone's death. At least not in open court. "I don't appreciate what you're doing *at all*."

"I'm proceeding as quickly as I can, Your Honor," I said, looking innocently up at the dais. It towered above my head, having been built in a time when we thought judges belonged on pedestals.

"That's not what I meant, Ms. Morrone." Judge Kroungold smoothed down a triangle of frizzy hair with an open hand. He wetted his hair down with water every morning, but after the second witness it would reattain its loft. "It's your *demeanor* I'm having a problem with, counsel."

Stay calm. Your mother's not even cold, poor baby. "I'm afraid I don't understand, Your Honor."

Judge Kroungold's dark eyes glowered. "Approach the bench, Ms. Morrone. You, too, Mr. Vandivoort."

"Of course, Your Honor," Vandivoort said, jumping up and hustling over. His mother's death had put such a spring into his step that he almost beat me to the dais. An inheritance, no doubt.

"Ms. Morrone, what the hell do you think you're doing?" Judge Kroungold asked, stretching down over his desk. "Is this some kind of stunt?"

Gulp. "I beg your pardon?"

"Don't act like you don't know what I'm talking about."

"Your Honor?"

"Please." Judge Kroungold looked around for his court reporter and waved him over irritably. "Wesley, I want this on the record."

The court reporter, an older black man with oddly grayish skin, picked up the stenography machine by its steel tripod and huddled with us at the front of the dais. A sidebar conversation is out of the jury's hearing, but not the appellate court's. The word *disbarment* flitted across my mind, but I shooed it away.

"Ms. Morrone," Judge Kroungold said,

5

"please tell me, on the record, that I'm not seeing what I think I'm seeing."

"I don't understand what you mean, Your Honor. What is it you're seeing?"

"No, Ms. Morrone. No, no, no. Nuh-uh. You tell me exactly what you're doing." Judge Kroungold leaned so far over that I experienced a fine spray of judicial saliva. "*You* tell *me*. Right now."

"I'm conducting my cross-examination of this final witness, Your Honor."

The judge's liver-colored lips set in a determined line. "So it would appear. But let me state for the record that you seem very tired today, Ms. Morrone. Very lethargic. One would even say that you seem *depressed*."

I didn't know he cared. "Your Honor, I am tired. It's been a long trial and I've worked this case myself. I don't have the associates Mr. Vandivoort does, from Webster & Dunne," I said, loud enough for the jury to hear.

Judge Kroungold's eyes slipped toward the jury, then bored down into me. "Lower your voice, counsel. Now."

Win some, lose some. "Yes, sir."

"I would never have expected to see something like this in my courtroom. For God's sake, you're even wearing a black suit!"

"I noticed that, too," Vandivoort added, as it began to dawn on him.

"Your Honor," I said, "I've worn this suit to court many times."

"Not in this trial you haven't," the judge spat

6

back. Literally. "And no makeup. Last week you had on lipstick, but not today. What happened to that pink lipstick? Too *bright*?"

Time to raise him. "Your Honor, why are we discussing my clothing and makeup in court? Do you make comments of this sort to the male attorneys who appear before you?"

Judge Kroungold blinked, then his eyes narrowed. "You know damn well I wasn't making . . . comments."

"With all due respect, Your Honor, I find your comments inappropriate. I object to them and to the tenor of this entire sidebar as an unfortunate example of gender bias."

His mouth fell so far open I could see his bridgework. "What? I'm not biased against you. In fact, I took great pains in my instruction *not* to tell the jury whose mother had died, in order to avoid undue sympathy for the defense. You, Ms. Morrone, are giving the jury the distinct and entirely false impression that it was your mother who died and not Mr. Vandivoort's."

"What?" I said, sounding as shocked as possible. At the same nanosecond, a quart of adrenaline dumped into my bloodstream and a familiar rush surged into my nerves, setting them tingling, jangling, and twanging like the strings of an electric guitar. *Believe.* "Your Honor, I would never do such a thing! I couldn't even begin to do such a thing. Who can divine what a jury is thinking, much less attempt to control it?"

Judge Kroungold's eyes glittered. "Oh, really.

7

Then you won't mind if I suggest to the jury that the death was in Mr. Vandivoort's family, not yours."

Shit. Was he bluffing, too? This game could cost my license to play cards—I mean, practice law. "On the contrary, Your Honor. I would object to any attempt to gain the jury's sympathy for male counsel, whom you are clearly favoring. In fact, I move that you recuse yourself immediately ·on the grounds that you are partial to defense counsel, sir."

Judge Kroungold reddened. "*Recuse* myself? Step down? On the last day of trial?"

Up the ante. "Yes, sir. I wasn't sure until today, but now you've made your sexism quite clear."

"My *sexism*?" He practically choked on the word, since he fancied himself a liberal with a true respect for women. Like Bill Clinton.

"Are you denying my motion, Your Honor?"

"I most certainly am! It's absurd. Frivolous! You'd lose on appeal," Judge Kroungold shot back, but he twitched the tiniest bit.

It was my opening and I drove for it. I had a straight flush and a dead mother. I *believed*. "With all due respect, Your Honor, I disagree. This sidebar is interrupting my cross-examination of a critical witness. Every minute I stand here prejudices my client's case. If I could proceed, perhaps I could put this ugly incident behind me. Mr. Vandivoort didn't object to my questioning, after all."

Kroungold snapped his head in Vandivoort's

direction. "Mr. Vandivoort, don't you have an objection?"

I looked at Vandivoort, dead-on. "Can you really believe I would do such a terrible thing, George?" The pot is yours if you can call me a liar to my face. In open court, on the record.

Vandivoort looked at Judge Kroungold, then at me, and back again. "Uh . . . I have no objection," he said, folding even easier than my Uncle Sal. Vandivoort was too much of a gentleman, that was his problem. Biology is destiny. It's in the cards.

"Then may I proceed, Your Honor?"

"Wait a minute, I'm not done with you, Ms. Morrone. Stay here." Judge Kroungold scowled at Vandivoort. "Mr. Vandivoort, take your seat."

What was this? Not according to Hoyle, surely.

Judge Kroungold signaled to Wesley as soon as Vandivoort bounced away, and Wesley got the convenient urge to stop typing and crack his knuckles.

What gives?

Judge Kroungold leaned over the dais. "I've been reading about you in the newspapers, Ms. Morrone, so I can't say I'm surprised by your showmanship. But I warn you. Play all the tricks you want. It might work in this case, but it won't work in *Sullivan*. You're in over your head in *Sullivan*."

It gave me a start, like he was jinxing me, but I couldn't think about *Sullivan* now. "Then may I proceed, sir?"

"Of course, Ms. Morrone," Judge Kroungold said loudly. "Ladies first." He leaned back and waved to Wesley to go back on the record.

"Thank you, Your Honor," I said, and turned to face my jury. But not before I remembered my bereavement and brushed an ersatz tear from my eye.

Which is when I caught a glistening behind the engineer's glasses.

Winner take all.

2

I shifted position on the stool that had been my perch in the butcher shop since I was a kid. Grayish stuffing puffed out of a rip in the green vinyl cushion, exposing the top of a steel pole. I didn't know which was making me more uncomfortable, the steel pole or my father's silent treatment. Frankly, I'd rather sit on the goddamn pole.

"Dad, you're not happy for me?" I asked.

Thwack! His stocky frame bent over a rack of fresh lamb and he separated two chops with a familiar cleaver and more vigor than necessary.

"I won four hundred grand, you know."

Thwack! Thick steel-rimmed glasses slipped down his bulbous nose. Gray chest hair strayed from an open button on his white uniform. His bald dome bore a constellation of liver spots, like a planetarium.

"The jury was only out for an hour. An hour, that's nothing."

Thwack! No lamb deserved this kind of treatment. Neither did the meat.

"Dad, if you don't talk to me, I'm going home to my boyfriend who doesn't talk to me."

He cleared his throat. "I don't like it, what you did in court. It wasn't right."

"Why not? I won, didn't I?"

"I didn't raise you that way!" He brandished the cleaver at me but I barely flinched, I've grown so accustomed to my father threatening me with sharp objects. You name it—boner, slicer, butcher's needle—I've had it an inch from my nose. It's good training for litigation.

"How did you raise me?"

"I raised you to be a good girl."

"Good girls make bad lawyers, Pop."

"Hah!" He returned to his work, squinting as he positioned the chops on a wooden carving block. It was dark with blood at its concave center and knifemarks scored its surface. "Hah!" he said again, but didn't elaborate. *Thwack!*

My victory champagne was wearing off. I crossed my legs in the offending suit, breathed in the spicy smells of the shop, and watched the sluggish traffic through the neon letters in the MORRONE'S MEATS sign, with its glowing orange pig. My father's shop was in the Italian Market, a city district of stores and outdoor stands hawking

11

fresh crabs, squid, and poultry alongside detergent, pantyhose, and sponge mops. Cars crept down Ninth Street, navigating between the stalls and debris like an urban Scylla and Charybdis.

"They should clean up here," I said to no father in particular. "Pick up the garbage. Don't you think?"

Thwack!

Wooden pallets and cardboard boxes were piled in the gutter; pictures of apples smiled from the boxes and the California oranges looked positively giddy. But the fruit pictures were the only thing smiling in the market lately. An arsonist had burned Palumbo's restaurant to the ground, tearing the heart out of the neighborhood, and a Vietnamese jewelry store down the street was robbed at gunpoint last week. My father's shop hadn't been hit. He thought the crooks respected him; I thought they knew he was broke.

"Dad, when are you going to sell this place?"

Thwack! His glasses, owing to their weight, slipped to the bumpy end of his nose. His eyesight was worsening daily; he was becoming the Mr. Magoo of butchers. He'd knife himself someday, if somebody else didn't.

"Come on, Dad. You're not mad at me for the trial, you're mad because of the *Sullivan* case."

"Right."

Vito speaks! "How long you gonna stay mad?"

"Forever."

Such a reasonable man. "Dad, you want to discuss this rationally for a change?"

12

"Fine, Miss Fresh Mouth."

My full name. Usually he shortened it to Miss Fresh. "Listen, Fiske Hamilton is a federal judge, one of the most respected on the bench. He needed a lawyer, so he came to me. What's wrong with that?"

"You're livin' with his son."

"Yeah, so?" I lived with Paul Hamilton without benefit of marriage. The fact still rankled my father, even though he didn't like Paul at all. Just one of the many paradoxes that made up Vito Morrone.

Thwack!

"Dad?"

"Like I said," he said cryptically.

LeVonne Bayson, who was sweeping up sawdust in the corner, smiled to himself. LeVonne was the shy black teenager who worked for my father. We all pretended LeVonne was there to help with the customers, but that wasn't the real reason. There weren't enough customers to keep even my father busy, or my Uncle Sal, who hung out in the shop from time to time.

"LeVonne," I called out, "do you know what this man is talking about? Can you translate for me? Would you tell the butcher I'm very happy to be in his country?"

LeVonne smiled like someone on a TV on mute and continued rearranging the sawdust.

Thwack! "What? What'sa matter, she don't understand English, Professor? Tell her it means 'like I said.'"

13

LeVonne shook his head, showing the wisdom not to referee. His skin was smooth, he was on the small side, and his features were still boyish as he looked down over the worn end of the broomstick. He wore his hair cut close to his head and a sparse patch of black fuzz was beginning to sprout under his chin.

"Why don't you just talk to me, Dad?"

"You shoulda said no. No. N-O."

"Turned down the *Sullivan* case? Why? It's the biggest sexual harassment case in the country, It's once-in-a-lifetime."

"That's why you're doing it?"

Partly. "Christ, what was I supposed to do? Say 'Look, Judge, I know you're in trouble and I'm a hot-shit lawyer *and* I'm practically engaged to your son, but can you just take your business elsewhere?'"

"Hmph." He wiped the cleaver on his apron and dropped it into the slot beside the carving board. Then he grabbed a well-worn boning knife, sliced a sliver of spongy fat from a chop, and threw the fat into a dented bucket. "Rita, did you ever think the judge mighta done it? Huh?"

I had, but I rejected it. "Fiske Hamilton? He's a class act, Dad. A Yale grad, a partner at Morgan Lewis for ten years before he went on the bench. He didn't harass her. I asked him and he denied it."

Milky brown eyes flared behind his glasses. "It said in the paper he was chasin' her around the

14

office, right in the courthouse. It was in the *Daily News*, did you see?"

"You gonna believe everything you read?"

"You gonna believe everything you hear?" He laughed, then looked over at LeVonne. "Mr. President, you like that one?" he shouted, and LeVonne smiled his secret smile.

"Dad, this woman's asking for three million dollars in damages. Intentional infliction of emotional distress, the whole works. She just wants to make a quick buck, that's all there is to it."

"No, I saw that girl's picture, I saw that girl's face, and I'm tellin' you, she's not doin' it for the money." He flopped the chop over and trimmed the remaining streaks of fat from the moist, pink flesh. A trickle of thin blood oozed onto the carving board, a lighter color than the Jackson Pollock bloodstains on his apron. This was why I became a vegetarian, no question.

"Dad, why are you still mad about this? It's a done deal. I take her deposition tomorrow."

"I don't care how classy the judge is, I don't like him usin' my daughter."

It stung. "He's not using me."

"The judge was screwin' around on his wife and he thinks you'll cover it up. He's bluffin' *you* and you don't even see it."

"He's not bluffing. I asked him, I watched him answer."

He wagged the knife at me. "Don't watch the player, watch the cards. You got the cards in

15

front of you and you're not lookin' at them. He's playin' you for a chump."

"But I know Fiske. He's Paul's father. He's family."

"Whose family? You're not married, so the judge ain't family. I don't know him, wouldn't know him if I ran over him."

I stifled a laugh at my father's choice of words. His eyesight was so poor he ran over two bicycles and a child's foot last year. Remarkably, the foot was fine, but the Schwinns were DOA.

"Dad, Fiske is a federal judge."

"Oh, yeah? So what's he got between his legs—a gavel?"

So genteel. My father loved to talk dirty; it was his favorite thing, after butchering lambs and running over the toes of small children. His coarseness drove my mother nuts until she fooled us both and had the last laugh.

"Mark my words," he said, making circles in the air with the pointy knife. "I've been around the block a few times."

"Not in the car, I hope."

LeVonne actually laughed out loud, or at least audibly. My father managed a smile, too, but I think it was at the lamb chops. There on the carving board, in carnal tribute to his skill, stood twelve pink chops, evenly sliced and arranged like a king's crown. "Ain't that pretty?" he said.

"It's art, Vito."

"Miss Fresh Mouth."

"You're the one. You."

16

Silence fell while we both cooled down. I knew we would, we always did. Coming apart and coming together, like pigeons fussing on a street-corner. It had been like this for as long as I could remember. He had raised me by himself, in this shop. I cut my first chicken at age eight and my first deck of cards the year later. An atypical girl-hood, we'll leave it at that.

"All right, the chops are pretty," I said finally.

He nodded. "So. You want something to take home? I got nice Delmonicos in the back."

"No thanks. I don't eat dead things, remember?" I watched him set the lamb on an old white scale. On its side were yellowed stickers from Licenses and Inspections and a gold star from some forgotten something when I was little. He peered down through his bifocals to read the numbers on the scale.

"Miss Priss. You need red meat. It's good for you, gives you protein."

Right. "Anyway, I want to go out and eat. To celebrate."

"Take the steaks, honey." He winked and wrapped up the chops. "Stay in and celebrate."

I forced a smile. My father didn't know Paul and I hadn't been getting along. I'd been trying not to worry about it, it happened in a relation-ship. I'd hoped it would change with *Sullivan*. Paul was close to his parents and was already showing an interest in his father's defense. We were talking more than we ever had. It was the reason I'd taken the case, even though judges and butchers apparently disapproved.

And it didn't matter, really, whether Judge Hamilton had harassed his secretary or not.

All that mattered was that I had to win.

 3

I sat at the dining room table next to a half glass of chardonnay, waiting for Paul to come home. The day's mail littered the table's smooth walnut finish. I had opened the bills and flipped through the catalogs, had read all the mail except for the letter that mattered. I wasn't ready just yet. I took a sip of wine, the crystal goblet knife-thin at the edge. The wine was cold, too chilled even to taste.

I looked around the room that Paul, a forensic architect, had designed. The walls were painted a slate gray with a creamy molding, harmonizing with a gray and burgundy Tabriz. Against the far wall was a walnut sideboard that had been in the Hamilton family since the Triassic, and above it hung a water-color of a still life. I was beginning to wonder if the furnishings were compatible in a way that Paul and I could never be.

The unopened letter was from my doctor. The envelope had a linen texture, its color was a stark, cool white. It made an almost luminous oblong on the table as twilight fell and the room dark-

18

ened. I didn't get up to turn on a light, though. There was nothing I really wanted to see.

I took another sip of wine and rolled it around on my tongue. It was developing a taste as it warmed up, it was too young. Paul had taught me what "young" meant as applied to the taste of wine, as he had taught me many other things you couldn't learn on a stool in a butcher shop. We'd been together for five years but were no closer to marriage than our fifth date. It was my reluctance; trying to build a practice, I had postponed the decision. Now it was upon us, and we were in trouble.

ALEXANDER EHRLMANN, M.D. I had almost forgotten about it during the trial, then *Sullivan* heated up. Dr. Ehrlmann had been one of the messages on my voice mail, but I hadn't had time to return the call. Hadn't made time to return it. Didn't know what to do with what he would tell me.

Most of all, I didn't know what to tell Paul, who was God-knows-where, way past dinnertime. I no longer felt like celebrating. I felt like sitting and drinking, so when he came in he'd feel guilty about being late on my big night. Then I wanted to open the envelope, throw it in his face, and make him feel guilty about that, too. But I knew I would do none of these things. I had kept it to myself since the initial finding, grown used to the idea. Accepted it, prepared myself to talk about it. If it turned out to be bad news, that is.

Maybe it would be good news.

My gaze fell on the unopened envelope. It challenged me to turn it over, like the last down card in a poker hand. Could be the worst news you ever had, could be the best. Come on, big shot, you're a player, turn it over. *Play.*

I took a last swig of wine and didn't care that it was underage. I picked up the envelope and inserted a taupe-polished thumbnail under the back flap. It only took a second to read. It would take longer than that to understand. Suddenly I heard Paul's Cherokee rumbling onto the gravel driveway. I put the letter back in the envelope and slipped it into the stack of catalogs.

In a minute Paul opened the front door and set down beside it whatever he was carrying. A tube of blueprints, a briefcase. Paul placed things down with care, he moved things aside to make room for other things. I used to watch him play chess with his father; they both handled the wooden chesspieces as if they would explode if dropped.

"Rita?" Paul called out. "Where are you?" He came into the dining room and turned on the sleek halogen light, then dimmed it when I shielded my eyes. "What's the matter, did you lose?"

Yes. "No."

He walked to the end of the table, his mouth a small circle of concern. It was his strongest feature, full and sweet, and then his eyes, a deep blue behind rimless glasses. An intelligent face with a strong chin, framed by sandy brown hair. And longish sideburns, at my request.

"I'm surprised you're home," he said. "I thought you'd be working late."

"Why would I do that? I worked all day, all month."

"But you have the deposition tomorrow in Dad's case."

"I get to eat, don't I? I thought we could go out to dinner. Maybe to Carolina's for a Caesar salad. And puffy rolls and butter shaped like flowers."

He sighed. "Sorry, honey. I ate already."

"Where?"

"On the road." He eased into a captain's chair and crossed his legs. Long, thin legs, with nicely defined knees. "Why are you looking at me like that?"

"Because I love you."

He smiled faintly. "I love you, too."

"Do you?"

"Of course. What's gotten into you?"

I almost laughed out loud, but it wasn't funny. "A virus, actually. HPV. Not H*IV*, H*PV*. Human papillomavirus. It's a whole different thing."

His smile faded. "Are you serious?"

"It's highly contagious. Some people even get warts, of all things. I don't have that strain, thank God. There are lots of strains, apparently. I know all about it, now that I have it for sure."

"Is this a joke? Rita?" He paled under the tan he got visiting job sites. Looking up at buildings,

21

figuring out why concrete cracked or glass panes popped out.

"Dr. Ehrlmann can't tell for sure when I was infected because the virus can remain inactive for months or years. Even ten years, in rare cases."

"A virus?"

"There's no real treatment. Ehrlmann tells me that 10 percent of his patients have it. It showed up in my last Pap test, then they retested for it."

"Are you okay? Are you sick?"

"I'm fine, but it's a risk factor for cervical cancer, so Ehrlmann says I'll have to have three Paps a year instead of one. He'll monitor it. I'll be fine."

He raked a slim hand through his hair and it flopped back into place. "Can I do anything?"

You already did, handsome. "Now that I have it, you probably do, too. But there's no risk factor in men, or the risk is so low it's insignificant."

"Risk factor for what?"

"Penile cancer."

"*What* did you say?" He swallowed hard, which I enjoyed. His Adam's apple went up and down like a little elevator.

"Penile cancer. Cancer of the penis," I said, at risk of putting too fine a point on it.

His forehead dropped into his hands.

"It's not going to fall off, Paul."

He shook his head in the cup of his hands. I guessed he was mulling over the falling-off part. *Clunk.*

"You okay?" I asked him.

He looked up and laughed, his face flushed. "Me? Oh, I'm just peachy." He reached across the table and grabbed my glass of wine. "May I?"

"Be my guest, but it's jailbait."

Paul downed the wine without noticing its youth. "You can make jokes about anything."

Almost anything. "People who have HPV generally don't know they have it. So they don't know if they pass it on."

"How do they get it?"

Did he really not know? If so, I hesitated to say it, because that would make it real. "It's sexually transmitted," I said anyway.

"Like gonorrhea?"

"Right, like gonorrhea, from the good old days when STDs didn't kill you. So there's only one outstanding question, as I see it. Where did we get a sexually transmitted disease when I have never been unfaithful to you?"

He set the empty glass down and his face fell, collapsing into deep lines around the mouth and eyes. Lines formed by forty-odd years of laughter and sorrow, both fraudulent and authentic. "What are you saying?" he asked, his tone quiet.

Watch the cards, not the player. "I'm asking you if you're having an affair. I want you to tell me the truth."

His mouth fell open and he was speechless. It reminded me of myself standing in front of Judge Kroungold. Suddenly I realized what had pissed my father off about my fake mourning in court.

I had cheated. It wasn't a bluff, it was a cheat. A fine line, and I hadn't seen it. Had Paul cheated? Had he crossed the line, too?

"How can you ask me this?" he was saying.

"Tell me the truth, Paul. It's not like we've been getting along so well, I know that."

"That doesn't mean I'm fooling around!"

"You work late a lot."

He stood up. "So do you and I'm not accusing you of anything."

Which is when it occurred to me. He wasn't accusing me. It didn't even occur to him to accuse me. Maybe because he already knew how we got it.

"Rita, I am not having an affair. I'm not, I swear it."

I didn't look at him. I was too busy looking at the cards.

"You must have contracted it before we met. You just said it could lie dormant for years, even ten years. You didn't cheat on me and I didn't cheat on you, so that's how you got it. From before. Didn't he say that was possible?"

"He said the odds were low."

"But it's possible. That's what happened, babe."

I nodded. I know a lot about odds. So much I still couldn't look at him. My mind was reeling.

"Rita," he said, touching my hand, "I love you, I swear it."

I looked up then. His eyes were stone blue and

24

desperate. His forehead seemed damp, but his grasp was dry and certain.

"I did not cheat on you. I would never cheat on you. You have to believe me. Do you believe me?" he asked, squeezing my hand.

I didn't answer him. Couldn't force out a yes, but couldn't quite say no. A feeling of exhaustion swept over me, telling me to fold. Making me toss even a terrific hand into the muck pile. Hoping he wouldn't turn them over like Uncle Sal.

"There's nothing to worry about, Rita. Nothing." Paul gave my hand a final squeeze, and oddly, I drew some comfort from it.

I needed the comfort. I had sustained a loss. I was in mourning, complete with black suit, black pumps, and black ribbon. It had been a long day. I had won and lost. And dressed right for both occasions.

Mother would have been proud.

4

I looked out the smoked-glass window of the conference room at the glitzy geometry of my hometown's skyline, glinting darkly in the hazy sunshine. The twin ziggurats of Liberty Place spiked into the sky next to the pyramid atop Mellon Center. The glass tent of the Blue Cross building reflected the squares balanced like bogus diamonds on top of Commerce Square. Philly was starting to look more like Vegas every day, and now there was talk of riverboat gambling on the Delaware River. Even I didn't think that was such a hot idea, everybody turning out like me.

I had arranged the seating at this deposition as carefully as any card game, giving myself the view of the casinos, with the court reporter at my left. I'd seated Patricia Sullivan and her lawyer on the opposite side, so they could stare at the wall behind me. I did not offer them coffee, nor did I show them a bathroom. You sue my client, you hold your water.

Patricia was reading Plaintiff's Exhibit 7 on her side of the table. She was an impossibly pretty young woman, with fair, curly hair, delicate cheekbones, and thin, creamy skin. Her perfume smelled like tea roses and her flowery jumper couldn't hide a chest in full bloom. The jury would think Michelle Pfeiffer, on Gregg shorthand. I wondered if I could pick an all-girl panel.

"Okay," Patricia said. She handed me the exhibit, which she had brought with her to the deposition. "I'm finished."

The exhibit was a Boynton greeting card that said HAPPY BIRTHDAY! YOU'RE ONE IN A MILLION! I glanced at it with a sinking sensation. Judge Hamilton had claimed their relationship was strictly business, and that was the only defense he wanted in court. Cards like this wouldn't help.

"Miss Sullivan," I asked, "on which birthday did Judge Hamilton give this card to you?"

"My last. November twelfth. I turned twenty-three."

She didn't look a day over sixteen. "How long had you been working for the judge at the time he gave you this card?"

"About two and a half months. I started the job in September."

"You were his secretary?"

"I was one of his secretaries, there were two. I'm not really a secretary, though. I'm a painter, but I couldn't make a living with only my painting."

"She used to paint all the time," said her lawyer, Stan Julicher. He was tall and brawny, with round brown eyes and a virulent sunburn he got from fishing weekends on his motorboat. I hadn't litigated against him before and didn't want to again. His papers were sloppy and intentionally delivered by messenger at the end of the business day, to give me less time to reply. A trick so dirty even I hadn't used it. "Her paintings were beautiful, flowers and all," Julicher continued. "And vases, with fruit and books. In one there's like a bowl with some fruit in it, and the apples look so real you could reach out and take a bite."

"Mostly I paint still lifes," Patricia said, by way of explanation. "Flowers, landscapes."

"Real pretty paintings," Julicher said, nodding. "But she doesn't paint anymore, since what happened with Judge Hamilton. Her career was just taking off. More and more people were discovering her art. She was like a rising star.

27

Who knows where her career could have gone if this hadn't of happened? The sky was the limit."

"Thank you," Patricia said modestly, mistaking the damages lecture for praise.

I decided to take the opportunity to explore her damages, even though I'd usually go through the complaint's allegations first. "Have you sold many paintings, Miss Sullivan?"

"Over the years, yes."

"How many per year, would you say?"

"Oh, a lot."

"How much income did you generate from these sales, per year?"

"We'll give you the tax returns as soon as they're ready," Julicher interrupted.

Right. "What's to get ready, Stan? They're past returns."

"They've been in storage, with my office being moved. I'm getting bigger offices on Walnut Street."

"You were supposed to have brought them today. I originally requested them in my interrogatories, and you said you'd provide them with your answers. Let the record reflect that my first request was made two months ago and plaintiff's counsel still hasn't supplied the tax returns."

"I'll supply them as soon as they're ready," he said with finality.

"And I'll reopen the dep when they're supplied, in order to examine the witness about them."

Julicher frowned and made a note on his legal

pad with a gold Cross pen. At the pen's top was a little Cadillac emblem that wiggled when he wrote.

"Miss Sullivan, just to get some idea of your income from your painting, how many paintings did you sell last year?"

"Three. I sell at sidewalk shows, out on the Main Line and Chestnut Hill." She sipped water from a Styrofoam cup. She'd be needing that bathroom any time now.

"Did you sell the three paintings at sidewalk shows?"

"No, I sold them privately."

"To whom?"

She paused. "Judge Hamilton."

Julicher made another note, and I wondered if this was news to him. It was to me, though the judge had allegedly told me the whole truth and nothing but. "How much did Judge Hamilton pay for the paintings?"

"Five hundred dollars each."

Yikes. "Were you sleeping with him at the time?"

"Objection!" Julicher shouted. "You're insulting the witness!"

Insulting the witness was my job. "I'm not insulting the witness, I'm asking a question of fact. This is a lawsuit, Stan. Not a picnic."

"I want that question stricken from the record!" Julicher said, turning to the court reporter, a freckled redhead who kept her eyes professionally downcast.

"Wait a minute," Patricia said. She leaned forward, agitated, and a muscle in her slender neck announced itself. "I can answer that. I *want* to. I was having a sexual relationship with him at the time, but it was coerced. I had to do it, to keep my job."

"That's enough, Patricia," Julicher said. "Listen to me, I'll tell you when to answer."

I cleared my throat. "Miss Sullivan, you were about to explain how you got the job."

"I read about it in the *Suburban & Wayne Times*, then I called and found out it was for Judge Hamilton. I'd heard of him."

"How?"

"From his being so . . . respected, I guess. And his wife, for her garden club. They were in the papers a lot."

"Is that why you wanted the job?"

"Objection," Julicher said.

"I'll rephrase the question. What made you decide to apply for the job, Miss Sullivan?"

"The pay, and I thought Judge Hamilton would be good to work for."

Julicher snorted derisively and I stopped short of telling him to save it for the jury. "Miss Sullivan," I said, "let's get back to the birthday card. You allege in your complaint that this card was the beginning of a course of sexual harassment by Judge Hamilton, is that right?"

"It's only one piece of physical proof," Julicher snapped. "Judge Hamilton sent her another greeting card, too."

Terrific. "Stan, are you the witness or is she?"

"I'll be damned if I'll sit here and let you confuse my client."

I turned to Patricia. "As I said at the beginning of this deposition, if you are confused, please feel free to ask me to clarify the question. Do you understand?"

"Yes," she said.

Julicher sighed theatrically.

"Now, Miss Sullivan, assuming this card is from Judge Hamilton, why do you think he signed it 'Judge Hamilton' instead of 'Fiske'?"

"If you know," Julicher added.

"I didn't call him Fiske," Patricia said. "I always called him 'Judge.'"

"You never called him by his first name?"

"No."

Not even in bed? I bit my tongue. "I noticed that the only other greeting card you brought today, the Christmas card, was also signed 'Judge Hamilton.'"

"'*Love*, Judge Hamilton,'" Julicher broke in.

"Stan, are you mistaking this for a conversation? Let her answer."

"I was."

"You were not!"

"I was too!"

Litigation can be so adult. "The record will speak for itself, Stan."

"Fine with me."

"Good. Let's try to act like grown-ups, shall we?"

31

He reddened even under his sunburn. "I will if you will!"

Enough already. It was our first fight and it wouldn't be our last. Julicher, a newcomer to Philly from New York, was trying to make a name for himself on this case. He'd hustled overtime to get it in the news and had even sent the complaint to the papers.

"Now, Miss Sullivan, assuming that this card is from Judge Hamilton—"

"He gave it to me himself," Patricia said. "By the coffeepot."

"The coffeepot? Are you referring to the first incident of harassment in your complaint?"

"Yes."

"Miss Sullivan, can you tell me what happened by the coffeepot that day? In your own words?"

"Well, we had a birthday party in chambers, all of us. The two law clerks, the other secretary, and me. Judge Hamilton had ordered a cake and we all ate in his office around the conference table. At three o'clock."

"And what happened by the coffeepot?"

"I was washing out the coffeepot at the sink next to the supply closet. We were alone and he handed me the card. When I was reading it, he touched my breast. Stroked it, kind of." Three deep lines furrowed Patricia's flawless brow and she seemed to withdraw into herself. The woman could sell an emotional distress claim, true or not. I thought I heard a jackpot in the distance, the quarters clanging into a metal tray.

"Did you ask him to move his hand?"

"Objection!" Julicher said. "What's the difference if she did?"

"That's no basis for an objection. I'm entitled to know exactly what happened. Answer the question, Miss Sullivan."

"No, I didn't," Patricia said nervously. "I was too shocked to. I didn't say anything, and he took his hand away and just walked out, into the office. And afterward, when I was taking dictation, he acted like nothing happened. I took a whole letter from him, two pages, and he didn't even look at me. I still remember the letter. Every word." She fell silent, looking upset.

Julicher had enough trial smarts to let the moment sink in. Even the court reporter swallowed hard.

"Did anyone see him touch you?" I asked quickly.

"No. No one else was around. It was like that, in the beginning. He would just touch me, never saying anything, until the time he kissed me, in his office."

"Were the doors open or closed?"

"Closed."

"You testified that he kissed you in his office. Did you kiss him back?"

"No," she said, her glossy mouth tightening. "I tried to tell him no, but he forced me. He leaned me backward over the chair and his hand went up my shirt. I should have stopped him, I know. It sounds silly now, but I felt embarrassed.

33

I felt like I shouldn't say anything, and that's what he said later. He said everything would be all right if I didn't tell."

"Did you tell him to stop or not? Yes or no?"

"Well, no. And then at lunchtime he would call me in and touch me that way, do that to me." Her voice cracked and she reached for her water, drinking it thirstily. "Then one day he went all the way."

It didn't ring true. "Do you mean he had sex with you?"

"Yes. Yes, that's what I mean. At noon, in his chambers. Sometimes he would have sex with me, sometimes he would want me to . . . do things, you know, to him. He told me he would take care of me, and I didn't have to worry about anything if I kept doing it. And didn't tell anyone."

A look of concern crossed Julicher's oversized features, and I knew why. It didn't sound like the typical pattern of sexual harassment. Still, there was something there, some kernel of truth. I took a flier. "Miss Sullivan, did Judge Hamilton ever send you flowers?"

"What?" Julicher said. "What's the point of that?"

"It's a question."

"I thought we were following the complaint."

"It's my deposition. I write the script."

"It's easier for the witness if you follow the complaint."

Because that's what you prepped her on? I

34

ignored him and looked directly at the witness. "Miss Sullivan, my question was, did Judge Hamilton ever send you flowers?" Some men are card senders, some men are flower senders, and some men are jerks. Fiske was a flower sender.

"Uh . . . yes."

Julicher looked at her, surprised. He evidently hadn't thought of that. Maybe because he was a jerk.

"Did he send you the flowers at home or at work?"

"At home."

I checked my notes. "In the roughly seven months you worked for Judge Hamilton, how many times would you say he sent you flowers?"

Her forehead creased again. "I don't know. I don't remember exactly."

"Would you say they came often or rarely?"

"Uh, often, I guess."

"Don't guess," Julicher said in a growl.

And don't lie. "Miss Sullivan, would you say that Judge Hamilton sent you flowers three times in seven months?"

"Uh, no."

"More times or fewer times?"

She shifted in her chair. "I don't remember."

She did remember, a fool could see it. "Did the judge send you flowers more than three times in seven months? Before you answer, I remind you that you are under oath."

"Objection!" Julicher said. "There's no call for that!"

"More," Patricia answered, agitated. "More than three times. But . . . I don't know how much. How many."

Julicher's thick lips formed an unhappy line and he scribbled another note on his legal pad.

"Miss Sullivan, which florist did the flowers come from?"

"Cowan's, I think."

The best in Wayne. I made a note to get a paralegal on it, to see if it was a standing order. Then I remembered something. Fiske had a thing about spider mums. He thought they symbolized true love and they were the subject of countless courtship stories told by his devoted wife, Kate. "What kind of flowers did the judge send you, Miss Sullivan?"

"Objection as to relevance!" Julicher shouted, tossing his pen onto the table, where it skidded into the stack of exhibits.

"Answer the question, Miss Sullivan."

Patricia looked from me to Julicher. "Do I have to answer? Does this matter, Stan?"

"Of course not," Julicher said. "Come off it, Rita. The line of questioning is irrelevant."

"It's highly relevant, and you can't object to relevance during a deposition anyway. Let her answer the question or I'll call Judge McKelvey and get a ruling."

Julicher scowled, then looked away, simmering. "Go ahead, Patricia. It's ridiculous, but you can answer."

She smoothed back her hair. "Well, the judge sent spider mums."

"What color?" Yellow.

"Yellow, I think."

"How many, each time?" Eighteen.

"Eighteen."

Eighteen, not twelve, because he wanted the vase to look overfull. "Why not a dozen, do you know?"

Julicher exploded. "What's the point what color, how many? This is a waste of time! None of this has to do with her allegations!"

"Why not a dozen, Miss Sullivan? I remind you again that you are under oath."

"I don't remember!" Patricia said, flustered.

Liar. So Fiske was having an affair. And it was a love affair, not just sex. Had he expected me not to find out? What the hell was going on? "Did Judge Hamilton give you anything else?"

"Yes," she said, looking worriedly at Julicher.

"What did he give you?"

"He sent me some oils and painting supplies."

Julicher frowned and the Cadillac emblem did the watusi. Maybe he had bought Patricia's sexual harassment story from the start, but more likely he wanted deniability too much to quiz her in any depth. Then again, maybe he anticipated Fiske wouldn't want to defend by proving they had a consensual love affair, and Julicher knew he had a winner either way. I was the one in the lose-lose position. And Fiske.

"Miss Sullivan, how many times did Judge

Hamilton send you paints and supplies in the seven-month period?"

"Once or twice. Uh . . . once."

But Fiske didn't paint, he played tennis. "How did he know what to send?"

"I don't know. I never asked for the supplies. Never."

"You didn't send them back, did you?"

"No."

"Did Judge Hamilton ever give you any money?"

Her eyes flashed defensively. "Absolutely not. He offered to lend me some, but I turned it down."

"Don't volunteer, Patricia!" Julicher shouted, loud as a school-yard bully. "I told you that!"

"Sorry. Sorry," she said, rattled.

"Miss Sullivan, did Judge Hamilton offer you the money before or after he bought the paintings?"

"Before."

So after she'd refused the money, Fiske bought her paintings. I put two and two together, unfortunately without the aid of my client. "Did he ever commission a painting from you?"

She didn't answer but reached for her water with a shaky hand. The court reporter remained poised over the stenography machine, its unlabeled black keys a mystery to everyone but her. The room got very quiet, and Julicher looked up from his notes when the silence caught up to him.

"The judge commissioned one painting from me," Patricia said finally. "A portrait."

"Of who? Whom?"

"Of you and the man you live with."

What? My throat caught. "The painting was of me?"

"It was from a photograph taken in Bermuda, I think the judge said. You were standing under a moongate."

Paul and me. Our first trip together. It was after we had dinner, the first night. A man from Iowa had taken the photo.

"You wore a white dress, like silk," Patricia said.

Paul had loved that dress. I bet him he couldn't unzip it with his teeth. Then he did.

"I think the portrait was supposed to be an anniversary surprise."

I remembered Paul slipping out of his jacket, then unbuttoning his dress shirt. *Why are you taking your own clothes off?* I had asked him. *Because I can do it faster*, he'd said, laughing.

There was laughter in the conference room. "Earth to Rita," Julicher said with a smirk, and I fumbled for my stride.

"Miss Sullivan, where is the painting now?"

Julicher leaned forward. "Now what's the relevance of *that*?"

None, but I wanted to know. "Miss Sullivan, where is the painting now?"

Julicher laid a hammy hand on his client's arm.

"Objection! You're asking her to speculate. It's absolutely irrelevant to this lawsuit!"

"Did you keep the painting, Miss Sullivan?" I asked, louder. If her own lawyer could bully her, so could I.

"I . . . don't know," Patricia said. Her thin skin was tinged pink, her voice sounded jittery. "Stan?"

"Objection!" Julicher shouted, slamming the table so hard Patricia jumped. "You're upsetting the witness!"

Time to raise him. "This is only the beginning, Stan. She's suing my client for a fortune. She had better understand what that means."

Julicher looked enraged. "It doesn't mean she has to take this shit!"

"Sorry, pal. That's exactly what it means!" I shot back, then heard a whimper. It was Patricia. Tears had sprung to her eyes and she was reaching into her jumper pocket for a Kleenex. Christ. The woman was either a perfect angel or a perfect actress. I decided to back off as she dabbed at her eyes. I'd made my point.

"I'm sorry," she said in a hoarse voice. "I didn't know—"

"It's okay, Miss Sullivan. Let's get back to the complaint," I said, and took her through her allegations while she recovered. The deposition went on without further incident while everybody calmed down, and my thoughts clicked away.

So Patricia and Fiske had been lovers, although neither would admit the truth in court. My problem was I had a case to win, and the best way to do it would be to prove there was an affair. But Fiske would never permit that. He'd be asked to resign from the bench, and it would kill Kate. I'd been dealt a garbage hand but couldn't fold.

I wondered if I could convince Fiske to settle. I wondered why I'd taken the damn case in the first place. And later, as I took Patricia through my final questions, I wondered about the silk dress Paul had loved so much.

Gone.

5

I ignored the stack of yellow slips on my desk, a pile of letters waiting to be signed, and the morning mail, still sitting in stiff thirds. Patricia's deposition had taken the whole day and I had a million things to do, but the first order of business was to call my favorite presidential appointee— the cheating, lying, deceitful judge who had manipulated me into this mess. Everybody hates lawyers, but they don't realize judges are just lawyers with a promotion. Think about it.

"Rita, how are you?" Fiske said calmly, when he picked up.

Pissed off. "Fine. Listen, we need to talk."

"Did it go well?"

"For a fistfight."

"What happened?"

"Her lawyer's a bastard and she's a liar. The whole lawsuit is a sham."

"I told you, she's fabricated the entire story."

How to put this respectfully? "Not exactly. You weren't forthcoming with me either, Fiske." In other words, you lied through your caps.

"What do you mean?"

Where to begin. "Patricia testified about the flowers you sent. They were spider mums."

"Oh?"

"So I know the truth."

He paused. "I see."

I almost laughed. This was how WASPs reacted to news that would trigger a Portabella mushroom cloud in Italians. "I can't defend this case without telling the truth."

"That's not an alternative."

"You're a judge, Fiske. The truth should at least be an alternative."

There was quiet on the other end of the line.

"I'm sorry," I said, without meaning it.

"Understood. But that defense is untenable, Rita. Any victory won that way would be Pyrrhic. I have a reputation, a judicial career, and a marriage to consider." His voice sounded tense but more honest than he had been. Finally, he was leveling with me.

"Then my advice is to make a settlement offer. She'd go for it, she doesn't have the stomach for litigation. She even cried during the dep."

"She did?"

Give me a break. "Let's settle it. I bet Julicher will call tomorrow with an offer, and if he doesn't I'll call him and feel him out. He can't be totally sure we won't prove the affair and if we do, he loses his case. And his contingency fee."

"No. No settlement. Out of the question. It's the same as an admission."

I rubbed my forehead. "No, it isn't. You wouldn't be admitting anything. You'd be making the case, and the girl, go away."

"No."

"You're putting me in an impossible position, Fiske. There's no solution."

"I don't agree. I'll find a solution."

Bastard. "Look, we need to discuss this later, in person." So I can smack you upside your head.

"Certainly. Kate and I are going out to dinner tonight at Samuel's. I think Paul will be joining us, but you won't, right?"

"Right." I had something better to do. As cranky as I felt, scratching my ass would be something better to do.

"Fine, then. I'll be home by ten. You and I can chat upstairs in my study."

Chat? "Good."

"See you then," he said, and hung up.

Paul, who called almost immediately afterward, sounded more concerned about Fiske than Fiske did. He phoned from his car, which he called his virtual office. "They're crucifying my father in public, did you know that?" he said,

43

angry. "I just heard it on the radio. They're trying to get the deposition transcripts."

"Don't worry, they're under seal." Not a hard order to get, one judge protecting another. "They can't."

"What did she say? How does she justify what she's doing?"

I couldn't talk about this with him. Not yet, maybe not ever. "She doesn't, really. How'd the job go, with the garage?"

"You want to talk about an underground parking garage on a day like this? Isn't her deposition important?"

"Yes, but tell me what happened with the garage. We have a life, too, right?" Ha.

"The salt got through the paving asphalt over the garage and damaged the membrane below. That's why it leaked."

"So you were right."

"It happens. Rita, give me the headline. How'd the deposition go?" The connection crackled, which gave me an idea.

"We can't talk now, over the car phone. It's not secure. Anybody can pick it up."

"Right. Damn. I talked to Mom, she's pretty upset."

I bet she is. What do they call it when a woman is cuckolded? Or doesn't that matter enough to have its own word?

"There were reporters in front of the house," Paul was saying over the static. "They tore up the garden, so she's fit to be tied."

She's got worse trouble than the begonias. "Where are you anyway?"

"Running errands. I'll see you at what time? Seven? At the restaurant?" His horn honked. "Pass me already, you jerk!"

"I'm not going to dinner. It's Tuesday, remember? Poker night."

"What? You're playing *cards* tonight?"

Here we go. "I'll be at your parents' by ten."

"I can't believe you're going to play cards! Dad got calls from the newspapers, even somebody from AP. All hell's breaking loose, Rita!"

There's no better time to play cards than when all hell's breaking loose. It clears the head. "I'll see you at home."

"Rita, it's a game! Shit!" he said, but I didn't know if it was at me or at the traffic. "Are you still upset about last night? Because if you are, we can talk about it. I want to talk about it."

I don't.

"This morning you were so quiet."

"I'm fine. I have to go."

"Sure. All right," he said. Unconvinced. Hurt.

Let it be. I hustled him off the phone and didn't respond to his parting line: "I love you."

I didn't know what to say.

The five of us—me, my father, Uncle Sal, Herman Meyer, and Cam Lopo—sat around the Formica table in my father's hot, cramped kitchen, waiting for a quorum. Seven is the optimum number for a poker game, but we never

45

had a full house. The average age of our group was seventy-two, so one player or the other was always in the hospital. Still, the Tuesday night game went on. Prostate would be the only thing that would end us for good.

"So where is he? He's late again," Herman said. He was a kosher butcher, compact and healthy even at age sixty-nine, with bushy gray hair. Herman was insane about poker and even collected chips. As usual, he wanted to get started. "What is it with that kid, he can't be on time?"

Herman meant David Moscow, a young copywriter who was trying to join us. David was gay, but the old men were past the age when such things mattered. They only cared that David was late. "He'll be here," I said, shuffling the cards. "Give him time."

My father, at the head of the small table, was fingering some plastic chips. "What's the difference if David's a little late? Mickey's late, too."

Herman frowned. "Mickey had a doctor appointment, he told us he'd be late. This kid, he's always late and he never tells us."

"Then that's the same as tellin' us, ain't it?" my father said. Water sweated down the sides of his brown beer bottle. "Same difference."

Herman shook his head. "No. He wants in, he should be here. What does it take? He lives a block away."

"Relax, Herm," said Cam, sitting next to him. "It's rainin' out. Everybody's late when it rains.

Forget about it." Cam had lost an arm in a machine-shop accident and always said nothing would ever bother him after that. At seventy, he was tall, gaunt, and his skin was pitted from teenage acne. Still, a ready smile redeemed his otherwise working-class face and he'd tell you proudly that his teeth were all his own.

"I can't forget about it," Herman said. "The kid has no responsibility. If he worked for me, I'd fire him."

Cam sat back in his chair. "Did you go to that show this weekend, for the poker chips?"

Herman nodded. "Yeah, but they're not all poker chips. Some are casino chips, some are dealers' chips. Some are markers. It's all different."

Cam smiled. "Oh, I see. Very complicated."

"Yes, it is, and to answer your question, I got some nice chips." Herman twisted toward the front door, showing the casino chip painted on his yarmulke. It was a gray chip that said CLUB BINGO in cheery red letters around the outside. I once asked Herman if this was sacrilegious, he said it depended on what your religion was. "Now where the hell is that goddamn kid?"

"It's not David's fault he's late," Uncle Sal said. "They work him because he's young. They take advantage." Sal was shorter than my father and frailer, with identical bifocals. His forearms were skinny, his elbows protruded from his short-sleeved shirt like chalky knobs, and he had a neck

47

as stringy as a baby bird's. Sal had never married, he was like a permanent little brother.

"What chips you buy, Herm?" Cam asked.

"I got some nice ones. One mother-of-pearl, a real pretty purple one, and I bought a new ivory. With scrimshaw."

"Like with a boat on it?"

"Nah, got a fleur-de-lis in the middle."

"Floor-da-what?" Sal asked.

Herman rolled his eyes. "Like a design, Sal. A French design. It's from 1870, like you."

My father laughed. "How much you pay for this French chip, Herman?"

"Like it's your business?"

My father smiled. "They're robbin' you blind, you know that." The plastic chips he'd been playing with fell to the table with a clatter I recalled from my childhood, when I'd go to sleep in the tiny back bedroom. They didn't let me join the game officially until I was thirteen and had paid my dues fetching beer and pepperoni.

"They're an investment," Herman said. "They're antique."

"Hah! They're used."

I pitched a card at my father and it sailed like a whirligig across the table. "Dad, play nice. He's got a hobby. You got a hobby?"

"Yeah, I read the obits, that's my hobby. I drink coffee, that's my hobby, too. Did you hear about Lou, Miss Fresh?"

"Lou who?"

"Terazzi, from Daly Street. Had a heart attack

48

in the middle of dinner. Dead before his face hit the spaghetti."

"You're a poet, Dad."

Cam shook his head.

"No kiddin'," Herman said, surprised. "Lou, huh?"

Uncle Sal patted his bony forehead with a paper napkin. "It's hot in here. The cards are gonna be sticky. I hate that, when the cards are sticky."

"Everybody's complainin' tonight," my father said.

Cam rose and got a box of Reynolds Wrap from the drawer. Not that he wanted to wrap anything, he used the box to hold his cards, in the slit behind the metal strip. "Stop your complainin', everybody. You're upsettin' Vito."

Sal looked down, examining his arthritic fingers. "I'm not complainin', I'm just sayin'. We should get air condition."

Herman rubbed his tummy through his T-shirt. "Vito Morrone, an air conditioner? You have to spend money."

"Hah! I spend money, I spend plenty of money. I just don't like air condition. I got enough time to be cold after I'm dead."

"It's the humidity," Uncle Sal said quietly. "The humidity, it makes the cards sticky."

My father frowned at him. "It's 'cause the windows are closed, we don't have the cross-ventilation. Every other time, we have the cross-ventilation. So stop your complainin', Sallie."

"I was just sayin'. It's humid, to me, is all."

Cam took his seat. "Stop fightin', both of you. We're okay without air condition. It's not that hot, just stop talkin' about it. So how's the meat business, Herm?"

"Lousy. Couldn't be worse. There used to be four hundred kosher butchers in this city. Now there's only a handful. A handful."

"Gotta make more Jews," Cam said.

Herman laughed. "Don't look at me, I did my part." He had three daughters he loved to the marrow. It was the middle one, Mindy, who'd painted the casino chip on his yarmulke. I'd met her at her son's bris, then later at a custody trial for the same child. She was a smart brunette, clever, and feisty enough to take on her lawyer husband and win.

"How's Mindy and the baby?" I asked him.

"Real good, real good. And she's makin' good money with the court reporting. Good money, Rita."

"Terrific. Tell her to send me more of her business cards. Now, what are we gonna play? Seven-card? No high-low?"

Herman and Cam nodded, but my father said, "That's all you ever want to play."

"Sue me. Mindy will do the transcripts."

"Seven-card it is," Cam said. He was the best player at the table, he liked to say he beat us with one hand tied behind his back. "If my Rita wants seven-card, it's seven-card."

"Thanks, handsome," I said, and he grinned.

Seven-card stud was my game. Four of the cards are showing, three are dealt facedown. It was harder than knowing none of the cards at all. Imagination, speculation, and fear rushed in to fill the gaps; the trick was to keep your illusions and reality straight. If I'd been losing my touch away from the table, I felt at home here, with Cam's stump and Herman's chips and Sal's complaints. I was glad I came.

There was a buzz from the door downstairs. "That's David," Uncle Sal said.

"No, I thought it was Santa Claus," my father said, getting up and shuffling downstairs.

Herman snorted. "Let him wait in the rain. I'm not going through this every week."

"They take advantage," Sal said again.

In a minute I could hear my father climbing the creaky stairs with David, then a *clang* as David dropped his umbrella into the metal can by the apartment door. I knew my father would like taking David in from the rain, I remembered him doing the same for me as a child. Unbuttoning my red boots, popping the loop of elastic around the button, then tugging off my damp socks. Laying them out on the radiator in the living room, where they dried into cottony arched backs, with a ridge down the middle like a spine.

"Sorry, I'm late," David said as he came into the room in a damp polo shirt and unstructured sport jacket. He looked at me in surprise. "What are you doing here, Rita?"

"Waiting to kick some wrinkly butts."

51

Cam laughed. "Oh yeah?"

"Hah!" my father said. "I got an ass like a baby."

But David kept looking at me. "I thought with the harassment suit, you'd be—"

"I took the night off."

"I just heard about that woman, the plaintiff."

"Siddown, kid," Herman said. "I'm waiting for the shoe to drop here."

"What'd you hear?" I asked. "That she was a Girl Scout, a budding Cassatt, or—"

"You don't know?" David pulled out his vinyl chair.

"Know what?"

"She's dead."

"Dead?" I said, stunned.

"She was murdered. I heard it on the radio in the car."

"Patricia Sullivan, murdered?"

David wiped rain-soaked bangs from his forehead. "They said her throat was cut. They found her at home."

It seemed impossible. Patricia, dead? My father's eyes met mine. They looked worried, which worried me almost as much as what I was hearing. "I have to go," I said, feeling a warm hand on mine.

It was Cam. "You all right, Rita?"

I would have answered him, but for the second time that day, I had no idea what to say.

6

Maybe it was because I had just left a poker game, but when I spotted the Hamiltons they struck me as the king, queen, and jack of diamonds. Satisfied and privileged, face cards all, nestled in a corner of this exclusive Main Line restaurant. They looked surprised as I dripped my way to their table, so I gathered they hadn't heard about Patricia's murder. The news had galvanized the city, but the staff wouldn't disturb their entrees. That was my job.

"Honey!" Paul said, and both he and his father stood up. "I'm so glad you're here. Did you leave the game early?"

Are you kidding? The game is just starting.

"Hello, Rita," said Kate warmly. Her face, though lined from the sun, was a handsome one, with high cheekbones and an almost mannish chin. Her hair, a polished silver, fell softly to her shoulders and her wide-set eyes were an unusual shade of gray, with dark eyebrows. Tortoiseshell half-glasses hung from a scarab lorgnette around her neck, for reading the menu. Everything so orderly, about to be disordered. I felt sick for her.

"Won't you join us?" Fiske asked. He was still standing, in a dark suit with his napkin in hand, and Paul was, too. I sat down and the men followed. "What would you like for dinner, Rita? The rack of lamb was wonderful, but we can get you a vegetable platter."

"Nothing."

"Nonsense," Fiske said. "We'll order dessert while you have your entree."

"No, thank you."

"You're not eating?" Kate asked.

"So you left the poker game," Paul said again, taking it as proof of love.

I wasn't supplying. "Not that I wanted to."

Fiske smiled. "I hope you weren't losing. I told Paul I'd bet on you any day."

Ha. He seemed only half-aware of the irony. I looked at him for a minute. His forehead seemed untroubled and his blue eyes were relaxed under eyebrows just beginning to silver. He had a large face, symmetrical and therefore appealing. But there was no warmth in it, just facial expressions that changed in increments. His was the perfect demeanor for a judge and the worst possible for a human being. Without knowing exactly why, I wanted to destroy his composure. So I said point-blank:

"Patricia Sullivan was murdered tonight."

Kate's hand flew to her mouth. Fiske blinked once, then twice. "Oh, my," he said. "Are you sure?"

What kind of question was that? "Of course. KYW news is sure. Channel 6 is sure. Channels 3 and 10 are probably sure, but I can't get them on the car radio. Her throat was cut. They think the murder weapon was a hunting knife, but they haven't found it yet."

"I don't understand," Paul said, leaning back into his Windsor chair.

I was only beginning to understand it myself. Fiske had lied to me, gotten me into the middle of something awful. "The radio said her jewelry and valuables were left alone. So robbery was not the motive."

"Oh, God," Kate said. She looked around the dining room. I read her mind: Does everybody know? Does anybody know?

"Did they say when it happened?" Paul asked.

"About six o'clock, they think. There'll be reporters waiting for us at the house, so I want us to go home together. They obviously don't know you're here, right?"

"I drove to the club first, then went out the service entrance in the back," Kate said.

"Good." A neat trick in a black Jaguar that matched Fiske's. They had his-and-hers Sovereigns, except that Fiske, an Anglophile, had bought his in England. "Fiske, would you take a drive with me? Paul and Kate can stay here until we get back."

"Why?" Paul asked. Kate looked equally puzzled.

"It's important," I said, but Fiske had already taken his napkin off his lap and was standing.

"Rita and I need to talk, Paul. The press will have a field day with this. We ought to make some sort of statement. What do you think, Rita?"

A practiced liar. "I agree. Kate, I need to borrow him for twenty minutes."

"I suppose we could go ahead and order dessert," Kate said uncertainly, but Paul frowned.

"Eat? Now? I can't sit here and eat as if nothing were going on."

Fiske, stepping away from the table, put a hand on Paul's shoulder. "You help me most by staying with your mother." He flagged down a young waiter, passing by.

"Yes, Judge Hamilton?" the waiter said, jerking bangs out of his eyes. He wore a tight leather choker around his neck, reminding me ominously of the way Patricia had been killed. One reporter said she'd been almost decapitated.

"My wife and son would like more coffee. And dessert."

I watched Fiske, so composed, and found myself wondering what time he'd left chambers for the day. Patricia's house was on his way home; he lived only fifteen minutes from her. And Fiske knew how to handle a hunting knife. He'd taught the whole family to hunt and even took hunting vacations in Texas.

"We'll be back by the second cup, dear," Fiske said. He bent down and gave Kate a dry kiss on her cheek. Her hand reached up for his and he squeezed it.

My thoughts raced ahead. Fiske had an obvious motive. Patricia and her lawsuit threatened

56

to expose him, to destroy his professional and personal world. And he knew the affair could come to light, I'd recommended as much as a defense on the telephone after the dep. Then he'd said he'd find a solution. I felt a chill, and it wasn't from my damp clothes.

"Shall we go, Rita?" Fiske asked.

"We'll take my car," I said, just as I allowed myself to think the unthinkable: Had Fiske killed Patricia? And could he actually have believed that would solve anything? We walked out of the restaurant and bolted in the rain for my BMW. We climbed in and I looked over at him coldly.

"Fiske," I said, twisting the ignition key, "you're taking this news rather well."

"It's not news to me."

"Say *what*?"

The engine roared to life. I hit the gas and tore out of the lot.

7

We parked on a private road next to the pond at Haverford College, which was dark except for the flickering gaslights along the road. The air inside the car felt hot and rain pounded on the taut ragtop. I could barely hear myself think over the thumping, but I didn't mince words with the man. "What the fuck is going on, Fiske? Level with me, because I'm in the middle of it."

"I knew Patricia was dead. She had to be."

"Did you kill her?"

"Of course not. How can you ask me that?" I couldn't see his expression, but I could tell by his tone he was shocked.

"How could I not ask you that?"

"You suspect *me*?"

"How'd you know she was dead?"

He turned away to look out the window, past the raindrops into the night. "I could never harm Patricia."

"You had an affair with her, right?"

"Yes. It lasted about six months."

So it was a love affair and she was crying sexual harassment. Why? A woman scorned? "How did the affair end?"

"She ended it."

"*She* did?"

He watched the rain. "I wouldn't leave Kate, Patricia knew that from the outset. I told her. So she ended it, one day. She's like that. An artist. Impulsive, unpredictable. Passionate." His voice sounded far away. "It was for the best. I had Kate."

"Why didn't you tell me any of this? Didn't you think I'd find out? A first-year law student—"

"Is she really gone?"

"Patricia? Of course."

He winced in the semi-darkness. "It doesn't seem possible."

Get a grip, pal. "It's more than possible. It happened."

"I saw the ambulance, the police cars. I couldn't believe it. There were so many." He shook his head slowly.

"What police cars? Where?"

"Out in front, on the lawn."

"In front of what?"

"In front of her carriage house."

"When did you see cars in front of her house?"

"Patricia wouldn't have liked that, right on the lawn. It was unnecessary."

I touched the wet sleeve of his trench coat. "Fiske, look at me. Are you telling me you were at Patricia's carriage house?"

He faced me, in a kind of shock. "I didn't kill her, Rita. You must believe that."

Jesus. Bullets of rain hit the roof. The car grew hotter, the windshield fogged with steam. "When did you go to the carriage house?"

"I stopped by on the way home, after you and I spoke on the telephone. After the deposition."

"Why did you go there?"

"To convince Patricia to drop the lawsuit. Our affair would come out, everything would come out. There was no other way to solve the problem."

I recoiled, letting go of his arm, and searched his face in the dark. "And when she wouldn't drop it, you killed her?"

"No! When I got there, police cars were everywhere. The neighbors were out. I knew something terrible had happened. I kept driving."

"Where did you drive? Did you go home?"

"No, I just drove around."

"Where?"

"Around. I don't remember exactly. Just driving, trying to figure out what had happened to Patricia. I was a little late to dinner. Kate got to dinner in her car, with Paul."

I didn't know what to say. I couldn't process it all fast enough.

"You know I didn't do it, Rita."

"How do I know that?"

"Because you know I love Patricia. Loved her. Only you know that. You know about the spider mums. Why would I kill her, if I loved her?"

"Pick a motive, any motive."

"Don't be so glib."

Fuck you. "Because she ended the affair."

"But I knew it would end. I knew it wouldn't last forever. I'm not a child."

"Because she was trying to ruin you, then."

"No, she wasn't."

"Of course she was! Why would she sue you?"

"I don't know. She is . . . was a very complicated woman."

"Oh, please." When will men stop calling manipulative women *complicated*?

"You don't think so? You met her."

"It's not as if Patricia and I had lunch, Fiske. I took her deposition because she was suing you.

60

She had your name and photo in every newspaper in three states. You need to think in realistic terms. Patricia's been murdered and you could end up a suspect. You have a big-time motive and a see-through alibi."

"You think I'm a suspect?"

Hello? Anybody home? "Yes. I would say the prime suspect, if I practiced criminal law, which I don't. You need a criminal lawyer, Fiske. You must know some, the best."

"You're my lawyer."

"Not anymore."

He looked angry. "You won't represent me? Why not?"

"You lied to me, for starters."

"I didn't lie. I just didn't explain the whole . . . I didn't think it would all come out. I'm sorry. But I want you to represent me."

"It isn't my field. I hate criminal law, it's dirty work. You want Leslie Abramson, not Rita Morrone."

"I want Rita Morrone." He shifted toward me, his shoulders bulky in the leather bucket seat. "We have time. I'm a judge, a prominent member of the legal community. They won't indict me unless they have their ducks in a row."

"What ducks, if you're innocent?"

"The same circumstantial evidence you have."

"You mean the paintings, the florist?"

"Yes."

"Are there hotel bills?"

"Never a hotel."

Like a judge's chambers is better? Your tax dollars.

"I went to her house, once or twice, at night," he said. "But she was never at my house. Our house."

What a guy. "How about your phone bills?"

"I don't think they show calls to her, but I didn't call her often in any event. She asked me not to, and I respected her time. She had to paint when she wasn't working." He paused. "But I did call before I left my chambers tonight. Before I went over."

"Why?"

"To ask if she would see me. I told you, I respected her independence."

Terrific. "That call will show up on a bill, now that the suburbs have a new area code."

"Yes."

"It won't look good, Fiske. A call right before she was murdered."

"I didn't know she'd be murdered! If I were going to drive to her house and kill her, would I have called first?"

I considered this, and evidently so had he, about ten steps before me. Fiske was a chess player, nationally ranked. He even played by mail, sending postcards that bore gobbledygook like Be3 and Bg7. Suddenly, something fell into place and I turned cold. "Fiske, you know what I think? I think you knew all of this was going to happen."

He turned toward me in the shadows. "I knew Patricia was going to be killed?"

"No, you knew that I would find out about you and her."

"I didn't plan for this to happen."

"Maybe not, but it was inevitable, wasn't it? Look, nobody in the family knows about the affair, do they?"

"No. Kate doesn't suspect anything. She thinks Patricia was an opportunist."

"And Paul?"

"Of course not."

"So you kept it from the family. But when you had a chance to hire a lawyer, you chose a lawyer close to the family. Practically in the family."

"Well, yes." Fiske acted only vaguely aware of his own mind, but I didn't believe it for a minute. My father had been right, which annoyed me no end.

"You hired me to use me, Fiske. You used me then and you're using me now."

"That's not true!"

"Then why let me be the one to find out about your affair? Because you thought I'd keep it secret?"

"Any lawyer would have done that. It would be privileged."

"You thought I'd be loyal to you no matter what, even to the point of keeping quiet about a murder. What other lawyer could you ask to do that?"

"I didn't murder Patricia!"

"Then why me?"

"I didn't think it would turn out like this, I tell you."

Liar. Cheater. Bastard. I reached for the ignition, but Fiske gripped my forearm.

"Wait. Maybe . . . part of me did. Part of me must have wanted you to find out. So that it wouldn't be a secret anymore."

"Bullshit. Two-bit psychology." I turned on the ignition despite his grip. "You wanted to destroy your life? Screw up your marriage?"

"I . . . think I must have," he said, his tone anguished. "Yes."

I looked at him while the engine rumbled. His face was obscured and he made no sound, but I had the sense he was about to cry.

"I think . . . I *wanted* to tell Kate," he continued, almost thinking out loud. "I wanted her to know. It just . . . got out of control. I loved Patricia, Rita, and somebody killed her. I want to know who."

It rang true. He sounded determined and bewildered, both at once. A natural reaction given the circumstances. Maybe he was innocent. Wrongly accused, or about to be. If so, his world was on the brink of falling to pieces, at his own hand. He slumped forward and rested his temple in his hand, inadvertently reminding me of a face card again. Not the king of diamonds this time. The king of hearts, the suicide king. Fiske was either that or a cold-blooded killer.

Why were men so damn *complicated?*

64

8

"They have no right," Paul said as he glared at the TV screen.

A black reporter stood on the wet flagstone path leading to the door of the Hamiltons' huge house, a three-story stone Tudor with diamond-paned windows, an arched front door, and spiky turrets on both sides. Any idiot could see the place looked like a minicastle, which wouldn't help public relations any.

"This isn't news, it's harassment," Paul said, naked except for the towel around his waist. He'd taken a hot shower but it hadn't relaxed him any. "*This* is harassment!" He aimed the remote control at the TV like a weapon and clicked up the volume.

The reporter fairly shouted, "We have tried to reach Judge Hamilton, but he has not been available for comment."

"He's asleep, you prick!" Paul shouted back. "Is he supposed to stay up all night to talk to you?"

"Relax, Paul," I said, but I knew this case was blowing up in our faces. It was all over the radio and TV news. Our answering machine tape had a slew of calls from the press and three from the managing partner of my firm. His final message was to meet him in his office first thing in the morning. I wasn't looking forward to it.

"They're showing it again," Paul said. "Can you believe it? The same goddamn tape over and over. My *family*, for God's sake."

I looked at the TV and caught the film of Paul, Fiske, Kate, and me, trooping across the front lawn under umbrellas. We'd left the restaurant in a homecoming I'd orchestrated, so I couldn't help objectifying the scene. Fiske, vital and self-assured, didn't look the part of a murderer, and projected like Blake Carrington with bona fide business acumen. When the reporters shouted questions at him from the sidewalk, he declined comment with a Windsor wave and the smile of a majority shareholder.

"People walking into a house is news?" Paul said. "I give up." He sank to the foot of the bed and lowered the volume. "My poor mother."

I squinted at Kate's image on the TV screen, but I didn't see his mother the way he did. Kate didn't look poor, in close-up. On the contrary, she looked wealthy and haughty, with cheekbones that could cut hard cheese. The kind of wife you would cheat on with your pretty young secretary, whose soft, windswept photo came on next. I looked at Paul's back as he watched TV. Beads of water glistened on his shoulders. His tan line peeked out from under the towel.

"Rita, look," he said. "It's you again."

A picture of me came on. Brown eyes with smudgy eye pencil, a strong nose that needed powdering, crow's-feet only surgery could improve, and a mound of long, dark hair exploding in the humidity. "Another bad hair year."

"Silly. You're beautiful."

Bullshit. I watched him watch me as I said from the screen, "We are all very sorry about the death of Miss Sullivan, and our thoughts are with her family at this difficult time. We have no further comment."

"You were great," Paul said to the TV. "You were wonderful, Rita. You've been wonderful. None of us could get through this without you." He turned suddenly toward me, and I didn't know whether he'd caught me looking at his tan line.

"Sure you could."

"Can't you just take the compliment? I'm trying to tell you how much I appreciate you." He edged closer to me on the bed and rubbed my instep, but I didn't want his touch or his words to warm me.

"Hey, stop."

"No, I'm going to compliment you. You ready?"

"Come off it, Paul."

"No. Hold still. This will only hurt a minute. I think you're a great woman and a great lawyer."

"Paul, stop. You just like the fee." I shifted away, but his hand chased my ankle and caught it.

"Oh, really? You think you're cheap?"

"Say what? I think I'm free."

"You, *free*? Just look around this room." He clicked off the TV as Patricia's attorney, Stan Julicher, came on, crying crocodile tears in front of his firm's large nameplate. Now that Patricia was dead, the harassment case was over. Julicher would miss his contingency more than he would miss his client.

"Hey, I wanted to see that," I said.

"How about this bed, huh? You think that came cheap?" Paul pointed at our four-poster, whose turned spindles stretched to a delicate arched canopy.

"This bed didn't cost anything. You built it."

"It still costs, honey. It's all cherrywood. The labor I threw in for free, because I liked you so much."

"What a guy." The bed was a birthday present Paul had built in his father's garage. I'd loved it the instant he'd taken me to see it, then I'd brought him wine and wrenches while he disassembled the contraption to get it out the door. He was never as good a planner as his father, which was part of his charm.

"And how about that armoire, huh?" He jerked his head at the cherry cabinet across the room. "Made to order, all by yours truly. With big drawers for my best girl's shirts and little drawers for her lovely undies. Just like you asked, right?"

I didn't say anything. I remembered him refinishing the armoire, hand-rubbing it with a chamois. I tried not to think about how good his fingertips felt on my leg.

"Wasn't it just like you asked? Wasn't it exactly how you wanted it? With the pull-out drawer for your extra decks of cards?"

I wanted to smile, but it caught in my throat. "Not for cards, you."

"For poker chips then. Poker chips to your heart's content."

"Not for chips, either."

"But it's a pull-out drawer, is it not?"

"Paul—"

"Your Honor, please direct the witness to answer the question." He caressed my leg. "My Honor says you have to answer. Yes or no." He liked to play lawyer and was good at it, from a lifetime of hanging around judges, lawyers, and courthouses.

"Yes."

"I rest my case. Call your next witness."

"Give me a break."

The light from the bedside lamp gave his amused expression a soft glow, and he rolled onto his side and played with my knee. "Do you still like this?" he asked softly.

I tried not to pay attention to the sensation of his touch or to his chest, twisted across the white bedspread toward me. I kept thinking of the doctor's letter.

"Huh? Do you like this, Rita? You used to like it when I did this."

I knew where he was going. I had a dim memory of it, growing more vivid with each stroke of his hand, like ember to flame. "I used to like a lot of things, Paul."

"I know. I remember them all." His hand traveled up to my thigh. "It wasn't so long ago, you know."

"Yes, it was."

"No, it wasn't."

"It was very long ago. When you liked me and I liked you." I heard bitterness in my voice.

He drew a line up from my knee with his forefinger. "I never stopped liking you. I like you still. But you stopped liking me, and I'm trying to get you back." He hoisted himself toward me, and his towel slipped down.

I averted my eyes as if he were a stranger. "You can't get me back."

He kissed my knee before I could object. "You wanted me on the first date, remember? I made you a salad for dinner and you were smitten, you said, and you wanted to make love. The first date, the very *first date*. A fast Italian girl, I thought."

I laughed, the memory was so unexpected. It dawned bright as daybreak, and as undeniable.

"Do you remember what I told you when you asked me, flat-out?"

I closed my eyes and remembered. His kiss traveled to the inside of my knee, slower this time, slightly wet.

"Miss Morrone, are you going to answer the question or do I have to ask My Honor to put you in jail?" His mouth moved along the inside of my leg, kissing me like he had that night in

70

his apartment. The lights had been off. I'd turned them off, the way I liked it.

"No," I said. "Paul—"

"I told you you had the most beautiful legs I'd ever seen, and as much as I wanted to know more about them, I liked you altogether too much to do that on the first date."

I kept my eyes closed, remembering. His kisses passed my knee and made a trail on the inside of my thigh. I felt myself easing back into the pillow while he kissed me, this first date that had so much promise. He had thrilled me. An architect with a pedigree and an open heart.

"I told you I thought I was falling in love with you, do you remember? That I was in it for the long run." I felt his kiss move up my thigh, under my robe. The notepad slipped from my lap and the sound it made as it fell to the carpet came from some other time and place. "I had to put you out that night, like a cat."

He always said that, *Like a cat.* I used to laugh. I felt myself warming.

"I love you," he said, and I let myself hear it. Let myself believe it for just a moment. It pushed my problems away, swept aside Fiske and Patricia, my managing partner, and my new HPV virus. I wanted to forget it all, get lost for a while. Slip away. No one had to know, no one had to see. Not even me. I reached up and switched off the light.

"Do you remember what else I told you that night?" he asked, his voice soft in the darkness.

Familiar. Like his sigh, and the throatier sound that would come later. "That it wasn't one night, it was forever." His mouth reached the top of my thighs, and he kissed them until my legs parted.

I remembered. It was the first date, then the first time we made love. Then the time after that and the time after that, too. All the times, all of the same piece, seamless. When the loving was still there and so palpable you could feel it like the bones on his back when he was on you. You could hear it in the sounds you made, and in his, too, deeper. You could feel it in the slickness between you, belly-level, in summer, and the way it warmed your feet in winter, no matter how cold it was.

That's what I remembered, all of it came flooding back, and in a minute it was inside me, filling me up, suffusing me with good feeling.

He was right about one thing. I loved him still.

If I could think back.

And the lights were off.

9

The office wall was crowded with diplomas and certificates and the slick desktop reflected the squat and omnipotent silhouette of a unique breed of high roller: the managing partner of a law firm. I'd first met Ed "Mack" Macklin when

I was a young associate and he had kissed off the last firm that wouldn't ante up every time he sneezed. Mack became my mentor, although I never realized before this moment how much he resembled Edward G. Robinson. But maybe that was because I was feeling like the Cincinnati Kid.

"Why are you getting out of the *Sullivan* case?" Mack said, relaxed in his cushy leather chair. His office was the largest in the firm, and well-appointed. An expensive leather couch and chairs clustered around a glass coffee table; a wall-length English credenza held some neat files and an expensive, albeit untouched, laptop computer. The virgin laptop was the hottest power prop, signifying that Mack had the juice to make the firm buy him a toy and also that he was too important to play with it. You had no power if you actually used your PowerBook.

"The *Sullivan* case is over. The plaintiff is dead."

"The judge called me last night, Rita. He was very disappointed. Said he expects us to stand behind him if he's charged with murder."

"Judge Hamilton called you at home?" Fiske was making all the right moves, and I was the sacrificial pawn. "What time did he call?"

"What's the difference? He's a friend."

"Of yours? Since when?"

"Since last night." Mack laughed abruptly. "Judge Hamilton is one of the most prominent members of the federal bench. He wasn't happy that our firm would leave him in the lurch."

"He'll get over it."

"I'm not happy when he's not happy. I'm not happy when any federal judge is unhappy, especially in our district. Don't you want to make me happy?" He spoke in the subdued tone of someone who expected an affirmative answer.

"No."

"You wound me."

"You'll get over it, too."

Mack gazed past me through one of three large, smoked-glass windows, which overlooked the offices of the law firm he had just left. He'd demanded this view because he wanted his old firm to see him making money for someone else. "So," he said, "I told the judge that he could rest assured that Averback, Shore & Macklin was his counsel at the beginning and we were going to remain his counsel to the end. Got it?"

"What's this? *Muscle*?"

He smiled, not unpleasantly. "I'm flexing. You like?"

"Be still my heart."

"Good. Then it's settled." He grinned like he wasn't kidding. I felt my temper rise.

"Not exactly, Mack. It's my practice. I'll run it the way I want."

"The judge is a client of this firm."

"No, the judge is a client of mine. He didn't hire the firm, he hired me. I was his lawyer, now I'm not. As of today."

He eased back into his desk chair. The gesture looked like resignation, but I knew better. Mack always recoiled before he struck, like a cobra. "You're right, Rita. It's your practice. You can run it any way you like. I can't make you do anything you don't want to do. But you know the Committee was delighted when the Hamilton matter came to you."

"I remember." A collective rubbing of soft, pasty hands.

"I don't have to tell you how disappointed they'd be if I had to report on your withdrawal."

I was breaking hearts everywhere. "A girl's gotta do what a girl's gotta do."

"You know, the Committee has been discussing the possibility of a midcourse correction in the partnership contracts. Were you aware of that?"

Firm politics was not my strong suit. The courtroom was where the action was, not the conference room. "Midcourse correction?"

"A couple of us have noted that the current distributions aren't adequately reflecting our contributions."

"You mean you're not making enough money, Mack?"

"In a word? Absofuckinglutely."

We both laughed, without mirth.

"It would affect all of our contracts," he said. "But your name was the only one from your class that came up for an increase. I could make it happen, Rita. You stand to skip two classes. Serious money."

A lawyer's trick; whenever possible, wave a

check. Since I grew up without money, I was almost impervious to this temptation. Almost. "You mean if I drop Judge Hamilton, I can kiss my raise good-bye?"

"In a word?"

Prick. "Very funny."

"Look, Rita, this whole situation is in your control. As I said, I can't make you do anything."

"Fine. No raise. I'm happy with my draw now."

Mack made a sturdy tent with his fingers. "Well, then, consider that your partnership draw may not stay as high as it is. If there's a midcourse correction, some of us will go up. But some will go down."

My mouth tasted bitter. "Don't tell me, let me guess. If I don't represent the judge, my draw will go down? In a word?"

He opened his hands. "I don't control the Committee."

"Who are you kidding, Mack? They don't take a dump without asking you."

"Rita—"

It pissed me off. "What you're saying is if I give up the representation, the Committee will recut the pie. And after they get done with my piece, I'll have to put the ice cream on the side. Think I'll be able to balance even a spoonful on my sliver?"

"You're overreacting. The whole thing is in your control."

"Then why am I feeling so controlled?"

"I have no idea. Big piece or little piece? The choice is up to you."

I folded my arms, looking no tougher than a petulant teenager. "Okay, I'm dieting."

He rocked back in his chair and stared at the ceiling lights, discreetly recessed. After a minute he said, "You're being stubborn about this and I'm entitled to know why."

"No, you're not."

"Look, this isn't a game. This is serious."

"Games are serious, Mack. You know that." Mack played big-time blackjack in Atlantic City and Vegas, to stay in shape for managing my law firm.

"Rita, this is a terrible decision you're making. The judge is your client, he needs you now. You're a terrific lawyer, a creative lawyer. That result last week at City Hall—"

"Oh, are you kissing my ass now? Because I like it a little to the left."

A buzzer sounded on the phone and Mack snatched up the receiver. "What? Send him in." The receiver clattered to the hook and he eased back again. "I called in reinforcements."

"Who?"

The door opened and in came a gray Armani suit, a silk paisley tie that ended in a knifepoint, and blue-black hair pulled back into a short ponytail, of all things. It was Jake Tobin, firm womanizer. His dark eyes looked faintly amused.

"You know Jake, don't you?" Mack said.

"Only by reputation."

"I'll take that as a compliment," Tobin said with an easy laugh, then closed the door behind him.

Mack said, "I asked Jake to join us because he's done extensive criminal work. He was a public defender before he joined us. Right, Jake?"

"For fifteen years," Tobin said. He leaned against the credenza and glanced enviously at the PowerBook. I was guessing he knew how to use it.

Mack said, "Jake, I was just telling Rita here that you've tried a lot of murder cases."

"About fifty jury trials, give or take some major scum. Most of them got out of jail free."

A career to be proud of. "I'm impressed. You want to represent Judge Hamilton? I hear he needs somebody like you."

Mack shook his head. "No, Rita. Wrong. My idea was that Jake could backstop you on the case. Judge Hamilton told me it's you or he goes to Goldberg's firm."

Tobin nodded. "Now *I'm* impressed."

"Don't be, I quit," I said.

Mack sighed. "Rita, I've had reporters calling from the *American Lawyer* and the *National Law Journal*. Joanne told me there were almost forty calls yesterday. And that plaintiff's lawyer, Julicher, he's all over the news."

"Julicher?" Tobin asked. "I never heard of him."

"I had his bio checked, wait a minute." Mack thumbed through a neat stack of papers to the side of his desk, pulled a sheet out, and skimmed it. "He's from New York, but not from any of the top-tier firms. A nobody. Graduated from a state university, then Fordham Law School, Class of '77, blah, blah, blah, blah. He's a slip-and-fall guy, does workmen's comp cases. A scrapper, a *nothing*, and he's on the tube all night last night."

"He's hustling referral business, Mack."

"Is he a good lawyer?" Tobin asked, looking at me.

"He's no scholar, but he's a fighter. If he still had a harassment case, he would've given me a run for my money."

Mack tossed the bio aside and stood up. "But it's a murder case now, it's getting everybody's attention. Everybody's watching. If you withdraw now, they'll all know about it. It'll make Judge Hamilton look guilty."

What if he is? "No, it won't."

"Well, I, for one, won't hang a federal judge out to dry. The networks are all over the story, so are the newspapers. Rita, we go back a long time. I'm asking you as a personal favor to keep the case."

"Why?"

"For the publicity, dopey," Tobin said.

I looked at Mack for confirmation, and his smile was already broadening. "I told you, I had forty calls yesterday. Forty—count 'em—*forty*. One was from *Good Morning America*. Federal Judge kills secretary? We're talking national exposure here!"

"*Allegedly* kills secretary," Tobin added.

Mack laughed. "We're on a roll with this, Rita. I even hired a public relations firm to manage it. It's a gold mine."

Wait a minute. The unsayable needed saying. "But what if Fiske really is the killer?"

They both looked at me blankly. "So what?" Tobin said, and Mack nodded.

I was dumbfounded. "It cuts both ways, boys. It could be bad publicity."

Mack laughed. "Ain't no such thing, kid."

"I second that emotion," Tobin said.

I looked at them and realized that as long as lawyers like this were around, I would always be second-best.

And I'd never even been to Cincinnati.

10

The tiny, cluttered kitchenette in back of the butcher shop filled with the smell of cholesterol as my father shook a crackling pan of homemade sausage. He was wearing his I'M ITALIAN AND YOU'RE NOT apron, but I couldn't read the front. All I could see was his thick back, which ended in a white ribbon tied over baggy white pants. The silent treatment again.

"So, Dad, explain this to me. You're pissed when I decide to represent the judge, then you're pissed when I want out? What is it? My aftershave?"

LeVonne, who had been rocking his fork by pressing on the tines, laughed softly. He ate with my father every morning at this ancient white drop-leaf, where they both pretended that LeVonne had eaten already and was just keeping my father company.

"You laughin', Professor?" my father said, without turning around. "I hope not, because it's not funny. Everything's a big joke with her."

"Who, me? Aren't you going to call me Miss Fresh?"

The only response was the sausage's. It sputtered, releasing an aromatic smoke of olive oil, fresh garlic, and green pepper.

"Come on, Dad, I like it when you call me Miss Fresh. Then I know it's you and not some Vito impersonator." I turned to LeVonne. "LeVonne, what do you think? Is it really him? It must be, who else would wear that apron?"

LeVonne's smooth lips tightened to hold back his smile. He looked fresh this morning in an oversized T-shirt with a faded picture of Kriss Kross on it. A gentle crease between the twins told me the shirt had been ironed. I wondered who had ironed it, for his parents were long gone and it was all his grandmother could do to get him to my father's. It occurred to me there was a lot I didn't know about LeVonne.

"LeVonne, will *you* talk to me at least? What grade are you in now? Tenth?"

He nodded and looked down at his heavy white plate. Being totally empty, the plate couldn't have held his interest for more than a moment, but he stared at it, saying nothing, while the sausage sizzled along with my father.

"You like school, LeVonne?"

He shrugged.

"Are you going to take a language next year?"

He shook his head.

I'm usually a better conversationalist than this. "LeVonne, I've been meaning to tell you I like your . . . uh, what do you call that, a beard? Are you growing a beard?"

He touched his chin, self-conscious.

"Do you call it a beard? Or what?" Just to see if he'd talk.

"S'whatever," LeVonne said.

"It's a goatee," snapped my father. "A beard goes all the way around."

Thanks, Dad. "Well, whatever it's called, I like it."

LeVonne hung his head even farther, until his chin was practically buried between Kriss Kross's steam-ironed backward-base-ball caps.

"I like it, too," my father said.

"I said it first, Pop. So that makes me a nicer person than you."

"Hmph." He jiggled the pan.

"In fact, I'm such a good person that when I have a guest to breakfast I do not turn my back on them until I get my own way." The sausage popped loudly. "Hear that, Dad? The meat gods agree."

LeVonne laughed, almost a child's giggle. He covered his mouth but the giggle persisted. My father pivoted and speared the air between us with the tines of the cooking fork. "It's not my own way, it's the *right* way."

"What's the *right* way?"

"The right way is you finish what you started. The judge could be charged with murder. You told him you'd defend him, you defend him."

"I said I'd defend him against sexual harassment, not murder."

He punched up his glasses with his wrist. "You said you'd be his lawyer, you're his lawyer. Finish what you started."

"But what if I shouldn't have started it? What if he was using me, like you said?"

"It don't matter."

"Can't I change my mind? Maybe you were right in the first place, Dad."

He straightened himself to his full height, which was five foot five. "I *was* right. I was right the first time and I'm right the second time, too. You don't quit just because it's tougher than you thought." He drew a horizontal line in the air with the fork. I had no idea what this meant, except maybe it was the thirty-eighth parallel and I was North Korea and he was South.

"It's not that simple, Dad."

"No? Why not?"

"It's not getting tougher, it's getting different."

He turned to LeVonne and pointed to him with the fork. "Do you understand what that means, Mr. President?"

LeVonne shook his head.

"It means it's not what I bargained for, Dad. I'm not a criminal lawyer. What's the matter with getting the judge a good criminal lawyer?"

"It's wrong!"

"Why?"

"General principles."

"General principles?" I smacked myself in the forehead. "How could I forget about general principles?"

"Go ahead, make fun."

"You should write the general principles down somewhere, Dad, like they do with the United States Code. This way we could all look them up and know how to live. We wouldn't have to come to Ninth Street every time we had a question. Think of the time it would save us!"

He shook the fork at me. "You could visit more. It's not the worst thing."

I rubbed my eyes and began to wonder why I had come. Had I really thought he could help? I didn't even eat sausage. "Now, getting back to general principles. Which general principle is it we're talking about? There are so many, and you can never find the index."

"You know which one, Miss Wiseguy."

"No, I don't. I didn't take general principles in law school. Maybe it was an elective?"

LeVonne turned around in his seat, facing

almost backward out the screen door to the tiny cement back of the store's lot. I don't know what he was looking at, there was nothing in the back except a cinderblock wall, two battered garbage cans, and a fig tree growing out of the concrete floor. Come to think of it, it was something to see.

"The principle, miss, is that you don't quit. I didn't raise a quitter. That's what I'm saying."

"Why does it come down to what you raised? This has nothing to do with you. Whatever decision I make, it doesn't reflect on you."

"Of course it does. Everything I do, everything *you* do—what did you say? What was that word?"

"Reflects?"

"*Reflects* on each other. On all of us." He made a circle in the air with the fork, and I figured we were talking the entire globe now, not just Korea. "It all *reflects* on us. Everything reflects on us. Our family name."

"Our what?" The concept was so ludicrous I couldn't repeat it. "We're the Morrones, not the Kennedys. Not the Rockefellers."

He slammed the fork down on the spoon rest. "Where did you get the idea that you have to have money to have a family name?"

His vehemence took me aback, and LeVonne shifted farther out the back door.

"Wherever you got it, it was wrong! We do have a family name—Morrone. It was my father's name, and he came and started this shop in 1914. He was one of the first to come over, to come to

85

the Market. My father, Vito Morrone, Senior. Your grandfather, you understand me?"

"Sure, but—"

"He had a name, and it counted as much as anybody else's, and everybody respected it. He never disgraced it. When he couldn't get hired at an inside job he started his own shop. He and my mother worked in it every day until they died. My father, he never gave up and never, ever *quit*. That's what I'm doing here and that's what LeVonne's doing here," he said, red in the face under his fresh shave.

"Dad, relax."

"We're all making our own name here. Nobody gave it to us, and we're making it every day. So are you. You don't disgrace it. You don't *run away*." He turned his back on me, picked up the fork, and jabbed it into the sausage. The meat spat in protest. Black smoke rose from the pan. Burned.

I felt a light touch on my arm.

LeVonne. His fingers were slim, his hand looked like a nimble spider against the white table. He shook his head, no.

"What?" I mouthed to him silently.

His almost-black gaze slid over to the left. I followed his eyes to the photographs on the wall, speared with steel tacks to a bulletin board of crumbling cork. I'd stopped noticing the pictures long ago: my father's old mutt, me at Holy Communion, my grandfather and grandmother, with maybe three teeth between them. But I sensed which picture LeVonne meant, and it was none of those.

Her hair was a white-gold swirl behind her head, her wedding dress was a white-gold swirl at her feet. My father towered over her in the photo, he must have been standing on a step-ladder. His jacket was a rented white, his hair two wings of pomade. He looked like a lovestruck young man who would never believe the lithe woman at his side would someday run away.

My father never spoke of her, and I'd stopped pressing him to. I didn't know why she left until one of the Espositos told me, when I was ten, that it was Another Man. Before that, I thought it was because she was Canadian, since Jimmy DiNardo said it wouldn't have happened if my father had married an Italian girl instead of a Canadian girl. My child's mind assumed that Canada was an exotic country, which accounted for my mother's singular looks and manners. Even her clothes were different; stiff linen dresses, orange capri pants, midriff tops that tied at the bellybutton. She was the talk of the Market, but I had not associated disgrace with what she did to my father until this very minute. He protected me from that, as he did from the fact that she died shortly after she left.

And it took LeVonne, who was stone silent, to explain my own father to me. I glanced back at LeVonne. His head was cocked as if he were listening. His dark eyes moved over my father's back, seeming to scan his posture and stance for clues.

I watched my father, too, then. I listened as he snapped off the gas and reshuffled the sticky sausage. And after he had tended the sausage forever and I couldn't stand wondering why he wouldn't turn around, I made a silent promise to him, or more accurately, to his back. I wouldn't quit the Hamilton representation, no matter what. There would be no running away. Not any-more.

After all, I had a family name to uphold.

Not Rockefeller. Not Kennedy. Morrone.

On general principles, no less.

When I got back to the office, my secretary, Janine, was sitting at my desk. Her black clogs were crossed on my mail and she was yapping away on my telephone. Janine Altman was a com-plete slacker except when a telephone receiver made contact with her triple-pierced ear. Then she'd twist her penny-red hair around a bitten-off fingernail and chatter away, animated as Ann-Margaret on the telephone in *Bye-Bye Birdie*. I kept Janine on because I was raising her to be a responsible adult, which was why I reached over and rudely pressed down the telephone hook.

"What's the story, morning glory?" I said to her. "What's the tale, nightingale?"

Her purple-lipsticked mouth dropped open. "Rita?" she said, scrambling to sit up straight. "Why'd you do that?"

"Child, I've asked you not to make drug deals from my phone. Can't you use your own?"

"It wasn't a personal call?" she said with her characteristic inflection. Every statement she made sounded like a question. It drove me nuts.

"Janine, are you asking me something or telling me something?"

"Telling you something? I was talking to Judge Hamilton on the phone? He says to come quick?"

I felt my stomach leapfrog. "What?"

"He's been arrested? He's in jail?"

Christ. "Where?"

She consulted a yellow message slip. "At the police station in Radnor Township?" She thumbed through the other slips on the pad underneath. "Before that the *Inquirer* called and the *Daily News*? And Jim Hart, you know, that reporter from Channel 10? The one with the hair?"

"The press? Do they know about the arrest?"

She nodded. "Yes?"

Shit. "You told them all no comment, right?"

She looked guilt-stricken under her alternative makeup.

"What did you do, Janine?"

"Nothing?"

"Tell me you didn't talk to the press."

"Just Hart?" She cringed, as if awaiting the blow I was actually considering.

"What did you tell him?"

"My phone number?"

I took in some oxygen, but not much. "Janine,

don't talk to the reporters. Don't date the reporters. Don't feed the reporters. The shit is about to hit the fan, *capisce?*"

"But he's so hot?"

Someday I would give up on her. "I'm sure," I said, and threw a legal pad and a copy of the Pennsylvania Crimes Code into my briefcase.

"I'm sorry?"

"Do something secretarial for me. Call Mack and tell him to assign some young genius to my cases. And tell him I said 'pay up.'"

"Okay?" She made a note in pen on the palm of her hand. Another thing I'd asked her not to do.

"Then cancel everybody today. And tomorrow."

"Tomorrow, too?"

I snapped my briefcase closed and grabbed my bag. "And tomorrow and tomorrow and tomorrow. You ever hear that before? You know what that's from?"

"Macbeth?"

I did a double-take. "Right."

She grinned crookedly and held up her hand. On her palm it said, YOUNG GENIUS.

11

The route to Radnor Township Police Station winds through the most expensive wilderness west of Philadelphia and is dotted with stone mansions set so far from their mailboxes it could be another zip code. Residents call this costly forest "hunt country" and I believe they hunt foxes here, not Italians or other critters.

If I didn't have a client arrested for murder, I might have enjoyed the drive, with the hand-stitched steering wheel sliding through my fingers and my car taking the curves like it was glued to the asphalt. Instead I was trying to remember the elements of the crime of murder as I whipped past the mailboxes, their tasteful white lettering echoing names on the SIGN HERE line of the Declaration of Independence.

Hancock, Morris, Lynch.

I tried to reach Kate on my car phone to tell her what was going on, but there was no answer, and no answering machine. Kate loathed them, lumping them with such abominations as VCRs, personal computers, and ballpoint pens.

Wolcott, Clark, Stone.

Kate would be tough enough to weather this, I'd seen her attack ivy like the Terminator. I guessed she wouldn't be at the police station.

Fiske protected her, by tradition and instinct, and she seemed content in this arrangement. I'd always thought their marriage had a comfy, natural-order feel to it, like a faithful pairing of loons. Shows you how much I know.

Adams, Ross, Smith.

I tried to reach Paul, too, but he wasn't at his office or at home. I called on the car phone, but no luck. I tried not to think about where he was, what he was doing, or who he was doing it with. I had to bail his father out of jail. I punched the End button on the car phone again for no reason at all.

Wilson, Taylor, Chase.

I caught sight of the police station at the fringe of the woods behind a huge, well-maintained baseball field. I came to a full stop when I saw the commotion.

ABC, NBC, CBS.

The baseball field was empty of Little Leaguers, whose families had fled the steamy tarmac of their circular driveways for beach houses. Reporters had taken their place, alleged adults with cameras and microphones. White TV news vans with flashy logos were parked in the station lot, their silvery satellite dishes reflecting the midday sunshine. Even the playground was overrun by the media and their shiny toys.

I took a deep breath, gunned all six of my Teutonic cylinders, and drove down the road and into the parking lot. I ignored the camera flashes and videocameras that recorded my car's excellent handling. I pulled into the first illegal space and the reporters were on me almost before I cut the ignition.

From a woman reporter with a dictaphone: "Miss Morrone, do you have any comment on the judge's arrest?"

How about shit, piss, and fuck? "No comment."

From a slick TV reporter: "People are saying the judge should step down from the bench. Will he?"

Are you kidding? "Why should he? Judge Hamilton is one of the best judges on the district court. We need him."

From a Connie Chung knock-off: "How will this affect the lawsuit for sexual harassment?"

She's dead, so it goes away. "I have no comment. Excuse me, I'd like to get through here without serious bodily injury. To you."

From a black reporter: "Will Judge Hamilton plead guilty?"

Does the Pope shit in the woods? "Of course not."

And a follow-up, shouted from the back of the crowd: "Is the judge guilty, Ms. Morrone?"

Your guess is as good as mine, bucko. "Absolutely not. My client is innocent of any and all charges against him."

I wedged my way through the throng, ducked a thousand more questions, and stepped inside the station house. I'd never been in a police station, but I didn't expect it to look like the home

93

office of an insurance company. The walls glowed eggshell white and the matching tile floor was buffed to perfection. The baseboards were done in teal, as were the doorjambs and other molding. The hall was quiet, no one was anywhere in sight. I figured all the insurance agents were out harassing people like you and me.

"May I help you?" said a gray-haired receptionist, who looked up from the mystery novel she was reading. Her back was to a large window, and reporters pressed against it like chimps at the zoo.

"Yes. Can you make those reporters disappear?"

"Certainly." She got up and dropped the Levolors in their faces. Mystery readers take no prisoners.

"I'm Rita—"

"I know, I saw you on TV. Have a seat in the waiting room. Lieutenant Dunstan is expecting you."

The color scheme of off-white and teal prevailed in the waiting room, and group photos of the Radnor police in the 1900s hung on the walls, displayed like family portraits. In each one, tall white men stood in front of a woodsy backdrop, sporting handlebar mustaches and greatcoats.

"You must be Ms. Morrone," said a deep voice. I stood up and shook the hand of Lieutenant Dunstan, a tall white man with a handlebar mustache. I avoided the double-take.

"Uh, yes."

"Would you like some coffee? We can have Hankie here get you some." He waved at the receptionist, who looked up expectantly.

"No, thank you. I'd just like to see my client, Judge Hamilton."

"So you're the one. I read about you," he said, his tone convivial. His face was open and earnest, with large blue eyes and a smile that said, The policeman is your friend.

"How is the judge?"

"He's fine. Fine. He's back in his cell."

"You have him in a cell?"

"Where else would we put him?"

My inexperience, showing like a bra strap. "Is he in handcuffs?"

"No, we usually use the cell or the handcuffs, but not both. Belt and suspenders, don't you think?"

I thought I heard Hankie sniggering, but it could have been my imagination. "Judge Hamilton is a federal district judge. He doesn't need to be in a cell."

"He's also under arrest for first-degree murder, Ms. Morrone. We can't give him special treatment here."

Not with the press watching, anyway. "Is he in a cell with other . . . detainees?"

"Nope. He's by himself. Don't have a lot of violent crime here, you know. Lower Merion Township acts as a buffer between us and the city."

Thanks a lot, I lived in Lower Merion Township. "How many murders do you have here in, say, a year?"

"Not a one, usually. Only a couple murders in the last five years, if you don't count that reporter I killed this morning." He laughed and Hankie did, too.

"Justifiable homicide," I said, and they both laughed again. "By the way, how did the press find out about the arrest?"

"They have scanners on all the departments. They know as soon as we do, there's nothing we can do about it. We're putting out a press release now. It says Judge Hamilton's been charged with homicide in the stabbing death of Wayne resident Patricia Sullivan."

"Have you recovered the murder weapon?" I felt silly saying it, like in Clue. Was it Professor Plum with the pipe in the conservatory?

"No, and we looked. That's all she wrote, I should say, Hankie wrote. She's good at English. She does all the press releases." Dunstan seemed inclined to brag about Hankie for a spell, but I was in no mood to shoot the shit.

"Can I see Judge Hamilton?"

"Sure. Follow me." He led me down another white hallway, then opened a teal door onto a small white room. At the far end of the room was a counter with a small brown refrigerator on it that said EVIDENCE ONLY, and a vacant desk with a new blue Selectric. Next to the desk was a skinny wooden bench with steel handcuffs locked to its legs. The handcuffs seemed jarringly out of place in this corporate setting, until I realized they weren't. This was a jail, Fiske was imprisoned, and it wasn't funny anymore.

"What evidence do the police have to support the murder charge against Judge Hamilton, Lieutenant?"

His smile faded. "Didn't you get a copy of the criminal complaint, the affidavit of probable cause?"

"No."

"I'll get you another, the judge has his. But I can tell you we have a witness."

"Who saw what?"

"She saw his black Jaguar in the driveway at the carriage house at about the time the murder occurred."

"Judge Hamilton's is not the only black Jaguar in Wayne, Lieutenant."

"It's the only one with a license plate that says GARDEN-2. She saw that, too."

Oh, no. The vanity plate, of Kate's choosing; her plate said GARDEN-1. "The witness is sure it said GARDEN-2?"

He nodded. "She also saw him get into the car and drive away, fast."

"Did she identify Judge Hamilton?" I said, my heart sinking faster than I could professionally justify.

"Yes, from a photo array, and we asked the judge about it when we brought him in for questioning."

"You questioned the judge without a lawyer?"

"He waived his rights, I was present when he did it. He said he didn't need a lawyer, he had nothing to hide. We weren't satisfied with his alibi or his answers to some of our questions, so we charged him. We feel confident we have the right man, Ms. Morrone." He sounded genuinely regretful, and was almost becoming the first authority figure I ever liked.

"Who was this witness?"

"I can't get into the details with you. I'll bring you the affidavit just as soon as Hankie gets it copied up. Preliminary hearings take place within ten days."

"When is the arraignment?"

"The district justice will be here within the hour."

"Here? At the station?"

"We can hold arraignments here, especially with the press outside. I don't want to fight them off, do you?"

"But where's the courtroom?"

"There is none. We hold it right here." Then he opened a door off the room and there were three jail cells side by side. Two of the cells were empty, but sitting on a skinny bed in the middle cell was the Honorable Fiske Harlan Hamilton.

Fiske looked up when he saw me, and I caught a tense expression, quickly masked. "Rita, how good of you to come."

"Of course I'd come," I said, taken aback at the incongruity of the scene. I'd seen Fiske most often in his library, now he was in a prison cell.

I'd seen him in a judge's black robes, now he wore a prisoner's white paper jumpsuit. It seemed unreal.

"Judge Hamilton, you okay in there?" asked Lieutenant Dunstan.

"Fine, sir," Fiske said. "Will Rita be able to come in with me?"

Lieutenant Dunstan hesitated. "We don't normally allow that. It's more a security matter. You understand, the procedures and all."

"Understood, sir," Fiske said. "Thank you very much."

"I'll come fetch you when the district justice gets here," Dunstan said, and closed the door with a harsh *clang*.

We were alone. At a moment like this in the Morrone family, a display of Academy Award histrionics would have taken place, if not some respectable summer-stock hugging and weeping. But the Hamiltons were not the Morrones, there would be no Verdi in the background today. I stepped closer to the bars, but Fiske stood motionless behind an insignia for VAN DORN IRON WORKS. We regarded each other for a minute.

"Do you know *The Mikado*?" Fiske asked.

"Was Ann-Margret in it?"

" 'Here's a pretty mess,' " he sang.

Singing? I searched his face. Close up, he looked grim, in need of cheering up. "I'm gonna bust you outta here, Mr. Big."

"Yeah?" he said, playing along as well as good breeding allowed. "How?"

99

I held up my briefcase. "See dis? All you have to do is eat it. I baked a file inside."

"What a plan." He dropped the accent, so I did, too.

"You get what you pay for."

"Does this mean I have a criminal lawyer?"

"No, you're stuck with me."

He brightened. "Are you staying on? Truly? I want to pay you, you know. I insist on it."

"Forget it. I'm yours despite the fact that you called Mack on me."

"Perhaps I shouldn't have done that."

"No perhaps about it, Fiske."

He paused. "Did he tell you to represent me? Is that why you changed your mind?"

"I'm here on one condition. We have to have an agreement, you and I. You have to tell me the truth from now on. With everything, every detail, no matter how small. The very next lie, I'm outta here and you get a lawyer who knows what she's doing." It sounded less threatening than I'd hoped.

"I agree."

"Pinky swear?" I held up my pinky. "Hold up your finger. I make all my felons do it."

"I swear to God, Rita."

"That'll have to do. Now what do I do at the arraignment? Act like I know what I'm doing?"

"Yes."

"My specialty. Did you get this affidavit they're talking about? What's it say?"

He repeated what Dunstan had told me, about

100

the witness ID, the black Jaguar, and the license plate. Then he mentioned the fingerprints.

"What fingerprints?" I asked him, surprised.

He retrieved some papers from his bed and thrust them at me through the bars. "My fingerprints were found at Patricia's carriage house. In the living room."

Shit. I skimmed the affidavit, which stated in general terms what I already knew.

"You know why, Rita, I told you Patricia and I had met there once or twice. But I wasn't prepared to tell the police why my prints were there. That's when they decided to charge me."

Stupid. "Fiske, how could you let them question you without a lawyer?"

He stiffened. "I am a lawyer, and I didn't commit a murder. I had nothing to be afraid of, I didn't need anybody to hide behind. And it wasn't my car either. It couldn't have been."

"GARDEN-2? A vanity plate on a vanity car?"

"It's my plate, but it wasn't my car. I took my car to work that day. I parked it under the courthouse, in the secured lot. Nobody could have gotten it out but me."

"But Patricia was murdered at the end of the day and you took it out around five o'clock. The police were underwhelmed by your alibi."

He faltered. "I went for a drive. I told you that."

So fucking lame. "Work with me on this, would you?"

"But it's the truth, I swear it! I went for a

101

drive. I needed to think." His voice rose, and I considered the wisdom of discussing his alibi here. Or discussing it at all.

"We'll discuss it later," I said.

He ran a veined hand through silvered hair. "Does the press know about the witness?"

"I doubt it, but they know you've been arrested. They're outside right now. I tried to run them over but there were too many."

"So it's public."

"Very."

"I can't believe this, Rita," he said, then looked down at his hands. On each fingerpad was a black smudge. "This is a nightmare."

"Buck up. Your mug shot's got to be better than your driver's license. Now, we have to get you out of here. Then I want to cram criminal law. You can quiz me."

"No. We have to get to the carriage house. I want to see it."

"What do you mean?"

"We should view the crime scene as soon as possible."

I knew that. "Wait a minute, Fiske. First I plan to get you out of jail, then I plan to get you acquitted. How I get from point A to point B I haven't figured out."

He squeezed the iron bars like a born convict. "But the best way to prove me innocent is to catch the real killer."

"Take it a step at a time. I'll bail you out, then

I'll go to the crime scene. You'll go home and take care of Kate."

"But I should go with you."

"Would you take a client with you, in my position? Of course not. At least not initially."

"But—"

"I call the shots, Fiske," I said sharply. He looked startled, and I admit I startled even myself. I make it a point to question authority, but I'd never yelled at a federal judge. "Look, I may not know exactly what I'm doing, but I will soon. The only way we can work this case is if you take direction from me. You can't play my hand for me, got it?"

"Play your hand?" he said, in a way that made it sound stupid and vulgar.

"You heard me."

He lifted his strong chin slightly. "But you won't mind if I give you my thoughts, from time to time."

"Your thoughts are welcome, your orders aren't. My job is to run the case. Your job is to tell the truth, smile for the camera, and get back to work. You're not stepping down from the bench, are you?"

"No. The Constitution applies to me as well."

"Fine."

"And I am innocent. Do you believe that?"

Sure, except for the witness ID and the license plate. "I'm going to get you acquitted. Isn't that enough?"

"No."

"It'll have to be."

"But how can you get me acquitted if you don't believe in me?"

"I'll act like I do and play the cards as they fall."

He looked puzzled.

"You don't play poker, do you, Fiske?"

"You know chess is my game. I dislike gambling, all games of chance."

"Get over it. It's time for the short course."

He looked none too pleased.

12

After depositing Fiske at home with a distraught Kate, I went to Patricia's. The carriage house was at the back of a property of at least six wooded acres, set well behind the main house, a white stucco mansion. A winding, paved driveway led from the street through the trees to the carriage house, a tiny clapboard cottage, painted ivory with blue trim. Just the sort of place that would appeal to artists, lovers, and plaintiffs.

I eyeballed the distance from the carriage house to the mansion. A hundred yards. Then the distance from the carriage house to the street. Seventy-five yards, through the trees. The driveway curved close to the back of the main house at only one point. A witness standing at the street or in the house would be able to spot a Jaguar, but would have a harder time identifying its driver with absolute certainty, especially in the downpour we'd had yesterday. I wondered who the witness was. I resolved to visit the owner of the main house as soon as I could.

I looked back at the carriage house. It stood two stories tall and was almost obscured by the grove of oak trees surrounding it. Its first floor was an ivy-covered garage, and a runner of English ivy over the door told me it hadn't been opened in a while. Maybe Patricia used the garage for storage. I flashed on the painting she testified about at her deposition, the one of me and Paul. Maybe she kept her canvases in the garage.

"Can I get a look in the garage, too?" I asked my baby-sitter, Officer Johanssen. Until the police released the crime scene, Lieutenant Dunstan had decreed I'd need an escort to inspect it, even outside. And each visit had to be logged in, recorded.

"Yes," Johanssen said.

We walked past the garage and around to the left, to a slate patio where the front door was tucked under a white trellis covered with purple clematis. The door was in good condition, except that its blue paint was alligatored with age and water. How did the killer get in?

105

"The door doesn't look damaged, does it?" I wondered aloud, intentionally.

Johanssen said nothing and took a key with a white tag on it from his pocket.

"Were you one of the officers on the scene, right after the murder?"

"No."

"Have you ever been here before?"

"No."

A buff Viking with a dark tan, the cop would make a terrific sperm donor if the egg brought the personality. He jiggled the key in the lock, pursing his lower lip. If I hadn't been there, I suspect he would have cursed. Finally the door swung open, revealing an entrance hall furnished simply, with a painted side table and a carved wooden lamp. A set of colored pencils sat on the table next to a stiff spray of dried pink statice.

"I guess the living quarters are upstairs," I said.

"Here are the stairs," Johanssen said. He walked to the left and I followed.

The stairway was narrow and uncarpeted. Johanssen trod heavily in his black shoes and the stairs groaned with each foot-fall. It was easier for me to watch his heels than to look up to the top of the stairs, wondering what I was going to find. Halfway up I had my answer, because of the smell. A smell I remembered from my childhood. I'd grown up with the scent of blood in the butcher shop, but this blood didn't smell like an animal's. It smelled different, primitive as menses. The hot air was thick with it. I felt queasy and leaned on the wooden banister.

Johanssen reached the top of the stairs and looked back over his shoulder. "Miss?"

"I'm coming." I swallowed my rising gorge and willed myself to climb higher.

What I saw at the top of the stairs horrified me. Patricia's living room, which also served as a studio, had been ransacked. Pencil sketches on white paper lay scattered across the unvarnished hardwood floor. Yellow tracing paper, curled at both edges, was strewn everywhere. A wooden easel had been knocked to the ground; it had a photograph of a meadow taped to it and held a canvas with a similar landscape. The painting had been slashed and there was blood splattered on the tear. Sunlight poured in through Palladian windows, illuminating the room obscenely.

"My God," I heard myself say.

"Remember, don't touch anything," Johanssen said. His eyes were focused on the right side of the room and his affect was flat. I followed his gaze.

A white line was taped to the floor like a Keith Haring outline. It was a jumble of arms and legs, as askew and berserk as the studio itself. No human, no woman, could lie in such a fashion. The neck was twisted back on itself. In the center of the figure, spreading over the hardwood floor, was a thin pool of blood, oddly a bright shade of red. Its primal scent was overpowered by a stronger odor.

"What is that smell?" I said, talking out loud, but Johanssen didn't reply. I stepped back, because whatever it was made my eyes sting slightly. A solvent, turpentine. I looked over and saw a clear liquid running like a tributary from an upended coffee can. It flowed into the pool of blood and the two fluids commingled grotesquely, so the blood stayed red, oxygen-rich. I recoiled from the sight and smell, almost slipping on a paintbrush as I stepped back.

"Miss?" Johanssen said.

"I'm okay," I said, regaining my footing if not my composure. I walked toward the window, where one of the screens was open. Outside was an expanse of grass in dappled sunshine, and the weathered slate roof of the main house peeked through the tree-tops. The air smelled fragrant and clean and I closed my eyes, inhaling deeply. Was Fiske capable of such savagery, especially toward a woman he loved?

"You done here?" Johanssen asked.

"No. I want to see everything." I had to.

We left the room and crossed the landing at the top of the stairs. Straight ahead was a galley kitchen that was undisturbed. A porcelain mug sat on a gray counter next to some dirty dishes. Nothing seemed out of the ordinary.

I peeked into the bathroom next to the kitchen. It was tiny, with a maid's sink and an old-fashioned tub with claw-and-ball feet. Everything was in order, down to the loofah stuck between the tub and the tile wall. Except for the toilet seat.

Its ring was up. Odd. Would a killer use the toilet? I wondered if the police had noticed, or if you had to be a woman to notice when the seat's been left up.

"The bedroom's here," Johanssen said, and I walked to the doorway.

It was beautiful. A queen-size bed with a lacy spread, in a disarray that looked sweet instead of merely unmade. The sheets were a soft, unbleached cotton, as were the pillows. Against the wall on the right was an oak bureau covered by a lace runner. "I guess there was no struggle in here," I said.

Johanssen said nothing for a change.

Against the far wall were windows with white lace curtains and a blanket chest stood between them. To the left was a bookshelf, but there were no clues announcing themselves anywhere. "Are there any other rooms, Officer?"

"No."

"Then I think I'd like to see the living room again."

"Suit yourself."

I tried to look at the room like a professional, now that the initial shock had worn off. I took a small legal pad from my purse and began to make notes. The blood didn't seem to fall in any particular pattern or spatter. It seemed likely that Patricia had been attacked in the studio, perhaps while painting, and had been stabbed there. I had no support for it, but it looked as if the killer had wrecked the place in a rage, possibly drug-or alcohol-induced, or in a struggle. I wondered if the cops had any theories.

"Looks like a struggle," I said, to no cop in particular.

Johanssen didn't reply.

Real helpful. I considered reminding the cop that I was a tax-payer and the least he could do was throw me a bone, but thought better of it. It wouldn't be very detectivey, begging for hints and all.

I stepped over to a shelf to the right of the room. Sketchbooks and pads flopped over on the shelves, next to a cigar box of pencils. Messy black smudges covered almost all of the surfaces around me. "Is this dusting for fingerprints?"

Johanssen nodded.

Hey, I was in the zone. I moved closer to the bookshelf. Untouched, except for the fingerprint dust, was a massive wooden paintbox that sat open on top of the bookshelf. It looked expensive, so I guessed this was the paintbox Fiske had bought Patricia. It was three trays deep and laden with silver tubes of oil paint. Cadmium Red, Prussian Blue, Viridian, said the black labels, and each tube had been squeezed in the middle like the nightmare tube of Crest, travel size.

But the paintbox hadn't been harmed. It seemed strange, especially if it was Fiske who had killed Patricia and ransacked the place. Wouldn't he have destroyed his expensive gift? And was the studio ransacked before or after she was killed? Was the killer looking for something? I stepped back and heard the rustle of paper underfoot.

"Watch out," Johanssen said. "We're not finished with the scene yet."

"Sorry." I reddened. Joe Cool at the crime scene, tripping over Exhibit A. I looked down at my feet, expecting yet another depiction of flowers in May, but I was wrong. Underneath my pump was a sketch of a young black man.

Nude.

I looked closer. He was reclining on some sort of sheet, and his handsome face, framed by short dreadlocks, was turned directly toward the artist. His body was young and strong; muscular shoulders,a broad chest, and nipples were suggested by delicate lines of black india ink. His hips looked bulky and powerful, and one leg was up, discreetly concealing what lay beneath his flat stomach. I wondered who he was and whether he was real or imaginary. I made a note to find out.

I glanced at the other sketches. All of them were fruits or flowers—peonies, cosmos, rudbeckia— like a Burpee's catalog in pencil. But I learned more about Patricia from the erotic drawing than I did from all the leggy cosmos, and I took the time to look at each painting, as well as the unfinished canvases that she had leaning against the wall. Then I remembered another unfinished canvas.

"Officer, can we see that garage now?" I asked.
"Yes."

I led the way down the stairs, relieved to leave the bloody scene behind, and walked ahead of Johanssen while he locked the front door. I made a note about the distance from the driveway to the mansion and confirmed my original conclusion that the witness's identification of the judge could be attacked. Except for that license plate part.

It gave me another unwanted thought, one I'd dismissed when I'd seen Kate at the house, looking so upset. Kate drove a black Jaguar, she had an almost identical license plate. And she had a motive—her anger at Patricia for bringing the lawsuit. If she knew about the affair, she'd have an even stronger motive. It sounded crazy, but could Kate have done it? And did I want to exonerate Fiske only to put Kate on the hook?

"Must not have used the lock," Johanssen said to himself, as he struggled to lock the front door.

"But she wouldn't leave the door unlocked." A woman, living alone? No way.

The lock fell into place. "Let's go," Johanssen said, and led me around the house to the front, where the avaricious ivy crept over the left side of the garage door. Johanssen tipped his hat back and frowned. "You really have to do this, lady?"

"Yep."

"This real important to the defense?"

"I doubt it, but the alternative is reading cases."

He looked at me sideways, then back at the door. "Must be manual."

"What?"

"The door." He bent over and gripped a rusty handle on the bottom of the garage door. It opened after four hard yanks, and a bare lightbulb in the ceiling shone down on the damndest thing. A motorcycle. It was a shiny turquoise blue with bright chrome pipes underneath and a leathery black seat. So Patricia had a motorcycle. There was no car in sight. I filed this piece of information and looked around the musty garage.

"Well, will you look at that?" Johanssen said with sudden animation, and glommed on to the bike as if pulled into its gravitational field. "It's a BMW."

"I didn't know BMW made motorcycles," I said idly.

"BMW? Are you kidding? They've been making them for years, since World War II. They made them for Rommel, the first shaft-drive bikes. He needed them because the sand from North Africa, it got in the chains on the old bikes. Abraded them. Motoguzzi copied it, and by the eighties everybody had the drive shaft."

"Really?" Like I care. Against the cinderblock wall of the garage was a shelf with tins of painting supplies, slim cans of brush cleaner, and linseed oil. So Patricia did keep her painting stuff in here.

Johanssen wolf-whistled. "Jeez, this is a 750."

"A 750?" I asked, keeping him distracted so he wouldn't see me snooping. "What does that mean?"

"Seven hundred and fifty cubic centimeters.

The displacement, the size of the engine. Like the horsepower in a car."

"Interesting." To others. I walked by the motorcycle to the other side of the garage. In the light from the window I could make out some suitcases, a pink steamer trunk, and some papers against the wall.

"My bike's a Honda," Johanssen said. "It's only a 550. They don't even make it anymore. They start at 650 now."

"I guess there's nothing down here," I said, trying to sound disappointed. "She must've used the garage for storage." I walked over to the cardboard boxes and peeked under one of the flaps, which was slightly damp. Inside was a pile of wool skirts and pullover sweaters. "Just a lot of old winter clothes. I wouldn't put my sweaters in an open box, would you?"

Johanssen shook his blond head over the bike. "Five hundred ccs just isn't enough, especially on an on-ramp when you need the acceleration."

Terrific. My usual communication with men. I walked softly to the steamer trunk. "I would never leave wool in a garage where the moths could get it, would you?"

"No. Half the time, the cars don't see you. That's the leading cause of motorcycle accidents, poor visibility of the bike. That's why you need the power, for maneuvering. You have to drive defensively on a bike."

"You know how I store my sweaters, Officer?" The latch on the trunk was a mottled brass. I

114

lifted it quietly with my best fingernail. "I get each one dry-cleaned, then I store it in the plastic bag they give you. You know the ones I mean?"

"Yeah. Lotta power in this baby. Lotta power." He squatted on his haunches to drool on the chrome pipes. "This needs a belly cowling. I'd put a belly cowling on it if it were mine."

"Then, after I have each sweater in its own individual bag, I slip in a couple of mothball crystal packets, the kind that come with the lavender sachets." Inside the steamer trunk was a slew of paperback books, Grateful Dead albums, old shoes, and sketchbooks. "You know the sachets I mean? The lavender? Purple?"

"Blue is nice. I think it comes in red, too. Like a maroon." His voice came from behind the motorcycle.

"This way you don't get that mothball smell in your clothes, you know what I mean?" Under the paperbacks were a bunch of spiral composition books. "I hate that mothball smell, don't you? I'll take lavender any day."

"Sure. And black. *Black* is something else. If I were gonna spring for one of these babies, I'd get the black."

"Black is nice," I said supportively, and closed the trunk. Behind it was a workbench made out of a door resting across two sawhorses. On top of the door were coffee cans and jars filled with paintbrushes and painter's knives, and a stack of small sketchbooks. Underneath were canvases, their rough white edges sticking out from between the sawhorse. Maybe the portrait of Paul and me was among them.

Johanssen had been quiet for some time, so I checked over my shoulder. He sat astride the motorcycle with his eyes closed. At least he wasn't making engine sounds. Not out loud, anyway.

I bent down and flipped through some of the canvases. More wildflowers, one after the other, then a portrait of the young black man, again nude. He stood and faced the artist almost obscenely. I passed by it quickly. There were three other canvases, each of different nude men. Patricia had a wild side, all right, despite her cherubic appearance.

I glanced back at Johanssen. His eyes were closed in orgasm. Again, mercifully silent.

I flipped over to the next canvas and swallowed hard. I was looking at a gorgeous portrait from our Bermuda trip. Paul was sunburned under the moongate, his jacket an idealized white. The garden behind us was lush, the sky shone a faultless blue. The only part unfinished was me. My face was barely sketched in, like a ghost.

"Find anything?" Johanssen asked. He was standing behind the motorcycle looking at me.

Bluff, girl. "Yes. Some beautiful paintings. I love art, don't you?"

"It's okay."

"You should really see this one, Officer. It's lovely. A still life of some Gerber daisies in a vase. You can see each brushstroke. Come on over and see."

116

"Uh, Gerber daisies?"

"Thick stems, a big bloom. Pinks, oranges, yellows. So perfect, so real. You'd love them. Come see."

"I guess I'm not a real good art fan," he called out, walking around the back of the motorcycle. "But my wife, she likes art. She grew up in Chadds Ford, so she likes Wyeth and those Brandywine guys. Sure is a nice bike."

"I like Wyeth, too, some of those meadows he did. And the snow scenes. I love those, don't you?" I flipped the portrait back in place and straightened up. I grabbed one of the small sketchbooks and quickly paged through it. They were pencil drawings of nude men, black men and white men, short men and tall men. The second sketchbook was more of the same, and I felt myself sweating by the third sketchbook, not knowing what I'd find. "Remember the Helga paintings?" I called out.

"Yepper, maybe I'd go with the maroon. I could live with the maroon. I bet I could pick one up, used. That shop in Montgomeryville, they'd have it."

I opened the cardboard cover of the third sketchbook and froze on the spot. It was a sketch of Paul. His eyes were closed, in sleep, on a lacy bed. He was naked, with a sheet draped carelessly over his thighs. I wanted to cry out but didn't.

"Maybe I should ask for it for Christmas?" Johanssen said.

I felt stunned. "Uh . . . worth a try."

117

"We could take long trips together. She's always saying we don't spend enough time, just the two of us. Be good for our marriage."

"Sure. Sounds like it." As if I knew what was good for a marriage. I tore through the other sketchbooks. Paul wasn't in any of them, but the young black man was, the one with the short dreadlocks. I returned to the drawing of Paul, holding the sketchbook in my hand. Deciding what to do with it.

"Yes sir," he said, and rocked back and forth on his heels. "I think I'll put it on my Christmas list."

"Good idea." I wanted to throw the sketchbook across the room, but I did something smarter. I shoved it into my purse.

"Can't blame a guy for trying," Johanssen said. Oh no? Watch me.

13

I almost came to understand Fiske's alibi because I drove for the next full hour with the convertible top down and the sketchbook in the backseat of the car. Hot summer air whipped my hair around and makeup melted off my face, but I didn't care how I looked. I didn't even care where I went. I just drove. Fast. Very fast.

That I got no speeding ticket is a miracle, but

that I did not rack up the car and kill myself stands to reason. First, I would never do that to my car. Second, I am not one of those women who turns her anger inward, the suicide prototype. I am quite proficient in turning it outward, and regard this as an improvement on the old-fashioned, Valium-taking, feminine-mystique model. After all, it wasn't me I wanted to kill, it was Paul.

For the first twenty-five miles or so, I actually considered this. How to commit murder, how to get away with it. You would think the fact that I had just examined a gory crime scene would counsel against my homicidal ruminations, but the opposite was true. It gave me a kind of permission. See, other people do it, you can, too. Like cheating on your in-home office deduction.

It took me thirty more miles to pass through the acutely felonious stage, but by mile fifty-five I had just enough high-octane bile left to make good company, so I roared home. I pulled into the driveway behind Paul's Cherokee, spraying its gleaming finish with gravel. I cut the ignition, grabbed the sketchbook, and slammed the car door, regretting only this last act. I never slam the car door, I care for my car. It pissed me off so much that when I got in the front door to the house, I slammed it so hard that the windows on either side rattled in their glazier's points and Paul came running downstairs into the entrance hall.

"Rita!" he said. His alarmed expression

reflected how deranged I must have looked, with my crayoned eyes, shiny face, and hair styled by Cuisinart.

"What's the matter, Paul? Don't I look like the woman you want to marry?" I did a model's pirouette and wobbled not at all.

"You look . . . fine."

I eyed him up and down in his pressed pants, black rayon shirt, and silk print tie. "So do you. All for me?"

"I was at Mom and Dad's. The police came and searched the house, the closets, even the garage. It took all afternoon to put everything back together. They took Dad's car, too. Where have you been?"

I brandished the sketchbook. "Tell me, does this look familiar?"

"I don't understand."

"But then again, maybe you don't recognize it. You were sleeping, as I remember. You must have been so exhausted."

"Rita, are you okay?"

"Why? Don't I look okay?"

"Well, you look a little—"

"Crazy?" I said crazily.

"No, but—"

"Boo!"

He took a step backward.

"Well, I'm not. Crazy, that is. I may drive a little too fast, I may bet a little too hard, and I may be committing malpractice on a murder case, but I am definitely not crazy." I held the sketchbook higher, like the Statue of Liberty on Ritalin. "I thought you were cheating on me and I was not crazy. I thought you gave me a virus and I was not crazy." I advanced on him with the book in the air. "Your Honor, may I approach the witness?"

"Honey—"

"Don't honey me," I said, which is something I always wanted to say. Then I took aim and hurled the sketchbook directly at his face. He shouted and his arms went up protectively—he was always so good at net—so the book bounced off his fingers and hit another of his treasured watercolors, knocking it askew. He looked over his shoulder at the painting, then back at me angrily.

"What is going on here?" he asked sternly.

"Pick up the fucking book and look at it! Chapter One is you asleep naked. Chapter Two is you asleep naked. Chapter Three is you asleep naked, too, so the book is not what you'd call plot-driven. Don't you just *hate* literary fiction?"

He didn't reply, and plucked the book from our pretentious carpet.

"It would help if you'd gotten up and done something, Paul. Poured coffee, made a drink. Nuzzled her ear, cleaned her brushes. But I guess you did clean her brushes. You must have or I wouldn't have this fucking virus."

He opened the tan cover of the book, then slowly turned the pages one by one.

"Now, you piece of shit, you have one minute

to tell me why you did this to me. Then you can pack your fucking bags and get out."

He couldn't meet my eye.

"Forty seconds." Boy, I felt as good as you can feel when you catch your lover cheating on you. "*Thirty* seconds."

"I can explain," he said quietly, still looking at the book.

"So can I. You're a piece of shit. A tall shit, a very handsome shit, but a shit just the same."

"That's not helpful, Rita."

"Fuck you! I'm not trying to be helpful!" I took off my jacket and threw it down on the rug. I cannot explain why I did this, except there was nothing left in my hands to throw. Paul watched my rage striptease with a sort of horrified confusion, then held up a hand.

"Stop," he said. "Just stop."

"In the name of love?"

"I had an affair."

"No shit, Sherlock! I may not know *The Mikado*, but I'm smarter than I look."

"That's not what I mean."

I found myself pacing. "Granted, sometimes you have to draw me a picture. Lots of them. Color would have helped, but I recognized you right off. I said to myself, I know that guy. He's the one who keeps asking me to marry him. That's what you wanted, right? A commitment? Give me a fucking break!"

"Do you want to listen to me or do you want to curse at me?"

"I want to curse at you, you asshole!" I was spitting at him as I yelled, and I did not care that this was unattractive. "And when I'm done cursing at you, I want you to pack your bags!"

"You said you'd listen."

"You had ten seconds and you blew them." I started to leave the room, but Paul grabbed my arm from behind.

"Rita, wait."

"Get off of me!" I wrenched my arm free. "Don't you dare. Don't you dare touch me." My whole body shook.

"Do you want to know why it happened?"

"You should be on your knees, begging me. You should be begging and saying you're sorry and groveling at my feet." I heard my voice grow thick. "Begging and saying you're sorry."

He sighed and stepped back.

I sighed, too, but only because I sounded so dumb. I didn't want to sound dumb, or be helpless. A victim. I wiped my eyes. We were silent for a minute.

"Why don't you sit down?" he said.

"Why don't you shut up?"

"I'll get you some water." Paul went to the kitchen, where I heard the cabinet door open and close and the water go on. By the time he came back with a tumbler in his hand, my body had stopped shaking. "Here," he said, but I only glared at him in response, so he set the heavy tumbler on the dining room table and sat down at one end. "May I explain now?"

123

I plopped into a chair at the other end. Between us was a runway of mahogany, a crystal vase of white roses, and the wreckage of our life together. "Don't ask me for permission. You didn't before."

He nodded. "The affair is over."

"Of course it is. She's dead."

"It ended a few months ago. It lasted about six months."

My stomach twisted. "So your father was sleeping with her at the same time? That's disgusting. That's *sick*!"

"I didn't know about that, about him. I broke up with her as soon as I found out."

So. "Does your father know?"

"No. Never. It was a game for her, just a game."

"What was it for you?"

He suppressed whatever he was going to say, then looked away. "I was unhappy."

It hurt inside, his saying it out loud. "You didn't say so, you dick."

He winced. "I didn't know until this happened. I didn't know why it started or why it ended until it was all over. Then she wanted me to come back to her, she said she was sorry, that it was over with him. That's when she filed the lawsuit."

"For sexual harassment?"

"She wanted to prove to me that she didn't care about him. That she loved me. So I would come back."

Jesus. "Why didn't you tell me that? It would have destroyed her case."

"Tell you? As Dad's lawyer or as my lover?"

Touché. I sipped some water. "So how did it start?"

"I met her at a sidewalk show. She wanted to know about design, and we talked. She called me later. It just happened. It was wrong. I should have told you I was unhappy."

"But you didn't have the balls."

He looked up sharply. "No. I didn't know then. I know now. I'm telling you now."

"Only because I found out."

"But I want to deal with it. Let's see what we have left. I can, Rita. Can you?"

Fuck you. I wanted to throw the glass right in his face, but I went one better. "She had other lovers, Paul. A regular United Nations."

"I know that. I told you, it was all a game with her. She was addicted to it, the excitement. She was self-destructive—"

"What a bunch of crap. You wouldn't have broken up with her if you hadn't found out about your father."

He leaned forward. "When I found out about my father was when I finally understood her. Knew who she really was, what was really happening. When the fantasy was over, what was left was a very empty, very damaged woman. And I wanted you."

Right. "How did you find out about your father?"

125

"I saw a photo from our Bermuda trip. Look, Rita, I'm sorry," he said, raking back his hair in a gesture uncannily like Fiske's. "I'll make it up to you, I swear it. I know why it happened. I didn't have enough of you, of your time. We need more time together."

"Maybe we should buy a motorcycle."

He looked at me like I was crazy. "Listen, you're always running, going off to work. And then there's poker. No matter what, you go."

"Don't you pin this on me! Take some fucking responsibility, would you? You cheated on me because I play poker? Because I work my ass off? It's not my fault you were running around!"

"It's not about fault, Rita."

"That's what people always say when it's their fault!" I saw a blur then, a kind of madness rising in my eyes, and I couldn't see anything else. I stood up. "*You* cheated and it's *my* fault? Are you crazy? Are you stone fucking *crazy*?"

He rubbed his forehead. "You don't get it."

"The hell I don't. You slept with her, you were living with me at the time. We're practically engaged—"

"Practically? That's the whole problem right there in a nutshell. We're either engaged or we're not!"

"Thank God I didn't marry you! Thank God that is one mistake I did not make! Now go pack your bags."

He looked as if I'd slapped him. "You don't mean this."

"I do too. I'll be back in two hours. Be gone by then. Leave your keys on the table." I turned on my heel and walked out of the room.

"Rita. Rita, wait. Listen," he said, but I kept walking. One foot in front of the other, out the front door.

My knees buckled slightly when I got outside, but I walked across the dry lawn and didn't fall, and didn't cry. My heart was a tight knot at the center of my chest. I strode to the car and got in, careful to close the door gently. I pulled out of the driveway and drove the speed limit to Lancaster Avenue. And I did not drive aimlessly, I knew just where I was going.

On the way I made a phone call to Fiske, whom I hadn't even called about the murder scene, so preoccupied was I with my personal life. I told him tersely what I'd seen, but not about Patricia's erotic renderings of the NFL or of his own son. He didn't have to know about that. And not from me.

I wondered how my father would react to the news, but I figured he'd handle it okay if I didn't spell out the cheating part. And if I told him about the virus, he'd take his sharpest cleaver and geld the man. I laughed to myself until I thought about what Paul said. About my not being home.

I pointed the car toward the city, and it struck me for the first time how strange it was that I had no friends my own age. No women friends, even close friends among my partners. We used to make lunch dates, but a deposition or trial would come up. Soon I'd stopped penciling anybody in. I realized I was speeding and eased off the gas.

I reached the Italian Market, but a sawhorse blocked Eighth Street about a block from my father's shop. The traffic was clogged and confused. A siren blared close by, and a blue-shirted Philly cop with a thick gut was waving a line up of overheated drivers down Christian Street. No way was I doing that. It would take me an extra twenty minutes to double back to the butcher shop, then another twenty to find a parking space. How would I get to cry on my father's shoulder by dinnertime?

I stopped my car in front of the cop and opened the window. "Can't I get over to Ninth, Officer?"

He shook his head and waved me on. "Not tonight. Keep it moving, lady."

"But I'll be late if I take the detour."

"You can't get through. There was a shooting and the perp took off. You wanna run into him?"

"A shooting? Where?"

"Lady—"

I felt my pulse quicken. "On Ninth? My father has a butcher shop on Ninth."

He looked down at me. "Which one?"

"Morrone's. The little one."

His face fell. "Pull over, honey," he said quietly, and waved the other cars past me.

14

"Right this way," said a woman cop, as she led me down a corridor in the basement of the hospital.

I felt drained. I had cried all the tears I could cry. My head was pounding. The only way to get through it was not to experience it. Keep it at a distance. And my emotions, too.

"You okay, Rita?" the cop asked, turning back as she walked. She had short brown hair, tight features, and no makeup. A hard face but for the kindness in her expression.

"Fine."

"It'll be over soon."

She picked up the pace and I followed. The floor slanted down, like a ramp. Down, then doubling back, and going farther down. We reached the very bottom of the hospital and passed through a wide brown door that swung shut behind us. MORGUE, said a sign on the door.

"Hey, Jim," the cop said to a man in a white coat like a butcher's. "You ready for us?"

I stood behind the cop to shield myself from the room. A formaldehyde stink filled my nose. The air was chilled. A chalkboard hung on the wall and it read, inexplicably: HEART, RT. LUNG, LT. LUNG, LIVER, SPLEEN, RT. KIDNEY, LT. KIDNEY, BRAIN, PANCREAS, SPLEEN, THYROID.

"All set," said the man, who stood beside a long table made of dull stainless steel. The table had slats across the bottom and a large round drain peeked from underneath them. I didn't want to think about what went down the drain. Next to the table was a scale with a steel tray hanging underneath its clocklike face. A butcher's scale.

"Cold in here," the cop said.

The man in white wanted to reply but thought better of it. He punched up his steel glasses with a deft movement, his arm a clinical blur of white.

"You want another Coke, Rita?" asked the cop.

I shook my head. No. This wasn't happening. None of it was happening. The man left for the adjoining room. There was the sound of a door being unlatched, a metallic *ca-chunk*, then a heavy *slam* as it sealed shut. I knew those noises from the shop. It was a freezer.

The man reappeared pushing a gurney. A steel bar surrounded the gurney and a black tarp was slung between the bars. On the tarp rested a white nylon bag with a zipper down the middle. The white bag was lumpy and formless. Smaller than I expected. I hadn't realized he was so short. Oh God.

"Why do I have to do this?" I asked them, fighting not to cry. "We know it's him. It has to be him. They saw."

The cop touched my shoulder. "It's procedure," she said.

"Actually, it's state law," said the man in white. He began to unzip the bag with a care that suggested he feared something would catch on the inside.

I covered my mouth and turned away. Behind me was a black counter and underneath it a bank of ugly green cabinets. The zippering sound reverberated off the cold walls. Then the noise stopped suddenly and there was silence.

"Miss?" said a professional voice. The man in white.

I wondered how many times he'd said this, and to whom. To mothers and fathers and daughters and friends. *Miss?* Look at the body of someone you loved. Or someone you know. Or someone you hardly knew but who has no one else to mourn him, or even to identify his remains. *Miss?*

"Is this him, miss?"

I made myself turn back.

It was a dark face that shone under the harsh white light, framed by the white body bag. He looked like a black child, sleeping in a snowy receiving blanket. He was a black child.

"Is this LeVonne Jenkins?" the man asked.

No, it's not LeVonne. LeVonne was only in tenth grade, so it can't be him. It shouldn't be him. I nodded, yes.

And began to cry.

Later, I waited in the ultramodern waiting room with my head against the cold glass wall, slouching in a mauve chair that promised more

131

comfort than it gave. The waiting room was empty except for a TV, and *Rescue 911* was returning from commercial. A woman, drowning, screamed for help. I felt raw inside, exhausted. I drew my jacket closer around my shoulders.

The operation had started an hour ago, and they told me it would be a long one. Difficult. A surgeon gave me the odds, like a gambler, and they weren't good. I picked up a battered magazine from the glass coffee table, looking for distraction. *Highlights*, a children's magazine. Hippos wearing Hawaiian leis danced across the cover, at an animal luau. I opened the magazine.

At midpage was a comic strip. GOOFUS AND GALLANT, said the title. In the panel, a young boy climbed a set of porch steps. In the middle of the steps was a roller skate. *Goofus leaves his toys on the step*, said the caption. The next panel showed another young boy rolling a bike down the sidewalk, heading for the garage. *Gallant puts his bicycle away, so no one trips over it.*

I got it. You could have a lobotomy and still get it.

I looked up. Nothing was there, except a face. Not *Rescue 911* or the chairs or the receptionist at a desk in the hallway. Just his face.

In life it was the face of a young boy, growing into a man. A boy with none of the glaring faults of a lout like Goofus, a boy with none of the bogus suburban qualities of Gallant. A boy who would have burst into laughter at the absurdity of Goofus and Gallant, even though he was a boy

132

who rarely burst into laughter. Who would have learned nothing from this inane pair, and who could have taught them volumes. I threw the *Highlights* across the room, startling the receptionist.

LeVonne.

LeVonne had died at the hospital almost as soon as they wheeled him off the ambulance. Two bullets had torn through his chest, one shearing the aorta. If my father lived through his operation, the first thing he would do is ask about LeVonne. Then the news would kill him.

"Rita," called a man's voice.

I looked up. Herman Meyer was thundering into the waiting room, in madras shorts and a thin white T-shirt. A bewildered Uncle Sal scurried next to him, almost identically dressed, supported by Herman's tanned arm. Cam Lopo was right behind them, holding a bouquet of sprayed mums. I got up to meet them and hugged Sal, whose bony back felt like a wren's in my embrace.

"He's gonna be all right, isn't he?" Sal asked.

"What happened?" Herman said. "They operating?"

"What'd they say?" Cam asked.

I released Sal and regained my composure. It was almost worse, their being here. Seeing how upset they were, Uncle Sal especially. "I don't know more than I told you on the phone. He got shot in the chest, it hit his pulmonary vein. They're going to stitch him up."

"You said nicked it, on the phone. Nicked it. That doesn't sound too bad," Sal said.

Jesus. How to prepare him? I couldn't even prepare myself. "It's a serious injury. He'd lost a lot of blood by the time they got him here."

"All I know is, they better catch the guy who did this to him," Cam said.

Sal blinked sadly. "He killed LeVonne. I can't believe it."

Herman shook his head. "The bastard. If the cops don't get him, I will. I swear it." They stood together, forming an aged phalanx of determination, but I didn't want to think about retribution just yet.

"Let's hope Dad gets better," I said.

Herman nodded. "Right, first things first. Did you see the resident yet?"

"No."

He scowled. "He shoulda been here. Or one of the fellows at least."

"What fella?" Sal asked, looking up nervously at Herman.

Cam gave me a hug, the flowers went around my back. "Rita, honey. How you holdin' up? We woulda been here before, but Herman wanted to get flowers. So stupid, flowers." He stepped back and tossed the stiff bouquet onto the coffee table but it rolled off the edge and onto the rug.

"Camille, what are you doin' throwin' the flowers around?" Herman said. He bent over with a grunt and retrieved the bouquet.

"Since when you care so much about flowers?"

Herman brushed off the mums. "They're Vito's flowers, not yours. Don't throw them on the ground."

"Vito don't even like flowers," Cam said.

"Get outta here, look in the shop window." Herman's voice rose. "Vito, he's got a plant, right there in the window. A green plant."

"Where?"

"In the window, you seen it. Under the pig."

"Which pig?"

"The pig, the pig—there's only one pig."

Cam stepped back. "Vito don't have no plant in the window."

"You wanna bet? He's got a plant right there in the window."

"What is it with you tonight? Flowers and plants. What is it with you?" Cam said, but I was coming to understand what was with them. If they were old women, they would have wept. But they were old men, so they bickered.

"Bet me, Camille," Herman said. "I need the money. I wanna go to the Deauville this winter like my brother." He turned to me. "Doesn't he, Rita? Doesn't your father keep a plant in the window?"

"I don't remember."

Herman stamped his orthopedic shoe. "You remember. The front window. Underneath the pig. With the tail goes like a curlicue."

"No," Uncle Sal said, sinking slowly into a chair. "No plant."

"See? No plant!" Cam said.

Herman shook his head. "What's Sal know? He don't know."

But I was watching my uncle, who was muttering to himself. Cam heard it, too, and we exchanged a look. "What'd you say, Sallie?" Cam asked, bending over and putting a knobby hand on Sal's shoulder.

"No plant," he said again.

Cam patted him. "Okay, Sal, we got it. No plant. If you say there's no plant, there's no plant."

Uncle Sal didn't seem to hear. "In the window Vito got a sign about the fresh sausage homemade daily," he said, counting on spindly fingers. "Then he got a picture of Rita at her college graduation, then he got a little stand-up calendar from the insurance company, then he got a sign about we accept food stamps, then he got a donkey made out of straw with a hat on his head. The hat is straw, too." He reached five fingers, then began knitting and reknitting his hands. "And there's no flies in the window 'cause Vito don't like that, when they have flies in the windowsills. It shows it's not a clean shop, Vito says."

Cam sank slowly into the chair next to Sal and put his arm around him.

"Pop used to say the same thing," Sal said. "No flies."

I realized then that Uncle Sal would surely die if my father did, like a domino effect, starting with LeVonne. One after the other in tragic succession.

Only Herman had any heart left. "Still no resident? Who's running this place, nuns?" He turned on his heel and locomoted to the receptionist in a wobbly beeline. The three of us watched numbly as he barked at her, then hustled back. "This place stinks," he said, even before he reached us. "They don't tell you nothing here. Now Hahnemann University, that's a hospital. My nephew, Cheryl's boy, he works there, in the OB. They shoulda brought him there."

"It's not the same thing," Cam said, but Herman planted his hands on his black leather belt.

"I know that. You think I don't know that?" Herman looked at me and clapped his rough hands together. "Now. Rita. Did you eat dinner?"

"I'm not hungry."

"You should eat something. I could get you from the cafeteria."

"No thanks. I'm not hungry."

"They must have a cafeteria in this dump." Herman squinted around him as if a cafeteria would materialize. "They should have a sign. Right here, where you need it. At Hahnemann, they got signs everywhere."

"It's okay, I'm not hungry."

"Everywhere you look, there's signs. If you're sittin' in the waiting room and you decide you want a cup a' coffee, you get up and go. For

Essie's gall bladder, we were in the cafeteria all the time."

"She's not hungry, Herm," Cam said.

"The portions were big, too," Herman continued. "They gave you a lot. This place is for the birds." He took off toward the receptionist again.

Cam laughed softly. "She's gonna kill him. Christ, *I'm* gonna kill him."

I couldn't laugh. I didn't want to think about anybody killing anybody. I sat down on the other side of Uncle Sal and rubbed his back through his thin, short-sleeved shirt.

"Vito's gonna be okay," Sal said, still playing with his fingers. I watched him make a rickety church and steeple, then look inside.

"Hey, Rita, isn't that your . . . boyfriend?" Cam asked.

"What?" I looked up. Standing at the reception desk was Paul, the last person I needed right now. He was shaking Herman's hand, then Herman pointed at us. Paul turned and his eyes met mine behind his glasses. He looked upset, concerned, and guilty as hell. Good.

"Is that him?" Cam said again, standing up and hitching up his Sansabelts with a thumb. "I haven't seen him in years. Full head of hair, still. He's a good-lookin' man."

For a cheater. Paul walked toward us, wearing a striped dress shirt, a charcoal sports jacket, and loafers without socks. He'd evidently had time to change; I hoped he'd had time to move the fuck out.

"It's Paul!" Sal said, rising to his feet unsteadily. He had only seen Paul a handful of times, but the tone of his voice told me he was grasping for all the family he had.

"Rita," Paul said, "how are you? Dad and Mom send their love." He grabbed me and hugged me, but I stepped out of his embrace stiffly.

"How did you know—"

"The police called the house. Your father had your name in his wallet for an emergency."

"Hey, how you doin'!" Sal said, then practically threw himself at a somewhat startled Paul.

"Sal, it's all right. Sal," Cam said. He put his hand on Sal's shoulder and gently pried him free.

"But he looks so good," Sal said. "So good."

Cam loped his arm around Sal's shoulder, half in embrace, half in restraint. "That's because he's young, Sal. It's easy to look good when you're young. You can drive at night, the whole thing."

"Good to see you, Cam," Paul said, nodding at him. I was surprised that he knew his name. "Sorry we had to meet again under these circumstances."

Herman walked over and he, Cam, and Paul began to make small talk. I felt myself withdraw. They batted around the crime rate and the judicial system; it reminded me of the conversation at wakes, where everyone lapses into group denial. I understood why it was happening now; there was nothing any of us could do for my father and we were all aching inside. Except for Paul. He didn't belong here. I felt my anger rising, and before I could think about it I snatched a fistful of his jacket.

"Paul, could I speak to you alone?" I said. Without waiting for an answer, I yanked him out of the waiting room, past a surprised trio of my favorite senior citizens, and to the elevator. "Go," I said, and punched the down button.

"Rita—"

"Get out. I don't want you here."

"But I want to be here."

"Bullshit. You don't even know my father. You never bothered."

"You never let me. There was never time."

"Great. Here we go again." The receptionist looked sideways at us and I lowered my voice. "Do you think this is helping me, to fight? Do you think I need this right now?"

"I think you need someone right now."

"Maybe so, but not you. Now go."

"Rita, let me stay."

The elevator arrived and the doors slid open. "Your stuff is packed and out of the house, I assume."

He sighed loudly. "Fine. You win. You're right, I'm not doing you any good right now."

"You catch on quick. Did you move out or not?"

He fished in his jacket pocket and handed me a piece of paper as he stepped into the elevator.

140

"I checked in at the Wayne Hotel. This is the number. If you need anything, just call."

I read the numbers, in architect's lettering, neat and boxy. I used to love his script. "Do me a favor. Hold your breath."

He stepped into the elevator. "I love you, Rita."

As the elevator doors rattled closed, I tossed the paper into the waste can and walked back to the waiting room. But before I walked in, I stopped without really knowing why. Herman was sitting uneasily next to Sal and Cam, and the three of them made a hunchy little row. They reminded me of a border of impatiens in autumn, clumped together and low-lying, petals curling and leaves cracking in the first cold snap. Their season was almost over. I felt a constriction in my chest.

I would lose them all, one by one. Lose their worn faces and their stuffy smells and their medical sagas. Their stories of stoop-ball and boxball, with spaldeens of pink rubber; their idolatry of Rita Hayworth and Stan Kenton; their wonder at the opening of Horn & Hardart's automat downtown and their joy at the ending of the war on VJ day. All the times they talked about at the card table—the times of their lives— vividly recalled and retold as the betting and the storytelling went round and round.

I'd spent a lifetime with these men. How could I lose them?

How could I lose my father?

15

By the next morning my father's condition had a name: stable. An intern told us the news and Cam was so happy he group-hugged everybody with one arm, shoving Mickey awkwardly into Herman's wife, Essie, and leaving Herman's yarmulke hanging by a bobby pin. David Moscow and his lover embraced openly and only a hospital orderly looked askance. Sal wept for joy and so did I, reveling in the resonance of the word. In the assurance of it, the reliability. Stable.

I sent them all home to shower and breakfast, and as they shuffled down the hospital corridor, clapping each other on their thin backs, they looked like an oldtimers' baseball team that had just won a championship. I realized that I'd never seen them so happy in victory, though I had seen them win at cards many times. Then it struck me; a win at poker isn't the same. A good night for you is a lousy night for your friends. It'd never occurred to me before.

I walked to the window that looked on to my father's room in intensive care and watched his chest heave softly under the thin hospital blanket. He hadn't come out of anesthesia, but he was breathing on his own. His face was a deathly white, his strong features oddly slack. A greenish tube ran underneath his nostrils, another one snaked under his bedclothes. Still, I counted his breaths, one shallow huff after another, twenty-seven so far, and thought the scene was the most beautiful I had ever seen. Except that his feet were uncovered again.

I checked my watch. Eight-fifteen. I would have to wait another forty-five minutes to go into his room under their stupid rules. "Tamika," I called to the young black nurse at the desk.

"What?"

"Let me go in. It's his feet."

"Again?"

"Please. It'll just take a minute. It's cold in there."

She shook her head. "We been through this, Rita."

"Come on, I promise I won't touch him or do anything that might speed up the healing process. Please?"

She sighed heavily. Tamika and I had dueled at dawn because she wouldn't let me and Sal stay in my father's room for more than the allotted fifteen minutes, and wouldn't let Herman and Cam in at all because they weren't immediate family. I'd threatened litigation against the hospital and Tamika had called me a bitch. You could see it had pained her to say this, she wore a thin gold crucifix and a frank expression that told me the truth: I was a bitch. So I had apologized, with the vague sense I was becoming a better person for it, despite my best efforts to the contrary.

"I'll just take a minute," I said to her in a conciliatory way. "I'll cover his feet and go."

Tamika got up. "*I'll* go in."

"Thanks a lot." I was learning to compromise. I was so proud of me. "I really appreciate it."

"Hmph," she said, apparently not trusting the metamorphosis in my inner lawyer. She sailed by me into my father's room, covered his feet efficiently, and walked out again. "Okay?"

I would have patted his foot, but never mind. "Terrific. Thanks a lot."

She returned to her station without another word.

I returned to watching my father through the window and counting. I lost count at thirty-five, when I noticed his breathing growing deeper. His chest was going up higher in the air. At first I couldn't believe it, but then I measured it by the windowsill behind him. His chest was going past the ledge when he inhaled. I called this to Tamika's attention as politely as possible and she seemed pleased, though she declined to let me go into his room for confirmation. Equally politely.

I checked my watch. Eight-fifty-five.

When I looked up, my father's eyes were open.

The skin of his hand felt soft and papery, but his fingers closed around mine with a strength that was surprising. His eyes were drowsy slits of brown, and without his glasses to obstruct my view, I could see the gray at the edges of his irises, edging in like storm clouds. Cataracts. Just like his father.

"Dad, remember Grandpop?"

He nodded, his eyes closed.

"Remember what he called his cataracts?"

He smiled weakly.

"Cadillacs. He had Cadillacs in his eyes." I laughed.

"My father, his English wasn't that bad," he said, his voice raspy, untested.

"Not that bad? Dad, come on, his English was nonexistent."

"He knew Cinemascope."

"True, he could say Cinemascope." My grandfather had learned the word from watching old movies. The same word, in white letters that got blockier as they stretched to the edge of the screen. He'd marveled at the word, all the time on the TV, and therefore very important. "Cinemascope. It's a good word. Not exactly a useful word, but a good word."

He smiled with his eyes closed.

"How do you feel, Dad?"

"You asked me already."

"So?"

"About fifty times."

"Okay, so I won't ask you anymore, Mr. Fresh."

His smile faded and he squeezed my hand. He didn't say anything for a long time, but the force of his grip showed me he hadn't fallen back

145

asleep. Finally, he said, his eyes still closed, "LeVonne."

It cut inside. I didn't know what to say, how to tell him. I decided to say the words. "He's dead."

He turned away. "I know. I was there."

God. I didn't say anything, just held on to his hand.

"He was at the counter. I was in back, in the kitchen. I heard shouting."

"I know, Dad."

"He tried to give him the money, but he killed him anyway. I always told him, give 'em the money. I thought that would save him."

There had been twenty-seven dollars in the cash register, the police had said.

"So I called to him, I yelled, and I come out with the spatula. He yells out, tells me not to come, and then this white kid, he shoots him. One shot. Two shots. I'm out, but I got nuthin' but the spatula." His voice grew fainter, almost to a whisper. "A spatula, Rita. Then the kid, he shot me. Just like that."

"I know, Dad. I know." I rubbed his hand and arm.

He didn't say anything for a minute and I knew he was trying not to cry. "LeVonne, he didn't call me in. He wanted to save my life, Rita."

"Dad, wait. You don't know that."

He turned and his watery gaze pierced into mine. "I know that boy. He didn't call me in the front for a reason."

146

"But what could you have done if he called you?"

His mouth opened slightly, his lips dry. It seemed to confound him. "I coulda done something. I coulda been there."

"It's all right, Dad."

He raked a hand over his bald head and the IV tube rustled. He looked confused suddenly. Disoriented. "I couldn't do anything for him. I wanted to help him. The blood. I couldn't."

"Nobody could, Dad. Nobody could save him."

"I tried. I couldn't do a goddamn thing. I got to him, I made it to him. Know what he called me, Rita?"

"What?"

His hand was atop his head like a madman. His eyes filled with tears. "Dad," he said, his voice cracking. "He called me 'Dad.'"

Then his sobs broke free.

16

I got out of the shower and answered the telephone dripping wet, because I was worried it was the hospital calling. It wasn't.

"It's Jake," said the voice.

"Who?"

"Tobin? Remember? Your partner?"

"Oh, yeah. The ponytail."

He laughed. "I hear you need me."

"Why? I got my own ponytail."

"You're walking into a preliminary hearing, aren't you?"

Christ. The furthest thing from my mind. I patted my face with a corner of my towel. "I guess."

"Criminal homicide ring a bell?"

"Sounds familiar."

"Murder of the first degree? Intentionally causing the death of another human being? And a total fox at that?"

"Like that makes a difference?"

"Not to you maybe. The newspapers are calling you a superlawyer. An experienced criminal advocate. They know something I don't?"

"I memorized the Crimes Code in the hospital."

"You studied? For a murder case?"

It could happen. "What are you calling for, Tobin? I've got things to do." I dripped onto the rug, but I'd be damned if I'd tell him I was wearing a washcloth.

"The preliminary hearing is Friday," he said.

"What? That's tomorrow! I thought I had ten days!"

"No, the hearing is held between three and ten days. They're pressing this one, they must think their case is strong. With the media howling, the pressure is on—"

"Wait a minute. How do you know when the hearing is?"

"The notice."

"A notice came to you?"

There was a pause on the other end of the line, except for a slight crunching noise. "Mack asked me to watch your desk, okay? He said you might need a hand."

"You read my mail?"

"I was trying to help."

"I don't need help. And don't open my mail for me. That's what my secretary is for."

"Oh, is that it? I was wondering." There was a crunching sound again.

"What are you doing?"

"Eating breakfast."

"Well, it's rude."

"Bear with me. I got Snickers, a cup of coffee, and a box of Goobers, but only if I'm good. And I'm good. That's why you need me."

"I'm sure. I have to go." I dripped onto my answering machine and noticed its green light flashing. If I had played the messages I probably would have found out about the hearing, but I had been too tired to listen to them when I got home from the hospital.

"Ask me anything. You must have questions."

"Tobin, look, I have a lot to deal with right now. My father is just out of the woods."

"I'm sorry," he said, between nougat and caramel. "Look, if you have to be with your

149

father, I'll take the preliminary hearing for you. Spell you. You'd stay lead counsel."

"No. I'll postpone the hearing."

"You don't want to do that."

"Why not?"

"It gives them time. Time to rehearse the witness, time to get the lab results."

"Lab results?" My head was full of blood cultures from the hospital.

"They test for blood, hair, fiber samples. They'll be doing all of that right now. A burg like Radnor, they're not like Philly, they don't have their own lab. They can do some fingerprint comparisons locally, but they have to send the other stuff out."

"Since when do you know so much?"

"Me? I've returned hundreds of sociopaths to a peace-loving society."

"I've been before a jury, too, Tobin. I win money. Lots of it."

"I know, superlawyer. You work too hard."

"Hold the lecture."

"I wasn't going to lecture you. I admire it, in fact."

"You make up this bullshit as you go along?"

"I mean it. I know how tough it is to try as many cases as you do. I give you credit."

It sounded almost convincing. "You trying to make nice after you opened my mail?"

"Can't fool you, can I? By the way, I heard about that stunt you pulled in court last week." He laughed. "I could tell you stories."

Maybe he could, but I'd be the last to admit it. I heard the sound of crinkling cellophane over the phone. "What are we eating now?"

"I'm eating Goobers, I don't know what you're eating. Why do you talk like a schoolteacher?"

"Because you act like a child. I have to go now."

"You want me to come to the hearing? I'll sit second chair. Subordinate to you, so you won't feel threatened."

"I don't feel threatened."

"Sure you do."

"Don't flatter yourself."

He laughed. "It's your funeral. My only advice is to hammer the witness. She couldn't have seen anything all that clearly. You could fit a fucking football field from the main house to the carriage house."

"I know that. How do you?"

"I scoped it out. Just the outside, I couldn't get in. Something about 'CRIME SCENE DO NOT CROSS.' They had a guard posted, he watched me the whole time. What a pain in the ass they are out there, nothing else to do—"

"Why'd you go to the carriage house?"

"I'm a helpful guy. You want my advice, the trick is to just listen at the hearing. The standard is low for the Commonwealth, so there's no way you're gonna win."

"You call this helpful?"

"Pay attention and take notes. Anything you learn, cross-examine, but don't try to score. Just let 'em know you're there. That you're comin' at them."

"Now who sounds like a teacher?"

"You can be a real bitch, you know that?"

"So I hear."

He laughed. "Women. Fear them."

"What?"

"Have it your way. Come back when you grow up, girl. In the meantime, DNFU."

"What does that mean?"

"DNFU? It's a term of art in criminal law. You must've heard it now that you're trying murder cases."

"Enlighten me."

"Do not fuck up."

Christ. I hung up the phone.

Later, standing in front of my closet in my robe, I realized I didn't need to put on a suit today. It left me with almost nothing to wear.

You work too hard.

Tobin had said it with approval, but my father hadn't. And neither had Paul, who had lectured me about it more times than I cared to remember. I found myself staring at Paul's side of the closet, which used to be full of sports coats and hanging shirts. It was empty. He had taken everything, evidently planning a long stay. Good. I slapped one of his empty hangers, sending it rocking back and forth, screeching.

I wondered what else he had taken and nosed around his bureau. His boar brush was gone from

152

the top, as was a tortoise-shell comb and the sliver-framed photo of us he kept on the top. It was the one taken in Bermuda, the one used for the portrait in Patricia's garage. I remembered the sketchbook with a vague uneasiness. Had Paul taken that, too?

I slipped into a shirt and khakis while I went through his drawers. Only some balled-up sweat socks and a pair of Jockey shorts. I padded downstairs in bare feet, the staircase creaking loudly in the quiet, empty house. The sketchbook wasn't in the entrance hall where I'd thrown it, or in the living room or dining room. I checked the kitchen and the trash cans but it wasn't anywhere to be found. I went upstairs to Paul's desk, the one in his home office, but no sketchbook. He had taken it.

Why?

I ran a hand through tangled, wet hair. The sketchbook was the only link between Paul and Patricia.

So what? What was I thinking?

I pushed aside my questions and finished dressing hastily. Then I grabbed my briefcase and prepared to do the only thing I was really good at, after poker.

Work.

17

This being the provinces, a scuffed Formica dais stood at the front of the small courtroom, flanked by cheap nylon flags of the United States and the Commonwealth of Pennsylvania. The counsel tables were wobbly, with peeling veneer, and instead of the typical fixed pews for spectators, there were chairs arranged in rows, like at an Amway demonstration. In fact, with the reporters and police milling around, the courtroom felt more like a Tupperware party than a preliminary hearing, at least until the judge took her seat on the dais and the bailiff shouted:

"The Commonwealth of Pennsylvania v. the Honorable Fiske Harlan Hamilton."

Fiske stiffened as he sat next to me in a dark blue suit.

The assistant district attorney launched into what turned out to be a histrionic opening statement; full of sound and fury, signifying no surprises. Apparently the witness ID, the license plate, and the fingerprints were all the Commonwealth had so far. Like they needed more.

"Ms. Morrone, are you representing Judge Hamilton?" asked Justice Sarah Millan. She was petite, with small features behind owlish glasses, and her short hair was clipped into salt-and-pepper waves. I'd never been before Justice Millan, but everyone called her a bitch. I figured we'd hit it off.

"I am, Your Honor," I said, standing up.

"Make your opening statement, but keep it short and sweet." Justice Millan looked sideways at the press clogging the perimeter of the courtroom. "I have a busy docket and I hate houseguests."

"Yes, Your Honor." I made my opening, keeping the table pounding to a minimum, but using the words *distinguished* and *innocent* a lot, and even throwing in a *rush to judgment* or two.

Justice Millan looked at the assistant district attorney. "Okay, Mrs. Ryerson, let's see what you got."

Assistant D.A. Maura Ryerson was a young, slim Villanova grad with bobbed reddish hair. She wore a coral-colored lipstick that matched both her hair color and her summer suit; it showed doggedness, if not taste. "Your Honor, the Commonwealth of Pennsylvania has an eyewitness in this matter."

"Good for you," Justice Millan said. "Get him up there."

"It's a woman, Your Honor."

"We take both. Call her."

Everybody chuckled, except for a stony Fiske, who stared rigidly ahead. I read his fixed expression as pure mortification. He had downed serial scotches last night when I told him I wasn't going to let him testify. I had no choice. His alibi had sounded worse with each retelling, and since the defense didn't have to prove anything, the safe bet was to stand pat.

"At this time," Ryerson said, standing up stiff-kneed, "the Commonwealth would like to call Mrs. Allison Mateer to the stand."

Justice Millan rolled her eyes. "So do it already."

"Mrs. Mateer, please come up now," Ryerson said, waving grandly, Bic in hand.

An older woman, Mrs. Mateer rose stiffly from the third row. She wore a white linen suit with a flowered scarf and smiled at me politely as she walked by. Funny, she hadn't smiled yesterday when she closed the door in my face. I'd gotten the gist of her testimony from the affidavit the police had turned over at the last minute.

Mrs. Mateer was sworn in and Ryerson took her through her identification and address, but I was distracted by a noise from the back of the crowded courtroom. I looked back to see Tobin leaning against the doorjamb, eating Jujyfruits. Who invited him? I gave him a dirty look, but Paul, sitting in the front row with Kate, thought it was for him.

Men.

"Mrs. Mateer, will you please tell the court where you were on the afternoon of June 18 of this year?" Ryerson asked.

"I was at my home."

"Where in your house were you, do you recall?"

156

"I was in the kitchen, at the back of the house."

"Facing south?"

"Yes, that's right. South. A wonderful exposure, plenty of sun, but you have to water constantly."

"Water?"

"My garden. If you don't, the flowers burn right up, and the lawn as well."

I made a note on my legal pad and edged it toward Fiske. *Are you sure Mateer doesn't know Kate? Maybe from garden club?* Fiske read it, frowned, and made a precise question mark with his fountain pen. I turned around to check with Kate. She was watching Mrs. Mateer but didn't appear to recognize her.

"What were you doing at approximately 5:30 P. M.?" Ryerson asked.

"Preparing dinner. A salad. I eat lightly, generally."

"Now, does your kitchen have a window in it, Mrs. Mateer?"

"Yes. Over the sink. It's a rather large window, because it's a double sink. I have a view of the backyard and the carriage house off to the right."

"You rented the carriage house to Miss Sullivan, is that correct?"

"Yes. My late husband and I, for the past two years."

"By the way," Ryerson paused, "did you know Miss Sullivan?"

"We were friendly, I suppose, as one would be. She was a lovely girl. A lovely young woman."

Mrs. Mateer's hooded eyes slid over to Fiske with a contempt the reporters picked up immediately. You could almost hear them scribbling away, and there was shuffling at the side of the room. I glanced back to see if it was the *Philadelphia Inquirer* duking out the *New York Times*. It was Stan Julicher, Patricia's lawyer, elbowing for a better view, pissing off a reporter with a steno pad. He was managing to stay in the limelight even without a client.

"Patricia Sullivan was a lovely young woman, wasn't she?" Ryerson asked.

Oh, please. "Your Honor, I'm willing to stipulate that the victim was lovely, and I sincerely hope the Commonwealth catches her murderer, because they don't have him yet."

The gallery laughed. Justice Millan caught my eye, amused, then said, "Overruled."

Not amused enough.

"I'll withdraw the question," Ryerson continued. "Mrs. Mateer, what did you see from your kitchen window?"

"I looked out the window to check on the garden. It had been so hazy that afternoon, and then the storm blew up. I remember thinking, well, I won't have to water tonight."

"And what did you see? At the carriage house?"

"I saw a man getting into a car."

Ryerson flashed me a set of head shots as quickly as legal ethics allowed, then approached the stand with them. "I move to have these photo-

158

graphs marked as Commonwealth Exhibits A through H."

"Fine, fine, fine," Justice Millan said.

"Did the police show you these photographs, Mrs. Mateer?"

The witness glanced down at the pictures. "Yes."

"And did you identify one of them as the man you saw running from Patricia Sullivan's carriage house?"

"Objection," I said, but Justice Millan waved me off like a fly.

"I picked out this one," Mrs. Mateer said. She held up a picture of Fiske, taken from a newspaper the day he was arrested. "Judge Hamilton."

Ouch. I tried to remain expressionless. Fiske tensed. The reporters scribbled and whispered.

"He was wearing a trenchcoat and hat when I saw him," Mrs. Mateer added.

Fiske was wearing a tan trenchcoat that day, but so was I, so was everybody. It was raining like hell.

"What sort of hat was he wearing?" Ryerson asked.

"It was dark brown, a fedora. With a wide brim. It was over his nose."

The hat still hadn't been found, and I'd never known Fiske to have a hat like that. "Objection," I said. "How could the witness identify this person if he had a hat covering his face?"

"She didn't say it covered his face," Ryerson said.

Mrs. Mateer sat forward on her chair. "I saw most of his face and chin, and I saw him when he drove by, too. I feel sure it was Judge Hamilton. I feel sure of that."

Give me a break. "Your Honor, I have to object. The witness *feels sure*? Since when is that enough to support a murder charge? I also object to this witness being trumpeted as an eyewitness. If she didn't see a murder being committed, she's not an eyewitness."

"Your Honor," Ryerson said, "Mrs. Mateer has given a positive identification of Judge Hamilton and is an eyewitness to events subsequent to the murder. Of course, the Commonwealth has additional conclusive evidence to support its charge, such as an identification of the defendant's car and license plate, and his fingerprints in the room where the victim was murdered." The reporters began to whisper as the weight of the evidence made its impact.

"Is the district attorney testifying now?" I said, but I was wondering how Kate would take the news about the fingerprints. We had prepared her for it by saying Fiske had been to Patricia's to drop work off.

"Overruled," Justice Millan ordered, banging the gavel loudly. "Quiet in the back, or I'll clear the courtroom. Ms. Morrone, save your objections for cross-examination. Let the witness tell me what she saw, ladies."

160

Ryerson looked at me sideways, like a driver edging a slowpoke out of the fast lane. "Thank you, Your Honor. Now, Mrs. Mateer, you are positive it was Judge Hamilton you saw?"

"Absolutely. Also he was quite tall, about six feet, and of muscular build, like Judge Hamilton. It was him."

"What did you see the defendant do next?" Ryerson asked.

"I saw him leave the carriage house and get into his car."

"Was he running?"

"No, not running, but kind of hustling, with his head down, as if he didn't want to be seen."

I made a note and heard Fiske shift in his chair.

"What did the defendant do then?"

"He got into his car and backed out of the driveway. It's rather long and curving, so you have to reverse quite a ways to get to the street."

"So you got a good look at the car?"

"Objection," I said.

Justice Millan smiled. "Relax, Ms. Morrone. She's young, she can lead a little."

Ryerson wasn't sure whether she'd been insulted. "Mrs. Mateer, do you know what kind of car it was?"

"I do. It was a black Jaguar, a newer model."

"How do you know it was a Jaguar?"

"I should know a Jaquar when I see one."

There was mild laughter from the gallery, and Mrs. Mateer drew her scarf closer to her throat.

"I see," Ryerson said. "Now, did you testify

that the back end of the car was facing you as you looked out the window?"

"Yes. It had to reverse."

"Did you see the license plate on the car?"

"I did. I saw the license plate the whole time. It said GARDEN-2, so I remembered it."

"And you saw that very clearly?"

Come on. "Objection, Your Honor," I said.

Justice Millan nodded. "Sustained. Mrs. Ryerson, don't push your luck."

"Mrs. Mateer, did you see the defendant do anything else unusual?"

I leaned forward. "Objection, Your Honor. The question assumes the actions described were unusual."

Ryerson leapt to her pumps. "There certainly is something unusual about a man scurrying out of a private home, jumping into a car, and driving quickly in reverse."

Justice Millan smiled tightly. "Oh, really? I had an ex-husband who did just that."

The gallery laughed, but I didn't. I was thinking of something. Something I couldn't put my finger on. Something was wrong, bothering me. I sat upright, listening.

"Then what did you do, Mrs. Mateer?" Ryerson asked.

"I waited a little, I wasn't sure what to do. It all seemed so odd to me. Then I decided to call the police. They came and found Patricia, dead. Murdered."

162

"Thank you. I have no further questions," Ryerson said, and sat down.

Justice Millan eased back in her chair. "Ms. Morrone, your turn."

I stood up to cross. "Mrs. Mateer, let me begin with just a few general questions, if I may. Do you know that the distance from your kitchen window to the carriage house is about a hundred yards?"

"I suppose."

"And there are trees in front of the carriage house, aren't there?"

"There are some trees."

I looked at my notes. "At least five large oaks, with very thick trunks, lie between your house and the carriage house, isn't that right?"

"I suppose."

"Also, there's a tall hedge between the two, isn't there?"

"Yes."

"It's about five feet, is it not?"

"Yes, but we keep it trimmed."

"But it hasn't been trimmed recently, has it?"

"No. It was due in early June, but the lawn service isn't overly reliable. Sometimes in the summer months, the service gets too busy, what with people spraying chemicals everywhere, willy-nilly." She shuddered.

"It was raining the afternoon of June 18, wasn't it?"

"Yes."

"The storm began about three o'clock, didn't it?"

"Yes."

"Objection," Ryerson said. "What's the relevance of this weather report?"

Fuck you. "Your Honor, the relevance will be clear if the young Mrs. Ryerson can be patient."

"Good. Overruled," Justice Millan said, and Ryerson flounced into her chair like Scarlett O'Hara. Fiddle-dee-dee.

I cleared my throat. "Do you recall that the sky became very dark as the storm came up, Mrs. Mateer?"

"Yes. It got quite dark. It was the tail end of that tropical storm. Wind was gusting, trees were knocked over. Conestoga Road was blocked for some time, by a branch, in fact." Her gold bangles jingled as she folded her hands on her lap.

"Mrs. Mateer, wasn't it raining hard when you saw this person?"

"Yes."

"It was a driving rain, was it not?"

"A drenching rain, I would say. I was pleased to see it, as a gardener."

I thought of asking her about the garden club but dismissed it. With what was to come next, it would sound like I was bringing Kate into it. "Did the person you saw have the hat down over his or her eyes?"

"Only partly."

"Do you remember if they held the brim of the hat, as if to shield themselves from the rain?"

"I don't think so, but I'm not sure." Mrs. Mateer closed her eyes, trying to remember, and her eyelids fluttered slightly. "Maybe, I don't know," she said, nodding, and Ryerson made a note.

"Did you notice any jewelry on his or her hand as they held the hat brim?"

She paused. "No. He may have been wearing gloves, I don't recall for sure."

"Did the person have the collar of the raincoat up around their face?"

"I don't recall."

Ryerson made another note.

"And you testified the person was rushing, too, so you only saw him or her for a short time?"

Justice Millan harrumphed from the dais. "Do we have to say 'his or her' every time, counselor? It sounds so politically correct."

The reporters laughed. Justice Millan gave good copy.

"Your Honor, this witness's identification of the defendant is sketchy at best. I can't concede it was even a man that she saw."

"Fine, fine, fine," Millan said. "But dump the 'his or her.' I'll remember you have a continuing objection. I'm a woman judge, if you haven't noticed."

The gallery chuckled.

"Mrs. Mateer, you testified that you saw this person rush to a black Jaguar?"

"Not exactly. I testified that I saw *Judge Hamilton* rush to the Jaguar."

Ouch. "And he got into the car and reversed out the driveway?" I tried to picture it in my mind.

"Yes."

And the car was backward. "He didn't turn around in the driveway and drive out with the front of the car facing you?"

"No, there's not enough room, one has to reverse out. It's quite inconvenient."

I paused a minute and the courtroom fell silent. A reporter coughed in the back, and there was whispering. I couldn't put my finger on it, but something was nagging at me as I pictured Fiske running to his car and jumping in.

"Mrs. Mateer," I asked, "did this person enter the car from its left side or its right?"

She paused. "What do you mean?"

"When the person got in the car, did he enter on the right side or the left?"

She blinked. "I don't recall. The driver's side, of course."

I was building on something, but didn't know exactly what. I got the same sort of hunch at the poker table, and followed it every time. "You say the driver's side, Mrs. Mateer, but was it the left or the right side of the car?"

"The right, I believe." She held up a bejeweled index finger. "Wait . . . it was the left."

"Objection, Your Honor," Ryerson said. "Defense counsel is trying to confuse the witness."

Not this time. "Your Honor, I'm trying to

understand exactly what Mrs. Mateer saw. The Commonwealth calls her an eyewitness, after all."

"Overruled." Justice Millan nodded, and Ryerson sulked in her chair.

"Mrs. Mateer, I need to know whether the person you saw got into the car from the right or the left. Please take a minute and think about it."

Ryerson sighed, making a great show of her exasperation, and Fiske tensed at my elbow. He knew where I was going and suddenly so did I.

"The left side," Mrs. Mateer said. "I'm positive now. The left."

GO FOR IT! Fiske wrote on my legal pad, but I shook my head. Better to save it for later. It wasn't a home run at a preliminary hearing but might be enough to constitute a reasonable doubt at trial. I didn't want to show my hand.

"Mrs. Mateer, you're sure that the person got into the car on the left in a great hurry, started it immediately, and drove off?"

"Yes." She drew a deep breath, now that she felt on safer ground.

"And the person didn't slide over in the front seat to start the car?"

"No."

"He jumped in and started right off?"

"Yes."

Fiske wrote *GO! GO! GO!* on the pad.

No, I wrote back. *Not today.*

He pursed his lips. He couldn't have been as good a chess player as I thought. I had learned

167

something, but the police wouldn't drop a murder charge on it. Fiske's Jaguar, being British-made, had the steering wheel on the right, so the driver would have entered from the right side of the car. Either Mrs. Mateer wasn't so good on the details or Fiske was being framed for murder by someone who knew his license plate but didn't know about his steering wheel. Or who had forgotten.

"Do you have any further questions, Ms. Morrone?" Justice Millan said. "Let's keep things moving."

"Just a couple, Your Honor. Mrs. Mateer, how often do you look out of your kitchen window?"

"Every time I'm at the sink. And other times, to check on my garden."

"I understand." You're *not* a nosy old bird. "Did you ever see people coming and going from the carriage house?"

"Yes."

"It was mostly men who came and went, isn't that right?"

"Objection, Your Honor!" Ryerson said. "What is defense counsel suggesting?"

"Your Honor, I'm hoping Mrs. Mateer can help me understand who visited the carriage house. That is highly relevant to proving who killed Patricia Sullivan, which is the only thing the Commonwealth should be concerned about."

"Overruled," Justice Millan said. "She's entitled to inquire."

168

"Mrs. Mateer, you said you rented to Patricia Sullivan for a two-year period. Did you happen to notice that men visited her during that time?"

"Well, yes."

"Would you say that many men visited her or just a few?"

She paused. "I would have to say more than a few."

"You would have to say 'many,' am I right?"

"Yes."

The reporters started yapping, as I knew they would. I wondered how Fiske would take this. Or Paul. "Mrs. Mateer, did you meet any of these men?"

"What?"

"Let's back up. You work in the garden out back, and you're a gardener, correct?"

"Yes."

"Are you a member of the Wayne Garden Club, by the way?"

"I was for many years, but no longer."

Hmmm. Kate's club. Did it matter? "When you were out working in your garden, did Patricia Sullivan ever introduce you to any of her visitors?"

"No . . . well, only one. I forget his name."

"Is he in the courtroom today?"

She scanned the crowd slowly. I held my breath, praying she wouldn't point at Paul. I'd normally never ask such an open question on cross, but I needed this answer. After a long time,

Mrs. Mateer said: "Well, I see a man I recognize, but Patricia never introduced us."

My mouth went dry. "Who would that be?"

She pointed a bony finger at the gallery. Heads swiveled frantically among the pews. I looked at Paul, who sat bolt upright, seemingly unafraid of her identification.

"In the back," Mrs. Mateer said. She aimed her finger at Stan Julicher, who raised his hand and smiled at the press.

"Besides him, is there anyone else?"

"No."

My mind flipped through the drawings I'd seen in the other sketchbooks in the garage, then the sketch I stepped on. "Mrs. Mateer, wasn't there one man who visited more frequently than others?"

"I have to object, Your Honor," Ryerson said. "This line of questioning casts aspersions on the character of the victim. This is the worst kind of—"

"Overruled. Get to the point, Ms. Morrone," Justice Millan interrupted. "I'm not interested in watching while you fish."

"Yes, Your Honor. Mrs. Mateer, there was one man who visited more than the others, wasn't there?"

"I don't know his name."

I thought of the front door, unlocked. "Did he live with Miss Sullivan?"

"I'm not sure."

"He was tall, wasn't he, about six feet?"

She nodded. "I suppose."

Ready, set, go. "And he was black, was he not?"

Mrs. Mateer cleared her throat. "Well, yes."

The gallery burst into excited chatter and Justice Millan pounded the gavel. "Now, children," she said.

"And he rode a BMW motorcycle, didn't he?"

"Why, yes."

And he left the seat up, too, but we won't go into that. I glanced at Fiske, who looked puzzled. Paul didn't. "Mrs. Mateer, I have one final question. You never saw Judge Hamilton visit the carriage house, did you?"

"No."

Thank God, Fiske had kept his trysts nocturnal. "I have no further questions of this witness."

I sat down and half listened to a repetitious redirect by Ryerson, then put myself on autopilot as Lieutenant Dunstan described in mind-numbing detail the police procedures for license-plate and fingerprint identification. He testified that they'd found Fiske's prints in the living room, which squared with what Fiske had told me. He'd confined his close encounters to the sofa. Why do you think they call it a love seat?

On cross-examination, I established that the police had dusted the carriage house and found no other fingerprints from Fiske, and had examined Fiske's Jaguar and had not yet found any evidence of the victim's blood, hair, or fibers from her clothes. But I couldn't resist a final line of questions, just to get the press salivating.

"Lieutenant Dunstan, did the police consider that one of the male visitors to the carriage house could have committed the crime?"

He nodded. "We investigated thoroughly, including the gentleman you referred to."

A shake, rattle, and roll emanated from the back of the courtroom. I looked back. It was Tobin, shaking his box of Jujyfruits, presumably warning me not to press further. Still, I couldn't resist a parting shot:

"Lieutenant Dunstan, how easy do you think it is to make a fake Pennsylvania license plate, one that would look real at a hundred yards, in the middle of a dark rainstorm?"

"I have no idea."

"What if I told you I made one this morning in only ten minutes, out of cardboard and indelible markers?"

"Objection!" Ryerson said, but the reporters responded predictably, salivating and scribbling, scribbling and salivating. Justice Millan banged her gavel again and again, to no avail. All the news that's fit to spin was being spun, like straw into gold.

"Never mind, I withdraw the question," I said. "I have no further questions."

I sat down and promised myself that someday I'd try to make a license plate out of cardboard and indelible markers. When I got a spare ten minutes.

18

After the preliminary hearing, we regrouped in Fiske's study. It was large, with floor-to-ceiling bookshelves and a rolling library ladder for reaching that emergency copy of Milton. Fiske kept the air-conditioning high so the first editions wouldn't molder and grow mushrooms in the dim room. The only light came from two narrow, arched windows, crisscrossed with leaded glass. It was a nice effect if you liked Early Medieval, but since I came from the serfing class I'd always felt uncomfortable here. Especially today, since I was wondering if I was sitting in this drafty castle with a killer.

Despite my link to these players, I felt suspicious of them. Fiske, who'd been framed for murder—maybe. Kate, who drove an identical black Jaguar with an almost identical license plate, and who was furious at Patricia for suing her husband. And my own beloved, who had slept with Patricia and taken with him the only thing that would prove he knew her. Had Paul killed her? Could he? Could any of them?

It was almost impossible to believe. I had known them for years and never would have dreamed any of them capable of such brutality. And Paul, never. Still, I had lots of questions and no answers, and any lawyer would have been thinking the same way. So I set aside my personal feelings, put on a poker face, and watched the cards. In this case, the face cards, all of which were, not coincidentally, two-faced. I started play with a gutsy opening bet:

"I think someone is trying to frame Fiske for murder," I said. "Any thoughts? Suspicions? Guesses?"

"Not a one. I don't have an enemy in the world," Fiske said. He sat at the head of a long table with six wooden chess games in various stages of play. Next to each chessboard was a stack of postcards. Fiske seemed to be looking at the closest chess game, albeit without much concentration.

"A judge without an enemy? Don't you make an enemy in every case—the loser?"

"Not really. I've been on the bench for almost twenty years and I run my courtroom fairly. Civil litigants know that."

"How about in the criminal cases, in sentencing cases? You sentence in the drug cases, don't you? They're federal."

"The guideline cases, of course. We're overwhelmed."

"Has anybody you've sentenced gotten especially upset? Screamed at you, threatened you?"

He shook his head. "Not that I can remember. I've gone over it and over it in my mind. All the possibilities."

"What about someone from the bar association

or your old firm? No old grudges? Nobody on the district court?"

"My colleagues? *Judges*? No, no." He fingered the White King, then set it back down. "It's this motorcycle rider that concerns me." He winced slightly and I knew he wasn't thinking about Kf8 and Kc7.

"I agree. I'm going to see if I can find him."

He looked up from the chess game. "How?"

"Investigate. I have some ideas."

Kate edged forward on the arm of a club chair, a stubby cigarette smoldering between her fingers, a Waterford ashtray in her other hand. She had apparently started smoking again. "Do you really believe Fiske was framed, Rita? That this was an intentional act? It seems the unlikeliest option to me."

"Why?" Fiske said to her. "How else would a Jag with my license plate appear in her driveway?"

She shrugged. "How indeed? I can think of lots of reasons short of someone actually trying to frame you, dear. Maybe Mrs. Mateer saw the license plate wrong. She simply could have misread it."

"You don't know Mrs. Mateer, do you, Kate?" I asked, but she shook her head.

"Besides," Kate continued, "it was a great distance, and with the thunderstorm, everything was gray and dark. Maybe she read it incorrectly."

"Mother, you can read a license plate in a thunderstorm," Paul said. He stood in front of the window, silhouetted against the sun, and it was hard to see his face. "Yellow letters on a blue background, like the Pennsylvania plate? It's easy to read."

"Then maybe she remembered it wrong." Kate blew a jet of smoke at the high ceiling. "How many times have you thought you remembered a number but didn't? Gotten one letter wrong or two? I always get phone numbers mixed up."

Fiske shook his head. "A mistake is more likely with a numbered plate, dear. Not a vanity plate."

"Oh, you just never liked those vanity plates. You put up such a fuss." She shaved her cigarette ash to a fragile cone on the thick edge of the ashtray.

I took a breath, then stated the obvious as tactfully as possible. "Kate, one letter wrong is your license plate. And of course it wasn't you."

Kate laughed abruptly, emitting a hiccup of smoke. "What are you saying, that—"

"Of course it wasn't Kate's car," Fiske snapped.

Paul's head swiveled in Fiske's direction. I wished I could see his expression. "Rita wasn't suggesting that it was Mom's car, Dad."

Of course I was. "Of course I wasn't."

"I confess I don't have much in the way of an alibi," Kate said, seemingly amused. "When I told the policeman I was gardening all afternoon, he looked at me as if I had taken leave of my senses."

Fiske smiled. "He doesn't know the time you

176

spend on that damn garden. Or the money." His tone was light, and if he suspected her, it didn't show.

"That reminds me," Kate said. "I did go to Waterloo Gardens that day, for a new hose. A soaker. I spent seventy-five dollars, but I didn't save the receipt, nor can I remember which clerk helped me. Will I get off the hook anyway?"

I met Kate's cool gaze through the screen of cigarette smoke. "Absolutely not. Anybody who spends that much money on a hose should be locked up. Go directly to jail and most certainly do not collect two hundred dollars."

The three of them laughed, relieved, and it got us past my bad manners in calling the Queen a killer.

"It had better be a nice hose," Fiske said. "A very nice hose."

"The mother of all hoses," Paul added.

Kate stubbed out her cigarette and set the ashtray on the tall end table. "Don't blame me, fellas. You know you can't get out of Waterloo for less than fifty dollars. I have to go back tomorrow to replace the geraniums the reporters trampled. Are they still out there?" she asked Paul.

He looked out the window. "The geraniums or the reporters?"

Kate smiled. "The reporters."

"Of course." Paul yanked at the curtain, but it was sewn open like in hotels. "The reporters will never leave and the geraniums will never come back."

Kate shook her head. "The police traipse through the house, the reporters destroy the gardens. The telephone rings off the hook all the time, and we're in every newspaper in town. When do we get our life back?"

Fiske glanced at her guiltily. "I'm sorry, dear. About all of this."

"Oh, phoo," she said, looking away. "It's not your doing."

I got up to go, and Paul stepped out of the sunlight and looked at me directly. His eyes looked slightly sunken behind his glasses; he hadn't been sleeping well. "You going home?"

Home? So he still hadn't told his parents. "No. I want to stop by the hospital. Then I've got some work to do."

"Like what? Maybe I can help. I've been thinking about it, about different approaches you might take. Logical ways of investigating the crime."

I picked up my handbag and briefcase, acutely aware that Fiske and Kate were watching this exchange. "I've got it under control, Paul."

"But, Rita, it's like forensic architecture. I look at the evidence, the clues, and try to find out what caused the problem. The leak, the crack, whatever. It's all deductive reasoning. Remember the underground garage? I can help you."

Fuck you. "I appreciate that, but—"

"I think Rita knows what she's doing, son,"

Fiske interrupted. I gathered he was trying to be supportive, but it left me wondering why he wanted me working alone.

"I'm not suggesting she doesn't," Paul said. "But I've cleared my calendar to help her find out who's behind this. Aren't two heads better than one?"

Not when I want to knock yours off. "I don't think so. If I need help, we have investigators at the firm."

"Then maybe I can start my own investigation and we can compare notes."

Did he want to help me so he could control what I found out? Lead me away from the clues? "Paul, I don't think we need some sort of parallel investigation."

"I think Paul is on to something, Rita," Kate said. "It sounds sensible to me. Paul may be able to help you. At the very least, you know he can be trusted."

Say *what*? "I have to go now."

"Then it's settled," he said. "We'll talk tonight."

Tonight? I fingered the note in my blazer pocket, from Tobin. He had pressed it into my hand after the hearing, as I fought the gauntlet of the press:

You were awesome! Dinner at Sonoma at 7?
Yours in saturated fat,
Jake

I flashed on the scene outside the courthouse after the hearing. The media had barraged me with questions, many about the mystery motorcycle rider. I'd practiced my "no comment" to the right and to the left, and had almost made it to my car when Stan Julicher had popped out of the crowd, his face tinged with righteous anger, like some avenging angel. "You know and I know the judge did it," he'd said.

"You're wrong, Julicher," I'd answered.

"Shame on you," he'd shot back, and I'd slipped into my car, feeling uneasy.

"I'll be home at six, okay?" Paul was saying.

"Actually, make it seven." By then I should be having dinner with another man and you can sit on the front porch and hold your goddamn breath. I'd already had the locks changed. "And by the way, Paul, maybe you could bring home that sketchbook we were looking at yesterday."

"Sketchbook?" Fiske said. "Are you sketching again, son?"

Paul shook his head quickly. "I threw it away, Rita. I didn't know you'd want it. Seven o'clock then?" He smiled.

They all did, except me.

My father was snoozing peacefully in his new hospital room. They'd moved him from intensive care and into a private room at my insistence. I'd thought he'd need the privacy to rest, but I could see now he didn't, since Sal, Cam, and Herman were playing cards on the table spanning his rounded belly. No money was visible to the naked eye, so I knew Herman would have the tote running in his head.

For a split second I wanted in on the game, but then I remembered I was working. I had to build the case for the defense and I needed the help of the only people in the world I could really trust. I let them finish the hand and explained the steps I wanted to take in my investigation. Then I opened the floor for questions. I should've known better.

"Why do I gotta wear this?" Sal whined. He held up a pair of gray wool pants and a navy Burberry blazer. "Why can't I just wear normal clothes?"

"Uncle Sal, I spent a fortune on those clothes. I'm dressing you better than you ever dressed in your life. You can even keep the outfit when we're done."

"I don't have no place to wear stuff this fancy."

"Then throw it away. Burn it. Use it to wrap pork chops."

"I don't like the shoes. They look funny."

"Cole-Haans with a tassel? What's not to like?"

"I like Herman's outfit better. He got the boots."

Herman, sitting next to him, shook his head. "You think I wanna wear cowboy boots? Look like those *goyim* in the Texas hats? I'm doin' it for Rita. Because she asked me."

"They're not cowboy boots, Herman," I said. "They're just black boots."

181

"So can I trade Herman for the boots?" Sal pleaded. "I got nothin' against black boots."

"I'm even wearing the leather jacket, all for Rita," Herman continued, rivaling any Catholic for martyrdom. "Why can't you just go along like me, Sal?"

Cam laughed. "Herman, how long you known Sal Morrone? Forty, fifty years?"

"Only thirty."

"Okay, thirty. So you know Sal has to find something to complain about."

Uncle Sal ignored them. "Maybe I can switch with Cam?"

"No," I said firmly.

"But I'll be hot in the jacket."

"It'll be air-conditioned."

Sal pointed to the brown work boots I bought for Cam. "Maybe I could just wear Cam's shoes? I like them things."

No kidding. He was already wearing the same shoes.

"Sal," Cam said, "what is it with you? It's like we're gonna be in a play or somethin'. I need my shoes, I gotta dress my part. I gotta act my part."

"A star is born," Herman said.

Sal put the blazer down. "I got an idea. Can't Herman do Cam's job and Cam do Herman's job and we switch all the jobs around?"

Cam shook his head. "He's confusing me."

"He's confusing himself," Herman corrected. "He's a confusing person. A confusing person to be around."

I rubbed my forehead. Halloween wasn't turning out the way I'd hoped. Remind me never to have a kid. Or an old man. "Look, Uncle Sal. Everybody has to go along with the plan. No trades, no switching!"

"Okay, okay. You don't have to holler."

"She wasn't hollering," Cam said.

Yes, I was. "Now go get dressed. We have to get going."

"Get dressed? Where?"

"In the bathroom."

"In the bathroom? Here?" Sal looked nervously at the door, he always looked nervous. I must have been crazy to think I could count on him. No one had ever relied on Sal for anything. I had no idea what he did all day, except play cards and watch old movies on television. My father had always taken care of everything.

"You can do this, Sal. You and me," I said, not believing a word of it.

"I don't know."

"I do. I know."

Sal picked up the blazer and disappeared into the bathroom with the clothes. I decided to wait to tell him about the accent he'd have to fake. Growing up is hard enough to do, and best done in stages.

19

The only sound in the empty showroom was the discreet hum of the air-conditioning, and the occasional squirt of a spray bottle from a man in a coarse blue jumpsuit, cleaning the windshields. Late-afternoon sun poured through mullioned windows that bordered the room. Reproductions of Chippendale end tables flanked the entrance, which opened on to five spanking-new, factory-delivered Jaguars of various colors. Each car gleamed under its own set of track lights, like babies in a multiracial nursery.

"But nobody told me about this," said the confused salesman. His navy blazer roughly matched Sal's and his loafers were almost identically tasseled. *Am I good or am I good?* "I should have been told."

"We sent the fax yesterday," I said authoritatively. "It would have mentioned me, Miss Jamesway." I had my hair knotted back and my glasses on, in case he recognized me from the newspapers. "And your name is Mr.—"

"Henry."

"Well, Henry—"

"No, *Mr.* Henry," he corrected. "I don't recall any fax."

"That's odd. The home office said they'd take care of it."

"The home office? You mean Detroit or Mahwah?"

"Mahwah." It was more fun to say.

"Then it would have come directly from Jim Farnsworth, the CEO."

"Yes, that's right. Jim said his assistant would send it."

"But we didn't get it." Mr. Henry patted his dark hair, which was combed and slightly perfumed, like a groomed Scottish terrier.

"No matter. We're here now. We don't want to keep Mr. Livemore waiting, do we?" I nodded at Uncle Sal, who was standing beside a sparkling Rose Bronze Van den Plas XJ12. His arms were folded imperiously over his skinny chest and he frowned at the Cream interior of the car in as British a manner as possible, as per my instructions. I'd ordered him to keep quiet because his English accent had proved to be a cross between Crocodile Dundee and Batman.

"Mr. Livemore? I don't recall that name."

"That's because he rarely leaves Coventry. He's the operations manager at Brown's Lane, and he hates to travel."

"Operations manager, you say? He's rather old for the job, isn't he?"

"Yes, but experience tells, don't you know. We really should get on with it. It'll only take a few minutes."

"But it's not procedure. We have our procedures, our channels of authority here—"

I leaned close to him and whispered, "It's my job on the line. Cut me a break, will you? I'd do the same for you."

His brushy black mustache twitched, his blue eyes were as bright as the XJS in front of us. Sapphire, they called the color, with an Oatmeal interior. Six cylinders and $66,200 of gorgeous. But since I was pretending to help build these beauties, I did not drool on the showroom floor. "I don't like this at all, Miss Jamesway," he said.

"Please? I need this job. I'm a single mother, trying to make a living."

He softened. "Oh, all right. Where do you work, Miss Jamesway? England or the U.S.?"

"I go back and forth." Between truth and falsehood. "Now, as I said, Mr. Livemore has been very concerned about the paint quality on the black models in recent years. Have you had any complaints about the black paint?"

"Exterior enamels? Not that I recall. Most of our customers are very satisfied, very loyal."

"Have you had complaints from your customers about chipping? Particularly around the doors? In the black models?"

He thought a minute. "No."

Out of the corner of my eye, I saw Sal run his finger along the polished side of a Kingfisher Blue XJ12 Coupe. His greasy fingertip made a streak like a slug's trail on the car's virgin surface. "Mr. Livemore would like to locate the owners of black

Jaguars in the area. He wants to contact these customers to see if they are as satisfied as Jaguar wants them to be. Do you have such a list?"

He blinked. "Not *per se*, no. We have a list of the cars sold in a year, but not by color. We sell many black cars, as you know. It's one of our most popular colors after British Racing Green."

Over my shoulder, Sal was opening and closing the long door of a Flamenco Red XJS Convertible with a Coffee interior. The *ca-chunk* sound echoed harshly, the only rugs in the room were squares under each Pirelli. *Ca-chunk, ca-chunk, ca-chunk.* The convertible door closed fluidly each time, but Sal grimaced like an Uberfieldmarshal.

The salesman caught Sal's expression. "He's very thorough, isn't he?"

"It's his job to be very thorough," I said, wanting to wring Sal's stringy neck.

"Maybe I should call my manager. He's at the dentist, but he has a beeper."

"No, you wouldn't want to bother your boss. You know what Mr. Livemore would do to me if I called him at his dentist?" I glanced at Sal, who was climbing into the driver's seat of the low-slung convertible. His puny frame vanished into the cushy leather seat. "Let's just get on with it, can we? Before Mr. Livemore starts testing the ashtrays."

"But the ashtrays are fine!"

"How about the electrical system?" The automatic windows on Fiske's car stuck constantly and the door locks were possessed.

"The electrics have improved since the quality controls we've instituted with Ford."

"Yeah. Right. This is me now, not *Autoweek*," I said, and he winced. "Look, I know how popular black is. That's why they're so concerned, back in England, that the paint on the black models is chipping and flaking."

"Flaking, too?" His face went white. Glacier White, to be exact.

"Mr. Henry, just so I understand the scope of the problem, I would guess there are hundreds of black Jaguars sold by this dealership."

"Hundreds? *Thousands* would be more like it, including the leases." His hands fluttered to the knot on his rep tie. "Chipping, really? You would think I would have heard about it."

"It occurs on very few models, but Mr. Livemore wants us to stay on top of the situation. Uphold the quality of the marque. Don't you agree?"

"By all means."

"And you're the only Jaguar dealer in the greater Philadelphia area, is that right? There's one in Cherry Hill, New Jersey, and none in Delaware?" I'd let my fingers do the walking.

"Yes," he answered, distracted by Sal, who had found the convertible's pristine shoulder harness and was snapping it back and forth. It retracted with a high-quality *craakkk* and the salesman flinched each time, like it was a rifle shot.

"Do you think I could see your list of cars sold or leased in the past, oh, three years?" Then I would have a list of everybody with a black Jag in the area. Maybe one of them had reason to frame Fiske. "I can pick off the black cars myself."

"That would take an enormous amount of time. It's a huge number."

"I have an assistant. In Mahwah. Mr. Farnsworth's assistant."

Mr. Henry shook his head slowly. "Maybe I should call my manager." He walked toward a desk located behind a glass partition before I could stop him.

Shit. "Mr. Livemore!" I called to Sal. "Perhaps you should come along. We may be phoning the manager."

Sal turned in the car seat, his eyes barely clearing the headrest, then began to climb out of the car.

"Come quickly, Mr. Livemore!" I said, panicky. I flashed on a scene of me manacled before the ethics committee of the Pennsylvania bar and hurried to Mr. Henry's desk, where he was reaching for the telephone.

"I'm shocked!" shouted a British voice from behind me. It was Sal. His face was Signal Red and his scowl was deep as the pile on a floor mat. "That's what I am, shocked! Put down that phone!"

Mr. Henry froze and the receiver clattered onto the cradle.

"How dare you!" Sal thundered. He stood taller and straighter, his scrawny shoulders squared off in their shoulder pads. Even his accent had sharpened up, he sounded like Pierce Brosnan as Remington Steele. I was dumbfounded. So was Mr. Henry.

"How . . . dare I?" the salesman asked uncertainly. "Call my own manager?"

Sal glowered at him. "This is shocking! You, my good man, you are in charge here, are you not?"

"Yes."

"Then why are you—as you Americans say—trying to pass the buck?"

"I'm not, sir."

"Do you have the information my client requested?"

Client?

Mr. Henry nodded. "But I need authorization to get the printouts."

"I'm giving you authorization!"

"But I mean from my own management—"

"I am your management, my good man. I am your management's management!"

Mr. Henry looked puzzled, rapidly discovering that Uncle Sal was a confusing person to be around. But this time it was paying off. "It will take at least a day to get that information."

"Right as rain!" Sal said, morphing into Rex Harrison. On steroids.

"And my manager would have to approve it."

Shit. I should have realized it. I couldn't get the records this way, but I could subpoena them now that I knew they existed. Time to fold 'em. "Mr. Livemore, perhaps we should go and seek the proper authorization. We can obtain it today or tomorrow, then come back."

"My word! How can you say that! And look at this man's desk! It's abdominal!"

Say what?

"This is a travesty!" Sal flipped inexplicably through the papers on Mr. Henry's desk, scattering them in a corporate hissy fit. I think he was trying to create a diversion even though nobody was breaking for the perimeter, and I gathered he had seen too many old war movies. "A mockery!"

"Please, Mr. Livemore!" Mr. Henry yelped, watching in horror as all of his papers flopped onto the floor, until the only thing on his desktop was a black three-ring binder and a cup of cold tea. "Please, sir!"

"What kind of order is this? What must our customers think when they come here? Disorder! Catastrophe! In short you have a ghastly mess!"

Sal was segueing into Mary Poppins, but I didn't have time to watch. I was intrigued by the salesman's black binder, which held a stack of forms filled in in a hasty pencil. There was a blank for the customer's name, address, and trade-in, and business cards had been stapled to the top right of the forms. As Mr. Henry bent over to pick up the papers, I read the top form upside-down. At the top of the form it said in a pretentious font: TEST DRIVES.

"But I usually keep it neater than this," Mr. Henry said apologetically, his arms full of slipping papers.

"I should hope so!" Sal said. "In England we keep everything neat and clean. The telephone booths are red, did you know that? They have windows. Clean windows!"

Mr. Henry nodded. "I saw. On a commercial."

Undoubtedly the same commercial Sal had seen. The ersatz Mr. Livemore was ad-libbing dangerously, leaving Alistair Cooke territory and entering the Irwin Corey zone. I wanted to get out before he blew our cover completely, but the notebook nagged at me. "Is this a log of test drives?" I asked.

Mr. Henry nodded.

"Do you go with the customers on the test drives?"

"Not usually. Most of our customers take the car out alone."

"Wot?" Sal exploded. "You just *give* a customer one of our Jaguars? You just let them drive away with it? As if it weren't worth nothing?"

Mr. Henry looked like he was starting to wonder. If he read the newspapers, he could catch on any minute now. "We *lend* the car. Our clientele doesn't need me riding along with them. We do ask for the customer's driver's license."

192

"Do you make a copy of the license?"

Two papers fell from the salesman's grasp. "I make a Xerox of it, then I throw it away after about a week."

Hmm. "Is there a time limit on how long you let the customer test-drive the car?"

"I should hope there is!" Sal interrupted. "I should hope so, for your sake! I should report this to my posteriors in Coventry!"

Eeeeek.

Mr. Henry looked from Sal to me, and back again. "Well, not usually. We trust our customers. Some of them, our manager lets them have the car for the whole afternoon."

"Shocking!" Sal said, and I shot him a warning glance.

"How long do you keep the log sheets for?"

"I hope they are disposed of right away!" said Sal the Major General. "And neatly! In the rubbish!"

"In fact, sir, I keep mine for six months," Mr. Henry said.

"That's an outrage! Disorder! Democracy! In short you will have a ghastly mess!"

Mr. Henry turned to me for succor. "But some people don't buy right away, and I keep the addresses that I log in. They make a good mailing list. No one I've dealt with ever mentioned anything about the paint chipping, if that's what you're wondering."

Not exactly. What I was wondering was whether it were possible to commit murder on a test drive. Patricia's carriage house was only fifteen minutes from here. "Do you let the customer test-drive any model they wish, Mr. Henry?"

"If the one they want is available. Usually I lend them a demonstrator. Our most popular model, the XJS Coupe."

"Is it black?"

"Yes."

Bingo. Except that Fiske's model was a Sovereign, so was Kate's. "Do you let them test-drive a Sovereign?"

"The Daimler? No, we don't usually have one on hand, they're scarcer. They look the same as the XJS anyway from the outside."

Boy oh boy. The jackpot.

"Well, I never!" Sal barked. *"Never!"* He was about to speak for the British Empire again, but I gave him the high sign when Mr. Henry bent over for more paper.

"Yes, Miss Jamesway?" he asked, not understanding. "Wot is it?"

Wot a whiz. You could draw a line across your throat and Sal would think you were talking necklaces. "Mr. Livemore, perhaps we should go. We can continue our investigation in Mahwah."

"Ma-what?" Sal said, more Ringo Starr than anything else.

I jerked a thumb toward the Chippendale entrance and stopped short of saying ime-tay to am-scray.

Sal nodded and gave me a jaunty thumbs-up,

game as any World War II doughboy. "All righty. Tally-ho! Pip pip."

Pip pip?

Mr. Henry and I stared at him in stunned silence.

Later, we drove back toward the city with the convertible top down, the sun so low in the sky it reflected in the car's outside mirrors. I was drafting a subpoena in my head for the dealership's sales and test-drive records, but Sal wanted rave reviews. "Didn't I do good?" he kept asking.

"Until you started chewing the scenery."

"What?" Wind buffeted his thin gray hair and his Adam's apple protruded like a figurehead. "What does that mean?"

"It means you did great. Terrific."

He grinned so broadly that the silver edge of his eyetooth caught the sunlight. "It was like I was in the movies. It was like I was a movie star."

"You sure were."

"I was like Cary Grant or something!"

If he were still alive. "Yep."

"Didja like what I did about his desk?"

"I liked what you did about the desk."

"Didja like when I told him I was shocked?"

"I liked when you told him you were shocked."

"He was gonna call and I *stopped* him!"

"You sure did. I don't know what I would've done without you." It was true, actually. "I mean it."

Sal squinted against the wind. "Why did we have to leave?"

"Because we found out what we needed to know."

"Oh."

"Okay?"

"Okay," he said, but he seemed to deflate visibly in his seat, like a child after all the birthday presents have been opened.

"You had fun, huh?"

He nodded.

"Fun is good, Uncle Sal."

He didn't say anything, just kept squinting as the wind blew his wispy hair around.

"What do you do for fun, Unc?"

He thought for what seemed like a very long time. "I like music."

"What kind of music? You a rap fan, MC Sal?"

"No, no." He didn't even smile.

"What then?"

"Big band. Glenn Miller, Tommy Dorsey. Like the old 950 Club."

"What's the 950 Club?"

"On the radio. In the afternoons."

"Like now?"

"Yeh," he said, without checking his watch. "They don't have Ed Hurst no more, but they got the music."

I turned on the radio and scanned until I reached the station. Even I recognized the song "Sing, Sing, Sing." "That's Benny Goodman, isn't it?"

"Yeh."

"I like this song."

"Your mother, she liked it, too."

Out of left field. "Did she like music?" I had no idea.

"Loved it."

"Really?"

He nodded.

I wondered. "What else did she like?"

"She liked to dance. She never sat still. She liked to go, your mother."

I guess. "That why she left, you think?"

He nodded again.

"Go where, though?"

"Anywhere. She liked action."

"Action?"

"Attention, like."

I considered this. A Canadian blonde among the dark Italian butchers, grocers, and bakers, like a yellow diamond on a coal pile. A woman who liked to go, married to a man who wanted only to stay. "She didn't really fit in, did she?"

"Like a sore thumb."

"She never would have stayed, would she?"

"Not for long. Vito was the only one who didn't see it comin'."

It hurt inside. For my father, then for me. "You don't think I'm like her, do you?"

"Nah. You got dark hair."

So he wasn't Phil Donahue. Morrones weren't known for their introspection. "I meant her personality, not her looks."

"Nah."

"Not even a little?" I almost hit a Saab in front of me for watching him, but Sal's only reaction was to shake his head. "Uncle Sal?"

"Can you turn up the radio, Ree?"

I laughed. "Is this the end of the conversation, Unc?"

He nodded, then smiled. "She was a wiseguy, too."

Our highway entrance came up suddenly, City Line Avenue onto the Schuylkill Expressway, and I turned onto the on ramp. I thought about pressing him on the subject, but let it go. It was the longest talk I'd ever had about my mother, and somehow it was enough. More words wouldn't make it any clearer, or any different. It was up to me to figure out anyway, for myself.

"The radio, Ree?" Sal asked again.

"Sorry," I said, and cranked the music way up. The clarinet and horns blasted in the wind as Benny Goodman hit the chorus and we hit the open road. At this hour, rush-hour traffic was going the other way. "You can at least catch the end of the song, huh?"

"Yeah. I like the end." The wind was stronger now that we had picked up speed. I pressed the button to close my window. Sal fished in his jacket pocket and found the Ray-Ban aviators I'd bought him, then slipped them on like a flyboy.

"Lookin' good, Uncle Sal," I shouted over the drums.

"You know, Ree, I kinda liked bein' a lawyer,"

he shouted back. "Maybe we'll do more lawyer stuff."

Like cheating and lying and perpetrating fraud? "Whatever you say, Mr. Livemore."

He paused. "Ree?"

"What?"

"Can't you make this crate move any faster?"

I smiled. Uncle Sal liked to go, too. Everybody did, a little. "Hang on, handsome. Hang on."

And he did.

Sing, sing, sing.

20

Tobin had chosen an upscale sidewalk restaurant on Main Street in Manayunk, a town along the Schuylkill River, on the outskirts of town. Twenty years ago, Main Street was a gritty strip of shoe and textile wholesalers that served as the backdrop for a hilly clumping of brick row houses. But Manayunk, like all of us, hippened up in the nineties, attracting an annual bicycle race to its hills, restaurants like this one, and countless boutiques vending black clothes. Now there were twelve-cylinder Mercedeses lining the street and ponytails who dressed like Tobin.

"I love it here," he said as he dumped ketchup onto a ten-dollar cheeseburger and a mound of french fries. "I got a loft down the street, above the interior designer's."

"We're too old for lofts."

"Speak for yourself, teach." He dug into his burger with abandon and didn't seem to mind being on display despite his table manners. More than one woman, walking by, cruised his Nautilus-powered Armani. "So, this is quite a little murder investigation you're running."

"You approve? That means so much to me."

"I knew it would. What's next?"

"I go motorcycle shopping with Herman tomorrow. We try to find out who bought that blue BMW motorcycle." I speared a salad composed of greens apparently picked from the shoulder of I-95. I should have asked what a mesclun salad was before I ordered this thing.

"You going with a kosher butcher, on a Saturday?"

"He's not that kosher."

He nodded. "Neither am I. So, let's see, you got Herman the butcher, you got Cam with one arm, you got your little Uncle Sal. It's a Dream Team."

"Watch it, pal. That's my family you're talking about."

"Interesting family."

"You don't get to define it, I do."

He wolfed down a canoe of a french fry. "Back off, I'm not criticizing. It's a big case and it's just starting. You should be getting your team together, before trial. Take all the help you can get."

"I am."

"Except mine."

I considered this. "I'm here, aren't I?"

"I didn't ask you to dinner to help you. I asked you to dinner to find out if you're gonna marry Richie Rich."

"Who?"

"That slice of white bread you bring to the Christmas party. I heard you live with him."

I can't say it took me aback, given his reputation, but I wasn't prepared for it before the crème brûlée. "You'll explain to me why this is any of your business."

"I'm your partner."

"So are thirty-five other people."

"And they're all talking about you behind your back. Is she really gonna marry the judge's son? They don't think you can do any better, but I do."

I guessed from his smirk he was kidding. "You defend me from vicious gossip?"

"At every turn."

"But then again, you eat Sno-caps for lunch."

He scarfed down another french fry. "So?"

"So what?"

"So you're not engaged or you'd have a ring."

I felt a twinge. "Not engaged."

"Not only are you not engaged, you're fighting with him."

"How do you know that?"

"Because you ignored him at the preliminary hearing and he spent the whole fucking time trying to get your attention."

I hadn't noticed. "He did not."

"And I hear you been together forever." He sucked ketchup from a finger. "So I'm thinking either Richie Rich won't marry you or you won't marry him. And since it's impossible for me to believe a man won't marry you, there's only one thing I want to know."

Christ. "My favorite color is red, but I won't tell you my age or weight."

He looked at me directly. "What's holding you back?"

"You're right, it's silly of me. Sexist, even. I'm thirty-two years old." Roughly.

"You avoid commitment, like all the other girls?"

"All right, I'll tell you. I weigh a hundred and five pounds." Or would, if I worked out.

"Or maybe you don't love him enough?"

Ouch. Maybe I do. "You're not getting the message, Tobin. This is none of your business."

"You want to tell me anyway?"

"Why should I?"

"Because despite the way I look or the way I act with my so-called partners, or the shit you've heard about me, I'm a pretty decent guy. And I'm very attracted to you."

I avoided his dark gaze and watched the candle on the table flicker in its frosted glass. His words were having some effect; my female ego must've been bruised more than I thought. "I don't want to have this conversation."

"But you are having it."

"No, I'm not." I looked away, but the people on the street were walking so close to our table they could see the ragweed in my entree. "Let's just drop it, okay?"

"You're telling me this is an arms'-length dinner?"

"Exactly."

"Professional colleagues? Not even friends? Like in high school, we're both in chess club or some such shit?"

"You got it."

"Wonderful." He drained the beer from its green bottle and looked around for the waitress. "I need another beer."

"You had three already. I hope you're walking home."

"They're Clausthalers, Mom."

"What's that?"

"Denial beer. Nonalcoholic, like me. It was not always thus."

I hadn't known. "Really?"

"Really." He gave up on the waitress and faced me. He suddenly looked tired, which made him look more human, worn in. "So, what's the status of the murder investigation so far?"

"I have some suspicions, but more questions than anything else. Nothing really logical."

"Murder is never logical. It's emotional."

"But you can use logic to solve it."

"No, you can't. To think like a killer you have to think emotionally. Murder is reactive, an emotional reaction to something. You have to figure out what set it off."

I remembered Paul, his confidence in deductive reasoning. "How do you know this, Tobin? The guys you defended were lowlifes. They committed murder on drugs or while they were drinking, right?"

"Don't be such a snob. Smart people commit murder. White people commit murder, too."

"I didn't say they didn't—"

"Murder is an irrational reaction to a given set of circumstances. It can be planned out, premeditated, or happen in an instant, but it's still emotional. And the emotions are strongest when it's a love relationship—boy meets girl, boy kills girl when she runs around."

I thought of Paul again, this time with a chill, and reconsidered what I was doing here. If Tobin was going to help me, and it seemed like he could, then I'd have to confide in him. Part of me didn't trust him, but part of me wanted to take the risk. So I took a deep breath and told him the whole story, about Fiske's affair with Patricia, and, because he listened so thoughtfully, even about Paul and Patricia. I told it as calmly as I could, and when I had finished, picked up my wineglass with a hand that shook only slightly.

"Holy shit," Tobin said.

"You got that right. So I guess what I have is Kate, Paul, and maybe Fiske, with motive out the wazoo and no credible alibi. Then I have a motorcycle rider to track down, the other boyfriends to question, and no murder weapon."

"That's one way to look at it. If you're blind. Willfully."

"What's that supposed to mean?"

"It means you have a prime suspect you don't want to deal with. Richie Rich."

No. "Paul?"

"Come on, Rita, look at the payoff. Whacking that girl solves everything for him. He silences the girl, the lawsuit drops out, and he gets off the hook."

"Why would Paul want the lawsuit ended?"

"Because it could expose him, too. Tell the whole world he was screwing his father's girl-friend. How would that play out in the vanilla suburbs? He has his own business, doesn't he? A reputation to protect?"

"But why would he kill her?"

"He pays her back for fucking around on him. For fucking up his life. Look, he lost you, didn't he?"

Did he? "Still, Paul is close to his father. He wouldn't frame his own father for murder."

"Not even if Daddy is screwing his girlfriend *and* cheating on Mommy? Maybe he's figuring you'll get Daddy off the hook. Wake up and smell the reality."

I couldn't believe it. "Tobin, I saw what was done to that woman. Paul is not capable of that. He just isn't."

"Almost anybody is capable of it, given the right set of circumstances. Where was Richie Rich that day?"

"Running errands."

"Sounds airtight to me," he said abruptly, then looked away at the passing traffic. The sun was gone, the crowd had died down. The diners had been replaced by couples holding paper cones of water ice, window-shopping up and down Main Street. Manayunk, being near the river and its own snaky canal, stayed reasonably cool at night. The candle on the table danced in its glass cup.

Tobin turned back and his eyes met mine. "I think you're in deep shit, good lookin'."

"Why? I have months before the trial."

"I'm not worried about the trial, you got the trial covered. If you prove what you told me about the Jab and raise the question of the motorcyclist, you got reasonable doubt. I could win that case. You probably could, too."

"I'm ignoring your arrogance."

"Everyone does."

Testosterone should be a controlled substance. "I want to find the motorcycle rider and question him."

"No. You're better off not finding him. Leave him wherever he is. Use him like a nice big question mark at the trial, to beef up the reasonable doubt. A black kid on a motorcycle on the run? He's more useful to you lost than found, especially with a white Main Line jury. It's like a gift. Happy Hanukkah."

"But what if he committed the murder?"

"Not your problem. You're the judge's lawyer. Get the judge off."

So much for justice.

"Listen, Rita, the biggest problem is that you're trying to catch a killer and you're way too up-close-and-personal."

"I can handle it."

He leaned forward on his elbows, gold-circle cuff links glinting like half-moons from beneath his sleeves. "I'm not talking about whether you can handle it, I'm talking about whether you're in danger."

"From what?"

"Let's say Richie Rich framed his father, knowing that he has his ace lawyer girlfriend on the hook for the defense. He knows the girlfriend is skilled enough to get his father off and also that she's too much in love to suspect him. He gets it all, and he gets away with murder. It's perfect. The guy's a genius."

I felt my heart beginning to pound. "But what about the Jag? The steering wheel?"

"Maybe he gets the car on a test drive like you think, maybe he borrows Mom's when she's fucking around with the roses. He forgot about the wheel on the right, but that's a detail. All he wants is revenge on the girl. Didn't he get you hired for the sexual harassment case in the first place?"

Paul had encouraged Fiske to hire me.

"I bet he was real interested in the case, too."

It had almost saved our relationship.

"He wanted you to stay with the representation, for murder?"

True.

"And he knew when you took the harassment case that you'd be prosecuting his lover? What a scam!"

"Fuck you." I rose to go.

Tobin laughed. "Oh, I see. You can handle it, you just can't discuss it."

I sat back in my uncomfortable chair and folded my arms. "Okay, discuss."

"I think Richie Rich set you up. I think if you get close to finding out that it's him, he'll kill you, too."

It seemed impossible. Paul hurt me?

"So I think I'll stick around for a while."

"What's that mean, 'stick around'?"

"Be your bud, check in from time to time. That's what chess club is all about. Aren't you glad you joined?"

I felt uneasy. Paul was probably cooling his heels on the porch at home. What would be his next move? "Do you play chess, Tobin?"

He smiled, his crow's-feet deepening. "Are you kidding? I suck at chess. I can't think two steps in front of me."

"You play cards?"

"No. I'm not a game player."

"Except with women."

"You got me all wrong. I don't play any games at all."

"Right."

"It's the truth. Whenever I play, it's not a game," he said, and this time he wasn't smiling. "Now, let's get a coupla sundaes."

After dessert, Tobin walked me back to the canal-side parking lot and put me into my car with a friendly pat on the back. On the short ride home, I thought about what he had said, trying to wrap my mind around it. It seemed possible only if you didn't know Paul. He'd always been nothing but peaceable, intellectual, and he rarely lost his cool. But then again, I'd never given him cause to be jealous. Until tonight.

When I pulled into the driveway the Cherokee was already waiting.

21

Paul's car was parked in front of the garage and its interior was dark. I guessed he was waiting on the front porch, having discovered his key no longer fit the front or back doors. I cut the ignition and got out of the car warily, despite my doubts about Tobin's scenario.

I headed across the lawn, which felt wet. Paul must have watered it, his mother had taught him to water after dark. I thought of what Tobin had said. Paul was close to Kate; he'd even been teased at school as a momma's boy. Would Paul have framed Fiske for cheating on her? I kept walking.

The outside and house lights were off. Our house, a stone and shingle colonial with a welcoming front porch, loomed large and dark. The neighborhood was quiet, probably most of my neighbors were out. A humid breeze rustled the trees shading the porch. I looked through the branches as I passed by but didn't see Paul waiting where I expected he'd be, on one of the white Adirondack chairs he loved. I climbed the stone steps to the porch and looked around. No Paul.

It didn't make sense. The Cherokee, but no Paul. He couldn't get in, maybe he went for a walk.

I checked my watch. It was 9:35. If he'd arrived on time, as he always did, he would've been waiting for over two hours. Enough time to walk up to Lancaster Avenue and grab dinner. I dug in my purse for my keys and opened the front door. The entrance hall was dark and silent. I closed the door behind me and clicked on the deadbolt.

"Lucy, you got some 'splainin' to do," said a voice, mock-Ricky Ricardo. It was Paul, his voice coming out of the darkness in the living room. I would've turned on the light, but it was closer to him.

"How did you get in?"

"You changed the locks on me, Lucy. That

210

wasn't very nice," he said, slurring his words slightly.

"How did you get in here?"

"We have one fight and you go and change the locks on me. You locked me out of my *home*."

"Paul—"

"Talk about hardball. You lawyers are somethin' else." I heard the chink of ice in a crystal tumbler. He drank scotch, but never to excess before.

"Tell me how you got in."

"I know this house better than you. I know which windows are loose and which aren't. I spend more time here than you. You have to go out and make the proverbial big bucks."

An old wound I thought we'd gotten over.

"Go ahead . . . say your line," he said.

"What line?"

"Whenever I say that, you say, 'Paul, you were born with more money than I'll ever make.'"

I didn't like the way he imitated my voice. "I think you should go. Now."

"Aw, come on, mang," he said, Cuban again. "You'll be happy I'm here when I tell you what I found out, Lucy."

"Stop calling me that."

"All right, you're the one who likes Lucy and Ricky anyway. All the time I'm hard at work, solving a murder. Where were you?"

"None of your business."

The lamp came on, illuminating Paul's face. He sat slumped in the leather Morris chair against the bookshelves, tumbler in hand, his head slightly to one side. "I know who murdered Patricia Sullivan."

Christ. "Who?"

"Tell me where you were and I'll tell you who."

"Come on, Paul."

"You'd like to have that answer, wouldn't you? Because you've been wondering. Maybe even about me, who's practically your fiancé."

"Who is the killer?"

"But your practical fiancé has no alibi, you've been thinking. He says he was doing errands, but what errands? Does he have the receipts? What store clerks will remember him? Like you were asking my mother. How stupid do you think she is?"

"Who is the killer, Paul?"

"Not yet. Tell me who you were with tonight."

I'd play a minute longer to get the answer. "My father."

"Lucy, Lucy, Lucy. I called the hospital. They said he was sleeping. I even called your friends the poker players."

Shit. "I visited my father, then I went to work."

"Tsk, tsk, tsk. Called there, too."

"I was in the library."

"You, not check your voice mail? Liar, liar, pants on fire. Are they, by the way? You're home early."

"I'm not going to play games with you, Paul. Tell me what you know or I go to the police." I reached for the deadbolt and twisted it loud enough for him to hear.

"Guess what I found out? I found out where you were tonight. I just wanted to hear it from your own mouth."

My throat tightened. I didn't know whether to believe him. "Who is the killer?"

"You lied to me."

"You lied to *me*."

"Oh, is that it?" he said, his tone angry. "Tit for tat? A retaliatory fuck?"

Don't get sidetracked. "Who is the *killer*?"

"Morrone's on the job, folks. All business. But she wasn't working tonight, was she?"

"That's it, I'm leaving." I turned my back on him and opened the door.

"Aramingo Avenue, in the northeast. Greater Northeast, as they say on the news."

I turned back. "Who?"

"Drives a blue motorcycle, paints. Plays guitar, of course. He ran a personal ad, that's how they met. Only he didn't mention he had a cocaine habit, even convicted of dealing, once. Or that he's a very, very jealous young man."

"What's his name?"

"Tim Price."

"How'd you get the address? Deductive reasoning?"

"'Fraid not," he said, half to himself. "I'm not a very good architect or I'd make more money, right? If you're so smart, how come you're not rich? Like Dad?"

I turned the knob. "I have to go."

"I saw a letter he sent her, with the return address. He was crazy about her, but he was just a toy to her. So were we all. She played games, that woman."

"Did they live together?"

"Sort of, but he was away a lot, and when the cat's away, well . . . you hate clichés, don't you? When I figured out the game, I broke up with her—when *he* figured it out, he killed her. Not a good game, was it? Not a safe game, like poker."

Fuck you. "If he killed her, why did he leave his motorcycle behind?"

"I don't know the mechanics of it, dear. No pun."

"Then why do you say he's the killer?"

"She told me she was afraid of him, that he'd hit her. Beaten her when he was high. Still, she let him come back. He had that bad-boy appeal some women like." Paul held up his glass, examining its facets in the lamplight. "Long hair, maverick type. That your thing, too, Rita?"

He must know about Tobin. Maybe I'd been spotted by someone we both knew, or maybe he'd followed me to the restaurant. I felt afraid suddenly and fumbled for the doorknob behind me. "Be gone by morning," I said, twisting the knob and walking out.

Behind me I heard the crash of a crystal tumbler hitting the wall. "Goddamn it! I live here, too! Rita!"

I started running to the car and didn't stop until I was inside.

I booked a night at the Four Seasons, in a cushy room overlooking the fountain in Logan Square. Not that I enjoyed the view, I spent the time making phone calls. I called a twenty-four-hour lock service to change the locks again and secure all the windows. For an extra fifty bucks, they'd deliver the new keys to the hotel. I flipped through the Yellow Pages for a burglar alarm company, but there was no answer. Then I called Herman and canceled our date to go motorcycle shopping, since I already knew the motorcyclist's address, and called my father. He sounded fine but wanted to know why Sal was so dressed up. Finally, I called Cam and told him our gig was moved up to tomorrow.

"Whatever you say, kiddo," he said.

Then I grabbed a hotel pen and began to draft legal papers on the king-size bed. I'd never practiced family law, but then I'd never practiced criminal law either. I alleged I had reason to believe I was in danger from one Paul Harlan Hamilton, my live-in boyfriend, who had appeared drunk and disorderly at our former home. I asked the court to keep Paul two miles from the property and requested a hearing forthwith. I had the papers photocopied at the marbled front desk, and mailed and faxed a set to Paul's office with a short note: *The next time I find you*

215

in the house, I file this. With copies to your parents, the police, and the newspapers.

It was my first protection order, both as a lawyer and as a client. One for the scrapbook. And it was undoubtedly the first time the Four Seasons had served as a women's shelter. I went back up to my room, chuckling. It was better than crying.

I flopped on the sea of bed and switched on the television. Spectravision, it said, which I guessed was a lot like Cinemascope. I muted the sound and the pictures flickered by in silence. A man and woman in jeans and sweatshirts clinked coffee mugs over a kitchen table. Dennis Hopper, still crazy after all these years, pushed Nikes. I was waiting for the eleven o'clock news, almost too sleepy to be curious about their coverage of the preliminary hearing, which seemed as if it happened ages ago.

I was still on the job, like Paul had said.

But I didn't want to think about him now. And it turned out that I couldn't anyway. After a fire in a Camden warehouse, Stan Julicher was the big news. His ruddy face, behind the black microphone bubbles, was animated by an almost religious zeal. Seated at a press table with him were a trio of TV feminists, angry women with no eyeliner and inmate hair.

"It's no crime to look good, girlfriend," I said to the TV. "No matter what Naomi Wolf says." I clicked up the volume.

"It's time for the citizens of this city to demand

that Judge Hamilton step down," Julicher was saying. "He is officially charged with the murder of a young woman, who may have died trying to vindicate her right to be free from sexual harassment. Yet the Honorable Fiske Hamilton sits in judgment of *us*."

Christ. Julicher was pissed because he'd lost his meal ticket, and he was about to ruin Fiske.

One of the feminists said, "We, too, call for Judge Hamilton to step down from his judicial duties, at the very least until the murder charge against him is resolved. He should not sit on cases of any type, civil or criminal, until his innocence is proven beyond the shadow of a doubt."

Of all the stupid, wrong-headed, knee-jerk reactions. "I'm not sending you girls any more money," I said to the TV.

The third woman leaned into the microphone. "We think it is ironic indeed that Judge Hamilton could tomorrow be sitting in judgment on murder cases when he is himself charged with murder."

I aimed the remote between her eyes. "Murder is a state crime, you idiot, and Fiske's a federal judge. Other than that, you're absolutely right." I nuked her with the off button and reached for the phone to touch base with Fiske, then had second thoughts. I was too tired to give any sensible advice. He'd have to weather tonight alone, and I'd deal with it in the morning.

I felt myself drifting into sleep with the clicker still in my hand. I thought of Paul, wondering if he had left the house, but my last thought was of Tobin, in his Manayunk loft. I wondered if he was watching the news.

And I wondered if he was alone.

22

I felt refreshed the next morning, even though the free *Inquirer* outside my door served up the headline I expected:

RESIGNATION OF EMBATTLED FEDERAL JUDGE EXPECTED

I scanned the article, which rehashed the press conference, including plenty of self-righteous quotes by Julicher. Fiske, wisely, "could not be reached for comment," and we all know where I was. The managing partner of Averback, Shore & Macklin, my favorite blackjack player, had managed to get in his share of hyperbole, dubbing me "one of the most prominent woman lawyers in the country." I figured we were talking at least thirty-five thousand dollars worth of prominence in my new contract, but Mack couldn't pay me enough for what this case had done to my life.

I gulped down my complimentary coffee and croissant and grabbed a shower using hotel shampoo, soap, conditioner, and moisturizer.

After I had consumed everything free, I settled down to call Fiske.

"Rita, where are you?" he asked.

"In town. How are you? And don't quote Gilbert and Sullivan."

"You've seen the news." He sounded tense.

"Of course. Want some legal advice?"

"I'm listening."

"Don't resign."

"The chief judge called. He asked me to consider it for the good of the court. He wants my answer tomorrow."

"Fine. Call him tomorrow and tell him you considered it and you're not resigning."

"Kate thinks I should. Lower my profile, all that."

"Hamiltons don't run, do they, Fiske? They don't quit. You have a family name to uphold, don't you?" I stopped short of explaining about general principles.

"I am innocent, goddamn it."

Works for me. "Then do your job. Stay away from the press. Leave the rest to me."

"You sound different, Rita."

"Do I?"

"Yes. Better. Are you making progress with the investigation?"

"I have the motorcyclist's address, and I'm on the trail of the black Jags in the area."

"Wonderful work!"

"And I lost some weight, too." About a hundred and ninety pounds, name of Paul. "But it's probably the creme rinse. Nothing like a good conditioner to give a girl some confidence. And a silky shine."

Cam swung the noisy electric hedge trimmers in a smooth arc from his perch on the stepladder. Above him was a hot midday sun and a mercilessly clear sky. His work boots were scuffed, he wore a sweaty Banana Republic work shirt, and his fifty-dollar khakis had grass stains at the knee. Camille Lopo was the best-dressed one-armed gardener-impersonator in Wayne.

"You're not getting tired, Cam?" I shouted, over the loud chatter of the trimmer's greasy teeth.

"Huh?"

"You okay up there?"

"What?" he shouted back.

"You sure you're not tired?"

He checked his watch. "Almost noon!"

Only Italians would persist in talking over a hedge trimmer. It takes more than Black & Decker to shut us up, even when one of us is almost deaf. "You sure you're not tired?" I fairly screamed.

"There's a lotta new growth! You can tell 'cause it's greener! Yellow-green instead of a dark green!"

"Spoken like a pro!" I yelled back, scanning the grass. I wanted to reexamine every inch of the grounds around the carriage house and Mrs. Mateer's house, and the newly incorporated

Lawns 'R Us was the only way to do it freely, without the official eyes of the Radnor police or their crime scene logs.

"This is our third lawn, kiddo! I *am* a pro!"

I felt a guilty pang, making a seventy-year-old do yardwork to serve my own purposes. "I owe you, big time."

"Baby, I'm busier than a one-armed paper-hanger." He swung the hedge trimmer on a plane as even as a card table. Sprigs of English hedge fell to either side and landed in mounds on the grass.

"YOU SURE YOU'RE NOT—"

"ASK ME AGAIN AND I'LL CUT *YOUR* ARM OFF!"

The clipper went back and forth, buzzing in my ear. I was posing as Cam's assistant, in identical outfit except for my Eagles cap, sunglasses, and Canon camera. I snapped another picture of the hedge. I wanted enlarged photos of the grounds for the jury, taken from my own uniquely distorted perspective.

"Don't forget to look at the ground!" Cam called out. "For evidence!"

So much for secrecy. I looked down but saw only the buzz-cut surface of Mrs. Mateer's newly shorn lawn. "You do good work, you know that?" I told him.

"What?" He switched the trimmer off and wiped his brow. The steely hair at his receding hairline was so damp it had returned to its original black. "Maybe this'll be a new career for me."

"You'd make more at the track."

"I don't know, I liked that sit-down mower. I liked it a lot." Cam had mowed the lawn with a rented Toro while I stayed out of sight. He was the one who went to Mrs. Mateer's door because she might have recognized me, even in my disguise. "Felt like a buggy ride, that mower."

"How do you know what a buggy ride feels like, city boy?"

"Are you kidding? I used to ride around with the iceman. We jumped on the back of the wagon to get the chips."

I took another picture, one of the house in the distance. Then a shot of Cam getting down from the ladder, just for fun.

"Look at it this way, kid," he said, tugging the ladder. "We had no problem gettin' work. We got three lawns right off the bat."

"That's because we're doing it for free, Cam. And you have your charms."

"It's the stump, it gets 'em every time." He flapped his empty sleeve. "Theresa married me because of this stump, I swear. Said she felt sorry for me. When we got in a fight, I used to tell her I got phantom pains, then—*bing*—it was all over."

I laughed, but I had banked on it. Who wouldn't accept a free lawn cleanup from a handicapped senior trying to start a new business? Especially when he'd just done the two houses across the street and they looked terrific?

"So what's the take so far?" he asked.

"You mean the defense evidence?" I reached into my fanny pack for my official evidence-collecting kit, a gold Lancome makeup case. I had plucked each item from the ground with a Revlon tweezers, put it in its own Baggie, and labeled it with a Clinique eye pencil. "Let's see, Exhibit A is a Fruit Stripe gum wrapper. Exhibit B is a cigarette butt. We have a plastic figurine of Garfield the cat, in mint condition, as Exhibit C. The smart money's on Garfield, Camille. He could crack this case wide open."

"The toy is from the Donovan place?"

"Yes."

He shook his head. "That Donovan kid was a brat. I never saw so many toys in a backyard in my life. And that castle thing with the green top and the sliding board? Did you get a load of that?"

"Little monster." I had tripped on the tetherball pole. "Turd."

He laughed. "When I was little I had a truck. A red truck. That was it."

"The rich get richer, Cam."

"Ain't it the truth."

He climbed back up the ladder and switched the trimmers on again. It buzzed away while I flipped through the thirteen bags I had collected. Each one contained apparent backyard trash, so I resumed my treasure hunt, walking along the hedgeline at the back of Mrs. Mateer's property, eyes to the ground. At the bottom of the hedges were dry dirt, crumbling brown leaves, and at the end, pricey bark mulch.

The sound of the trimmers grew more and more distant. It took me five minutes to reach the property line, where the hedge abutted the equally vast grounds of Mrs. Mateer's neighbor. The end of the line. Maybe I was wasting my time. And poor Cam's, who was sweating away, with one arm, on a ladder. I would burn in hell and it would feel a lot like this.

I thought of trying to call Price, the motorcyclist, again, but I had already left three messages on his machine. I had packed a flip phone in my pants pocket in case he called back. If he didn't, I'd visit him unannounced after this escapade was over.

I pivoted on my sneakers and saw the carriage house in the distance. It was crisscrossed with yellow police tape, sealed but unguarded. Still, I had to be subtle about my snooping because of the neighbors, and the suburbanites who slowed their Range Rovers to gape at the house where a woman bled to death.

I walked all the way back to Cam, nose to the ground like a bloodhound with a law degree, and retrieved a new blue-enameled Ames rake. Lawns 'R Us was not only the most fashionable fraud on the Main Line, we were the best-equipped. I avoided thinking about what I was going to do with this stupid equipment later and concentrated on raking the hedge clippings into piles that I rolled toward the carriage house.

I looked everywhere as I raked and bagged any trash I found. An hour later, Cam was almost at the end of the hedgerow bordering the Mateer driveway, and my work shirt was drenched with sweat. On the lawn in front of me lay rolls of hedge clippings, like hoagies on a party tray. I' had collected two more gum wrappers, both Doublemint, and yet another cigarette butt. Either it was a trashy backyard or a killer with a major oral fixation.

Picture time. I glanced around to make sure I wasn't being watched, but everybody had gone to buy more things they didn't need. I took some shots of the Mateer house from the vantage point of the carriage house, snapping away like a hungry realtor. When I looked through the square window of the Canon, I saw Cam, waving at me with his arm.

What a ham. I snapped the picture he was begging for and shifted the camera to get a better view of the Mateer house. Cam kept waving. It was a cute photo, but I didn't think it would enlighten the jury. I took another picture of the Mateer house, showing how the view from the kitchen window was partially obstructed by the trees.

"June, June!" I heard Cam shout. It was the alias we'd agreed upon for me, since it was, after all, June. Plus I liked sounding like a centerfold for a change. "June!"

I looked at him over the camera.

Cam was waving again, but something in his movement was odd. Jerky. Either he'd found something or he was having dyspepsia. I looked

225

through the lens and zoomed it up to telephoto so I could see his face. It was streaked with grime, strained and anxious. He was pointing excitedly to the ground at his feet.

Baby, baby. I broke into as subtle a sprint as possible, the camera swinging around my neck. Cam was standing on Mrs. Mateer's asphalt driveway, where the end of the hedge reached the white stucco of the house.

"Rita, look," he said, in a hushed tone.

I looked. Nestled among the hedge trimmings, a soggy green tennis ball, and a chubby pink begonia was a knife.

I blinked, but it was still there. I'd handled more than my share of knives in my father's shop, but I didn't know what kind of knife it was. It had a dark brown handle and its dull bronze blade was scarred by brownish stains. The stains could have been any kind of goo, but what it looked most like was dried blood. I couldn't believe my eyes, neither could Cam. We stood over the knife like kids who'd found a garter snake in the back-yard. Too afraid to touch, but too amazed to turn away.

"Way to go, Camille," I said.

"I'm lucky today, kid. Maybe I shoulda gone to the track."

"Then you would've missed playing junior detective."

"You mean senior detective." He smiled, then stared down at the knife. "What are you gonna do?"

226

An excellent question. Should I bag it? Should I call the cops? Can you pluck a knife with an eyebrow tweezers? "Damned if I know. Garfield I can handle, but this?"

"We can't take it, can we?"

Hmmm. "Let me think about that." Meantime, I grabbed the camera and fired off shots from every angle. From close up, from far away, I finished an entire roll on the knife alone. And the more I looked at the knife, through the white viewfinder inside the camera lens, the more I believed Cam had found what I hadn't dared hope we'd find. The knife that killed Patricia Sullivan.

But I needed to learn more about the knife, so I could draw some conclusions about its owner.

As it turned out I knew a knife expert, rather well.

23

My father, propped up slightly in his hospital bed, squinted through his bifocals at the photo. "It's a knife."

My expert. "I know that, Dad. What kind of knife is it?"

"All-purpose, like a buck knife."

"But it's not a buck knife?"

He held the photo closer. "No."

"Told you," Cam said, sitting on the other side of the bed, still in dirty gardening gear.

"Could it kill someone?" I asked.

"This knife? In a New York minute."

It sent a shiver through me. "Who would own this kind of knife, Dad? What would it be used for?"

"Anything, everything."

"Like what?"

He peered at the picture. "Hunting, fishing, working in the garden or somethin'. Even around the garage. You could cut boxes with it, maybe wire. Anything."

My heart sank. "Really, anything?"

"General purpose." He set the photo down on his tummy and picked up the next one by its edges. "You think it's the killer's knife?"

"Yes. Who would have this kind of knife around?"

"Anybody."

"Shit."

He wet his lips, which looked parched. "It's a good knife to have around, what can I say? I have one just like it in the back kitchen, even old like this. I use it on the fig tree, to trim it."

"I never saw it. You never pointed it at me."

He smiled weakly. "Maybe it's not the murder weapon."

"It looks like blood to me," I said, gathering up the photos. "What do you think? You're the hematologist here."

"Yeah, maybe." He closed his eyes, suddenly fatigued. "What'd the cops say?"

Cam laughed. "We didn't wait around, Vito. We hadda see a man about a horse."

It had taken an hour to get the pictures developed but far less than that to summon the Radnor police to the Mateer property. I had called them from the flip phone but opted not to stay on the scene until they arrived. No need to tell them I was perpetrating a fraud in a work shirt, not to mention corrupting the morals of a major.

"What I don't understand is why the cops didn't find it," Cam said. "It was right there."

Which is what was bothering me. Cam and I had gone back and forth about it in Thrift Drug, while we waited for the pictures. The technician kept looking at us funny, he didn't hear many conversations about murder weapons in front of the Midol.

"I mean," Cam continued, "how come I could find it and they couldn't?"

"*You* found it?" my father asked. "With *your* eyesight?"

Cam looked offended. "My eyes are good. Right, Rita?"

"Right, Cam. It's your hearing that sucks."

"Bullshit," my father said. My heart warmed to hear him regain his profanity. "Your eyes are lousy. Half the time you're asking Herman whether it's a club or a spade."

"I did that once," Cam corrected.

"Come on, more than once."

"I can still see better than you, Vito."

"That's not saying much," I said, and my father nudged me with his foot. His color had improved and the nudge felt strong, but I noticed his lunch had barely been touched. He felt terrible that he couldn't go to LeVonne's funeral. It had been set for tomorrow because the coroner had just released the body. "So why do you think the cops didn't find it, Pop?"

He set the photo on his belly with a sigh. "Who knows? Cops. They can't find who killed LeVonne either, even though I gave 'em a good description."

"Still no leads?" Cam asked.

"That's what Herman says. He calls 'em all the time, the detectives. He gives 'em hell."

Cam chuckled, but my father didn't. He sank deeper into the thin pillows. I worried he was becoming depressed. "You sleeping okay, Dad?"

"Fine."

The nurses had told me he slept only off and on. "You eating okay?"

"Like a horse."

What a load. "The nurses say you're not."

"The nurses think they know everything," he said, his eyes still closed. "They love to boss you around. Except that little one with the red hair that Sal likes. Betty."

"Are people still named Betty?" I asked.

"This one is," Cam said. "*Madonne,* she's a tomato."

Va-va-va-voom. "Do men still say that? What is this, a time warp?"

My father smiled. "Sal likes her, but he's too chickenshit to talk to her."

"Where is Sal?" Cam asked.

"Out with Herman." My father opened his eyes and reached for my hand. His felt rough and warm, familiar. "You all right, kid?"

"Fine."

"You all wrapped up in your case?"

"Yep."

"Don't work too hard now."

"Me? Never."

"Miss Fresh." He closed his eyes but hung on to my hand. "I can hear that brain of yours, workin' away."

I laughed, but he was right. I was arriving at one explanation why the police hadn't found the knife during their investigation: It hadn't been there. Did the killer plant it after the fact, and why? It was a risky, risky thing to do.

So if I couldn't learn anything from the knife itself—because I was guessing the killer was too smart to leave his fingerprints all over it—I learned something from the fact it had just been deposited beside the begonias. This killer wasn't afraid of risk any more than I was. He was playing a game with the police, or even with me.

And he was upping the ante.

It used to be that the billboards along I-95 North had directions to Sesame Place in Langhorne, and Big Bird pointed the way with a feathery index finger. Now the billboards advertised the casinos in Atlantic City. POKERMANIA. HIGHROLLERS. QUARTERMANIA. The casinos took in $350 mil last month. Bigger business than Big Bird, any day.

I was still in gardening disguise, driving to the home of my favorite motorcyclist, Tim Price. He'd been ignoring my calls, but the shorter tone on his machine signaled he'd been retrieving his messages. I was hoping I could scare him with a pruning shears during my interrogation, and if that failed, federal court litigation. I was organizing my threats when I got a call on the car phone.

It was Lieutenant Dunstan, from the Radnor police. "I'd like you to come in to the station, Ms. Morrone."

I had expected he'd still be unhappy with me. The radio news was already reporting that a lawyer had found the murder weapon. "Look, Lieutenant, I'm sorry about this morning. I know I should have notified you I was going to the crime scene—"

"It's not about that, Ms. Morrone," he said tightly.

"What then?" I passed the billboard for Trump Castle. SLOTS OF ACTION. SLOTS OF MAGIC.

"We have some information for you."

"About the knife?"

"No, as I told you, the testing will take some

time. It's about the shooting at your father's store."

My pulse quickened. "Is there a lead?"

"The Philadelphia police called here, after they couldn't reach you. They found the man who they believe did it. He was found dead, out by the airport."

Dead? "Who was he?"

Papers rustled on the other end of the phone. "A thug, in and out of jail."

"How do they know he's the one who did it?"

"He had a gun on him, a nine-millimeter Beretta, that ballistics matched to the bullet found in the young man who was killed."

Poor LeVonne. "They can do that?"

"Sure. When a bullet lodges in soft tissue, it maintains its integrity. They match the markings, like engravings."

So they had LeVonne's killer, who was himself dead. I felt a bitter sort of satisfaction.

"The shooter's name was Danny Suri. His last known residence was in Port Richmond."

Also in Northeast Philly, not far from the motorcyclist's. "Could this Suri have known Tim Price? Have you met with Price, Lieutenant? Have you questioned him?"

"We haven't been able to locate him for questioning, but we investigated him thoroughly. He has no prior criminal record."

"Did you know he was living with Patricia Sullivan?"

"Sure we did. We checked him out, Ms.

Morrone, regardless of what you suggested at the preliminary hearing. We knew about Price as soon as we found the motorcycle. A woman couldn't drive a 750, not in a BMW."

Sexist. "Why not?"

"She wouldn't be strong enough to hold it up at a stoplight."

Oh. "Could Price know this Suri? Is there a connection?" I passed a billboard that said BET THE PONIES BY PHONE—PHILADELPHIA PARK. Underneath was an 800 number.

"We have no evidence of any connection. Suri was a thug with a long criminal record. Assault, aggravated assault, two robbery convictions by age twenty-five."

"But why would Suri rob a butcher shop? My father made next to nothing, and it showed."

"There's evidence of drug use. He was in and out of rehab, for cocaine use."

I remembered what Paul had told me. "Price did cocaine, too. Maybe they met each other in some rehab place?"

Dunstan paused on the other end of the line. "The Philadelphia police say Suri's services were for hire."

"What services?"

"He roughs people up."

"But who would hire somebody to hurt LeVonne?" It didn't make sense. Then I thought of what my father had said in the hospital. "LeVonne gave his life for me." "LeVonne didn't call me in." Of course. "Lieutenant Dunstan,

234

what if Suri was hired to hurt my father? Rough him up? Even kill him?" I heard my voice sounding panicky.

"Why don't you come to the station? I prefer not to discuss this over a mobile phone."

A stall, I'd used that trick myself. "Do you have evidence that connects Suri to my father in any way, Lieutenant? Or to me, or the Hamilton case?"

"We have no evidence like that at this point. That would be speculating, Ms. Morrone."

"So speculate."

"I wouldn't jump to conclusions."

But I would. "It's not your father, Lieutenant." My hand knotted around the steering wheel. Had somebody tried to harm my father and killed LeVonne in the process? Did somebody want me distracted, warned off the case? Was my father in danger, even now? Rage swept through me, and fear. I floored the gas pedal, cut a swath through the grassy median, and picked up the highway going south, back toward the city.

"Ms. Morrone?" It was the lieutenant, right in the middle of my felony-level moving violation.

"I have to go, Officer," I said, hanging up. My thoughts raced along with the car. Would Paul do such a thing? Would Fiske or Kate? And how did Price know Suri? How did any of them know Suri? I couldn't puzzle it out anymore and I didn't want to. It was time to end it.

Time to flush the killer out. Nobody would

threaten my father again. Nobody would kill another innocent.

I flew toward the city and in no time got a bead on William Penn, standing atop the clock tower of City Hall, one of the most beautiful buildings in my hometown. I'd known that clock tower all my life, visited it with my father as a child. He used to take me up the skinny elevator inside the tower and we'd pass behind the huge yellow clock face, past the oiled brass gears as they ground time forward. The dark innards spooked me, and I would hold tight to my father's hand. Now someone had attacked him, threatened him.

I had to do something about it, but the first order of business was to make sure he was safe. I called his room and told Cam to stay with him, that I'd explain later. I hung up the phone, lost in thought, blowing past billboards and exits. The speedometer needle edged upward and the engine surged in response. I wished my brain worked as good as this car. I needed a plan.

YOU GOTTA PLAY TO WIN, read a billboard for the Pennsylvania Lottery.

"Damn straight," I said, but the slogan stayed with me. Resonating.

You gotta play to win. I knew how to play games. I knew how to win. If the killer was playing a game, then I would play, too. And I would win. It took me until the Callowhill exit to figure out how. I would go with my specialty.

A bluff.

24

My father snored loudly as Sal, Cam, and Herman watched over him, like the three wise men in retirement. I sat down and explained my plan to them, scanning their tense, lined faces for the resistance I had expected, but they proved me wrong. They had lived through Depression and World War. Herman had even survived the Bulge. There was steel in them, no matter how frail they appeared, and they were ready to avenge my father and LeVonne. They thought the bluff would work.

"Then Monday it is," I said.

Herman folded his arms. "Why wait 'til then? Why not now?"

"I want it to happen at the busiest time. It's dead there on the weekends."

"Bad choice of words," Cam said, without mirth.

Herman nodded. "All right, Monday. We got LeVonne's funeral on Sunday anyways."

We fell silent a minute. Only Sal hadn't said anything yet. His forehead had fallen into customary creases of anxiety and he'd shed his Burberry in favor of short sleeves and chalky elbows.

"You in, Mr. Livemore?" I said to him. "You said you wanted to do more lawyer stuff."

"This ain't exactly what I meant, Ree."

"I know. Still, you game?"

"I don't think this is such a good idea. You could get hurt."

"That's what I need you for. You three are my protection. My backup."

"You don't want to tell your father?"

"Are you kidding? He hates when I work late, you think he'd want me to do this?"

"How about the police?"

"I don't think they'd go for it. Besides, we're all we need. Sal. You know anybody who plays better poker than us?"

Cam smiled, so did Herman. Sal's eyes lingered on my father, but he didn't say anything.

I couldn't wait for an answer. I picked up the hospital phone and dialed what I knew would be the motorcyclist's answering machine. The tone was short, the kid was still retrieving his messages. I left the message laying out the bluff. This message he wouldn't ignore, if he were the killer. I hung up the phone and Cam smiled.

"Way to go, kiddo," he said, and Herman nodded.

Sal folded his knobby arms, still looking at my father.

"Uncle Sal?" I asked.

"I'm in," he said after a minute. "I'm in."

"Good." I got up to go. "Then I'm outta here."

"Where you goin'?"

"The Hamiltons. Let the game begin."

25

Kate answered the door, distracted. Her half-glasses perched precariously atop her nose and a Nikon Sure Shot hung around her neck. "Oh, Rita. Come along, dear. Come see what I'm up to."

Planning another murder? This woman needs a job.

"You've never seen this, I believe," she said. "Not all of it anyway." She led me into her large country kitchen with custom pine cabinets and sparkling white countertops. Stacked everywhere were decorative plates, vases, and cups in the same colorful pattern as those displayed on the kitchen walls. No bloody knives were in evidence, so I relaxed.

"What are you doing, Kate?"

"How's this for a project?" Spread out on a rustic pine table was a piece of black velvet, and on top of it sat a plate. "I've been wanting to get to this for a long time," she said, then leaned over the plate and snapped a picture.

"You're taking a picture of a dish?" Definitely needs a job.

"Not just any dish, it's Quimper. French

faience. Pottery that's made in Brittany." She picked up the dish, turned it over, and showed it to me. On the back was a black squiggle. "See this mark? It's a *P*, for Charles Porquier. He introduced the first mark of the house. This lone *P* is an extremely rare signature."

"Why are you photographing it?"

She set the plate down with care and took a picture of the *P*. "For insurance purposes. I have a hundred and fifty pieces, if you include the knife rests, the wall pockets, everything." She waved at a hutch crammed with plates. "The collection is worth, oh, sixty thousand dollars."

If I had been drinking coffee I would have spit it out, but she hadn't offered me any.

"You seem tired, dear." She removed the plate from the velvet and returned it to the hutch. "How is your father? Improving?"

It reminded me of my purpose. "He's fine, thanks."

"I'm so glad. This must be quite a stressful time for you."

"For you, too. The reporters everywhere, Fiske in trouble. Actually, I've been working on a way to solve this murder. I came to tell you and Fiske about it. Is he around?"

"Upstairs in his library." She removed a plate from the wall, dislodging it slowly from its hooks, and set it down on the velvet. "Fiske got himself in trouble, dear. He'll get himself out of it. He's formulated a plan of his own, he'll tell you about it."

I didn't know if I'd heard her correctly. "What?"

"Isn't he the one who started this? With his little affair?"

I didn't know what to say. "Affair?"

She smiled tightly over her glasses. "He has a midlife crisis, so he trifles with his secretary. It's not exactly unheard-of."

So she knew?

"Don't look so surprised, dear. Of course I knew he was having an affair. I've lived with the man for forty years, married him right out of Bryn Mawr. Never even finished my degree." Her tone sounded bitter, but I couldn't read her expression because she bent over and stuck a Nikon in front of her face. "This piece is my absolute favorite," she said from behind the camera.

"You knew, but you never let on?"

"No. In fact, when he told me about it this morning, I acted very surprised. Aren't men foolish?"

"He *told* you, this morning?" What was going on?

"Oh yes. It's all part of his grand design. Endgame, he calls it. Will you look at the work in that plate? It's all hand-painted, you know." She picked up the plate and held it up. Orange and blue flowers ringed the border and in the center was a peasant woman in a white cap and full orange skirt. "Isn't she lovely?"

Frankly, no. The woman's face was crudely painted, with only one or two lines to represent her features. "She looks kind of blank, don't you think?"

"Naïf."

"What, she looks naive?" I was projecting.

"No. It's the style. Naïf. Primitive."

Enough with the fucking dishes. "How did you know about Fiske?"

Her face dropped even its tight smile and she set the plate down. "He was like a young man again, happy as a lark. That's why I think it was the first time he . . . strayed, because I hadn't seen him so happy."

Ironic. I thought of Paul. He'd cheated and he still wasn't happy. "Did you tell Fiske you knew?"

"No."

"You weren't angry?" Angry enough to kill?

"No." She shrugged in her thin cotton sweater.

"You didn't think about breaking up?"

She snapped another photo and looked up at me. "Why would I, dear? Fiske and I grew up together. We've built a life, a home. Why would I throw that away? Why would he? I knew he'd get over it." She turned away and flipped the plate over, back to business.

So Fiske didn't tell her he'd loved Patricia, and she wouldn't admit it to herself anyway. I eyed the plates hanging on the kitchen walls, seeing them as if for the first time. Each one depicted a man or a woman standing in profile, with the men facing right and the women facing left. Kate had hung the dishes in pairs, so the men and women faced each other. Still, their faces remained unsmiling and expressionless. She could put them together, but she couldn't make them happy couples.

Nobody could.

"Ah, Rita," Fiske boomed as I entered his library. "Good to see you."

I hadn't seen him this happy since his arrest. What a screwy family. "Fiske, how are you?"

"Fine, just fine, thanks. I'm in control now. I'm not stepping down. I told the chief judge."

"Good. I stopped by because I have something to discuss with you. Kate said she'd be up in a minute—"

"Do you know why I like the Royal Game, Rita?" He waved exuberantly at the chessboards resting on the long polished table.

Huh? "What?"

"Chess. I like it because of what it teaches us about battle, about conflict. It originated as a game of war, you know, in India, in the sixth century. One of the grandmasters, Lasker, said that chess was a fight in which the 'purely intellectual element holds sway.'"

"Really." Between him and Kate it was a regular university around here.

"It didn't occur to me until today, until I saw the headline calling me 'embattled.' I thought, that's what I am. In battle." He looked up and smiled. "In battle."

I get it. "Fiske, listen—"

"There's power in these pieces, properly used.

243

Take this one, for example." He held up the White Queen. "She has the greatest range, the greatest striking power, on an open board. A full twenty-seven squares at the center of the board." He twisted the piece between his thumb and forefinger. "She may take from one or two squares away, but she may also take from a great distance. Then she is the most effective. You don't see her coming, she *blindsides*. Just like a woman, eh?" He set the Queen down and laughed, but I didn't.

"Fiske—"

"Do you know what Ben Franklin said about chess, Rita? That it can teach us life lessons."

Wrong. Chess is not life, poker is life. When games collide.

"I have Franklin's essay right here. I was reminded of it after I saw the headline." He reached for a book on the shelf behind him and thumbed through it. "Here we go. Franklin, in *The Morals of Chess*, writes that chess teaches us perseverance, for one 'discovers the means of extricating one's self from an insurmountable difficulty' and 'one is encouraged to continue the contest to the last.' Isn't that wonderful, Rita?"

"I guess."

He snapped the book closed. "Well, I'm extricating myself. The King is powerful, too, and although his striking distance is shorter than the Queen's, he takes justly. Face-to-face, not from a distance. Each time he attacks, he places himself at great risk, simply because of his proximity. Nevertheless, he looks his enemy in the eye—

and he *takes*." Fiske inhaled as if inspired. "Did you know that in the endgame, the King cannot be mated in the middle of the board? He must be driven to the edge. Now I ask you, why should I permit myself to be driven to the edge?"

"You shouldn't." It had finally happened. Fiske had turned into a White King.

He slammed the book to the table so hard the chesspieces wobbled. "But I have, Rita! By the press, by the chief judge, by Julicher, by every women's group in the city. By every *minor* player on the board. And I've had it! So I'm fighting back, and I've already made the first move."

"Telling Kate?"

He paused. "Why, yes. She told you?"

"Yes."

"An aggressive gambit, my own application of the Sicilian defense. Do you know what she said, my lovely wife? She was terribly hurt, but she said she'd forgive me."

I still couldn't believe Kate would react so calmly, no woman would. At least I didn't. "That's all she said?"

He smiled. "What else was there to say? People are not chess-pieces, they move unpredictably. I would never have guessed that Kate would understand this, but she has. She's promised to stand by me, and she will. My next move was to invite Patricia's lawyer, Mr. Julicher, to the house—he should arrive at any minute—and I intend to deal with him. Honestly. Justly. Face-to-face."

"Stan Julicher? Here?"

"I'll tell him the truth and ask him to back down. If my own wife has no cause for complaint, why should he?"

What? Fiske was making a bad move and ruining my own game. "Wait a minute. Julicher won't let up."

"Even after he's made aware that he's persecuting an innocent man?"

Talk about naive. "Come on, he's a publicity hound! He couldn't care less."

Fiske's mouth made a determined line and he folded his arms like a regent. "Then he'll be made to understand whom he's dealing with. He'll understand if he doesn't cease and desist this harassment in the media, I'll make my next move. We'll exchange pieces, I'll take King for Pawn."

"What do you mean?"

"I'll file suit for libel and defamation. Julicher has gone far beyond any privilege to discuss this matter. I'll join in suit every radio and television station on which he appeared, every newspaper that carried the words. Checkmate!"

"Fiske—"

"Don't fret now. My initial strategy is to take the high road. I invited him here, with his women's groups to boot. But no press, that was my stipulation. He agreed."

I shook my head. Things were happening too fast. I didn't know whether to go forward with my own plan or not. Then I remembered my father, and LeVonne. "Fiske, listen to me. I have something to tell you and Kate."

"I'm right here," said a clipped voice from the door. It was Kate, followed by Stan Julicher. "Look what the cat dragged in," she said drolly, and showed Julicher to a wing chair. Then she perched on the arm of her club chair and lit a cigarette.

"Mr. Julicher, I don't believe we've met," Fiske said, extending a hand. "I am Fiske Hamilton. It's a pleasure to meet you."

Julicher shook it, glancing around at his elegant surroundings. "Good to meet you, sir."

Fiske cleared his throat. "As I believe I mentioned, I called you here to discuss the *Sullivan* case as frankly and freely as possible."

"Fiske," Kate interrupted, "Rita said she has something to tell us." She cocked her head toward me. "Don't you, dear?"

An awkward moment. I didn't want to tell them with Julicher here. "What I have to say is privileged, Kate."

"Attorney-client privileged?" Fiske asked.

"Yes, of course."

Fiske squared his shoulders. "But I have absolutely nothing to hide, Rita. I see no need for secrecy anymore. I'm about to tell Mr. Julicher the truth about Patricia and me. I am innocent of any other wrongdoing. So, please, speak as freely as if we were alone."

Unthinkable. "Fiske, you're still a murder suspect. Anything we say here is discoverable if you waive the privilege. Mr. Julicher, if he wanted, could testify—"

"I told you, so be it. Let it come out that I called Mr. Julicher here to clear my name. Let it come out that I met with him, man-to-man, to settle this thing once and for all."

Julicher edged forward on his chair. "Anything I hear in this room stays in this room."

I almost laughed. "Come on, Stan. You won't tell the press as soon as you hit the driveway?"

His eyes went rounder. "I swear it."

"Bullshit." There was no reason to trust him. Then I remembered what my mentor Mack had said about publicity, and it gave me an idea. "Tell you what, Stan. You can tell the press everything you hear in this room, but not until Monday afternoon. And I'll give you an interview about it, an exclusive interview. Imagine it, you interviewing me—former adversaries—on how we broke a murder case."

Julicher almost fell off his chair. "An exclusive?"

"Yes, on the condition that you can't breathe a word until I call you on Monday afternoon. If you do, I'll deny the whole frigging thing. There'll be egg all over your face."

"Agreed."

It would stick, I felt reasonably sure. I glanced at Fiske. Time to start play. "This conversation is confidential, then, to everyone but Paul."

Smoke curled around Kate's silver hair. "We haven't seen Paul today," she said. "Have you?"

Did she know about us or not? It didn't matter anymore. "You'll see him for Sunday brunch, as usual?"

Kate nodded. "Sure."

"I can't come, I have LeVonne's funeral. Tell him about it, will you? I want him to know, see if he thinks it's logical." I had planned it this way. I didn't know if I could bluff Paul, I didn't want to try.

"Of course."

"Good. Here's my plan—"

"A plan?" Fiske said. "To do what?"

"To catch a killer, of course."

So I took a deep breath and lied, lied, lied. Not too much detail, not too little. Just a single playing card, laid facedown, and a high bet. All the while, a poker face. Adrenaline surged into my veins and my nerves tingled with tension. As best I could tell, they bought the whole damn thing. It felt like the best bluff ever, for the highest stakes.

After all, I was betting my life.

26

By nightfall I was exhausted, but the game was on. I hated waiting until Monday, but I had no choice. Maybe it was better this way, the time would give the killer a chance to stew. Let him simmer and twist, wondering what my cards really were. Fear would seep in, imagination would dominate reality. If I read the killer right, he was a gutsy player. He would take one risk too many and lose it all. All I had to do was believe. I could do it at the card table and in the courtroom. Could I do it on Monday?

I was more scared than I wanted to admit.

I drove past my empty house but didn't want to go in.

I checked the hospital, where my father was asleep, under the vigilant eyes of the Pep Boys.

I parked at the Four Seasons, but they had given my room and all the others to a dentists' convention.

I stopped by the Italian Market, which smelled overripe on this humid night. Saturday was the Market's busiest day, and the muggy air was dense with the fetid odor of rotted fruit and vegetables. The stalls were dark, closed up. A Mafia trash hauler screeched in the stillness. I pulled up in front of my father's shop, closed since LeVonne's murder. A residual strip of crime scene tape hung limply from the door. The neon pig flickered orange in the dark.

I went into the shop and quickly got what I needed, then locked the door again, leaving the CLOSED sign rocking silently. I avoided thinking about how it used to be, with me sitting on the vinyl stool watching my father trim fat or LeVonne smiling silently, over his broomstick. I put my mind on cruise control, and the car as well.

When I finally cut the engine, I was only partly surprised where I ended up.

"You look like you need a drink," Tobin said. He padded to the kitchen in his bare feet, DREXEL UNIVERSITY T-shirt, and gym shorts.

"Cold water would be fine," I called after him, sinking into a black leather sofa. The living room was expensively furnished, with exposed brick walls and Japanese black-and-white photographs mounted gallery-style around the room. Legal pads and Xeroxed cases were spread in a semi-circle on the maroon rug, next to a Rosti bowl full of candy. "You having M&M's for dinner?"

"I'm out of Snickers."

"You ever eat anything without sugar, Tobin?"

He returned with a Pilsner glass of beer and handed it to me. "No, I watch my diet. Especially when I'm working."

"You were working?"

"I do that, you know." He eased into a matching chair opposite me. "Drink your fake beer."

I sipped the beer, which tasted bitter and cold. "It's too young."

He rolled his eyes.

"How come you're alone?"

"I do that, too."

"On a Saturday night?"

"Did you come here to give me shit or to say hello?"

I didn't know why I came, in truth. "Both?"

251

He smiled. "You're tired."

I smoothed back my hair and wondered vaguely how bad I looked. "I am. I worked hard today."

"Too hard to return my calls, I guess."

"I haven't been home."

"I was worried about you. I called you all day. I felt like Lesley Gore. I even waited for the three rings."

"What are you talking about?" I sipped the beer, and he watched me drink.

"The three rings? Didn't your mother ever tell you to leave three rings when you got home?"

Let's not get into it. "No."

"So what happened? I heard you found the murder weapon. How'd you pull that off?"

"It's a long story."

"So tell me." He leaned forward over his bare knees. "You're alive, so I guess Richie Rich didn't kill you."

I didn't want to get into that either. "Not yet."

"You're talkative tonight."

I set the beer down. "I just don't want to talk about Paul."

He slipped back into the sofa. "What do you want to talk about? Work? Criminal procedure?"

"No."

"Jujyfruits? Sno-caps? I like Baby Ruth, don't you? I like New York in June, how about you?"

"No."

"Then what do you want from me?"

An honest question. I thought of Fiske saying

252

that the Queen took from a distance, by blind-siding. I didn't want to be that kind of woman. But I didn't know what kind of woman I wanted to be. "Tobin, I only know one thing for sure."

"What?"

"I only know what I don't want from you."

"Which is?"

"I don't want you to play any games with me." Like Paul did.

"I never played games with you, or any woman."

Sure. "I've seen you at office parties. It's a different date each time."

He looked stung. "So what if I've dated a little?"

"A little? You're pushing forty."

"Or a lot? I haven't met the woman I want to commit to yet. How about you? You bring the same man to the parties, but you're not committed to him either. So what's the difference?"

There was none.

"I can't hear you." He laughed, cupping a hand to his ear.

I hated to admit it. "Not much, in that regard anyway."

"In that regard! You know who you remind me of, more than anybody?"

"Cindy Crawford?"

"*Me.*"

Please.

"We're alike, you and me," he continued. "We have a lot in common."

"We both have ponytails, that's it."

"Are you kidding? We have similar backgrounds, we grew up here. We work too hard, we like to laugh. We're loners. And we've never been married, which doesn't mean we can't commit."

Maybe.

"What?" he asked.

"I didn't say anything."

"I know. You have a bad habit. You think a lot of things you don't say. You're too internal. It all goes on inside your head."

It took me aback. "Thanks a lot."

"But it's true. I watch you. I notice things." He leaned over, closing the space between us. "Why don't you tell me what you're thinking. Right now."

Fine. "I was thinking, maybe it *does* mean we can't commit."

He winced, but it softened into a smile. "Maybe it does. Want to find out?"

Gulp. "I don't know."

He touched my cheek gently.

"I'm not sure."

He nodded. "That's honest."

"I don't want to play any games with you, either."

"You don't have to. In fact, you shouldn't, because I don't like that."

Women talking indirectly.

"Rita, spit it out."

I remembered Patricia's high-risk game, then what Paul had said, about poker being such a safe game. Patricia and me; how much were we alike, how much were we different? And my mother, too. "Don't you like women who play games, Tobin? Women who like action? Don't you find them exciting? Adventurous? The thrill of risk, all that?"

"No," he said flatly.

"Tell me why."

"It's obvious, isn't it?"

"Not to me."

He reached for my hand and took it in his. It felt warm, different. Not as refined as Paul's, but still strong. "The way I see it, risk—real risk— is not playing any games at all. Real risk is you, coming here. Real risk is you and me."

It made me edgy.

"If you really want to take a risk, then you have to start telling me what you're thinking. You have to stop playing games." He paused, tracing a bumpy vein on my hand with his forefinger. He was so close I could smell the summer heat on his brow. "I hope you can do that, because I would really like to try. With you."

I listened to his words, heard the timbre of his voice near my ear, the slight roughness there. It was all new, this, and everything about him was new. The rules were different now, there was no game at all. I wanted to avoid the mistakes I'd made with Paul. I wanted to be different, too. So I did the first thing that came into my mind.

I leaned over and kissed him.

It turned out to be exactly the right thing.

And later, when we made love in his soft bed, that was all different too. His smells, his sounds. I let him touch me, and take me, and I closed my eyes and took pleasure in him without pretending I was anywhere else, or in another time. I didn't have to hide any doubts about him. I didn't have to avoid any feelings of distrust or anger. Or pain, and fear.

In the end I cried a little, and he held me close and made me laugh. Tumbled me around, handled me. Then hoisted me up and onto him with both arms, steadying me. Held me fast to him with his hands at my hips, moving me, encouraging me. I took him freely then. Justly. Directly. And every time I tried to turn out the light, he stopped me.

But I like it that way, I told him.

Learn a new way, he said. He wouldn't be denied.

So I learned about that, too.

27

I didn't ask Tobin to come with me to LeVonne's funeral because I didn't know how, or even if, he'd fit into my life. Nor did I tell him about the plan I had set in motion for Monday. It was my thing with Cam, Herman, and Uncle Sal. They sat next to me in an oak pew toward the back, their gray heads bent during the service.

It was an overcast morning, muting the rich colors of the stained-glass windows. The church was spacious and dignified, but spare and dim. The only light was afforded by hanging brass fixtures, mounted too high to do much good. Oak beams braced the vaulted ceiling and there was a decorative carved arch over the altar. In front of the altar, elevated from the floor, was a coffin. In it lay a small, dark figure.

LeVonne.

He rested in a cushion of soft, ivory muslin, and his fine hands had been placed one over the other. He was dressed in a gray suit and black tie, with a white shirt that was too big in the collar. His lips were pressed together, as they had been so often in life, but without his eyes open, the warmth of human expression was gone from his features. As the service began, the funeral director draped a white cloth over his face. I don't know why. It didn't help any.

LeVonne's grandmother wept in the front row, supported by her lady friends and a heavyset nurse in a white dress and starchy cap. Only a handful of mourners were present, fanning themselves with cardboard paddles that advertised the funeral home. An uncle and two cousins were there, but no mother or father. There were neighbors, but only one or two boys from LeVonne's class. His teacher said the turnout would have been better if he had passed during the school year, like a boy killed last month in crossfire between gangs. I told her I understood, but I didn't.

I listened to the organ music playing softly and watched the women weeping, rocking, holding their right hands high in the warm air as the preacher gave the eulogy. He spoke in a subdued baritone about how LeVonne had attended church each week with his grandmother, although he'd been too "soft-spoken" to sing in the choir. The preacher talked about how LeVonne worked hard in school and at Popeye's Fried Chicken, then how he got a job at the butcher shop, where he seemed to "find a home." And how he loved *Star Trek* and *Batman*, though he always got stuck playing Robin.

At the end, the preacher told us to celebrate LeVonne's life and to take comfort in his death. To believe LeVonne's death happened for a reason only God could know. And when he said that, I stopped crying and wiped my eyes. I knew better, you see.

I knew the reason for LeVonne's death, and it had nothing to do with a divine plan. It was a matter of ballistics and bullet markings and soft tissue. It wasn't about faith, it was about science. It was knowable, and proven. LeVonne died because a man fired a bullet into his heart, and this man had been promised money by another man to do so. And ultimately, the reason for LeVonne's death traced back not to my father, for whom LeVonne had given his life, but to me. I was the reason LeVonne was at the front of the church, under a bower of small white roses.

And though I couldn't bring him back or change any of that, I could take responsibility for it. I could set it right.

And I would. Tomorrow, at noon.

28

City Hall is a massive Victorian building hewn of white marble, with a slate mansard roof and dormers. Built in the center of the grid that is Philadelphia, it contains eight floors of court-rooms and administrative offices that wrap around an enclosed courtyard.

Municipal workers, just released for lunch, chattered past me in the courtyard. Attorneys with briefcases whispered as they hurried by, coaching their clients on the noon break from trial. Police strolled in groups of two and three, at City Hall to testify in criminal trials. I figured this courtyard would be the safest place in the city to meet a murderer. I may sleep with lawyers, but I'm not totally crazy.

Underneath my sturdy pumps was the black center of the huge compass that was painted on the floor of the courtyard. The compass's black directional spikes, limned with crackling gold paint, pointed at the four arched entrances to the courtyard. I faced south toward my father's store and waited for the killer, suppressing the sensation that I was standing in the middle of a target. Smack-dab on the bull's-eye.

People poured through the south arch of the courtyard, but no one looked familiar. No one approached me. Could the killer be watching from the building? I scanned the windows. In some the blinds were drawn, in some they were slightly askew. Two women workers stood in a large window on the first floor, chatting. No killers in City Hall unless you counted the budget deficit.

Beyond the top tier of windows, the sky was a clear blue. A hot sun glinted on the large mirrored ball suspended over the center of the compass. The mirrored ball was an unusual sight, a sparkling globe oddly incongruous in the marble courtyard. The object of the ball was to see yourself as part of the whole city in its fish-eye lens, but the lesson was lost on the kids who made toothy faces into it.

The lesson was lost on me as well. I valued the mirror ball because I could see all four courtyard entrances in it at the same time. I checked my backup in the ball as it swung slightly in a warm breeze. Cam lurked under the south arch, slouching under a Phillies cap. Herman leaned against the west arch, fake-reading the *Daily News*. Sal stood under the north arch in his Ray-Bans, eating a soft pretzel. No one had the east arch because I'd run out of senior citizens. I'd had to enlist David and his friend to watch my father in the hospital.

I shifted on my feet and glanced at my watch: 11:55.

I scanned the crowds coming through the courtyard. If the bluff worked, the killer would come through one of the entrances at noon. Then one of the backup men would tail him, ready to grab him and scream bloody murder as soon as I gave the high sign. I hoped the killer turned out to be the rasta-haired motorcyclist. I didn't know how I would feel if it were Paul, now that the time had come.

11:58. I fingered the plastic Baggie in one of my blazer pockets. It held my father's knife, the one that looked like the murder weapon. Then I checked the Polaroids in the other pocket, pictures I'd taken yesterday of my father's knife in a lablike setting. I gritted my teeth. I was ready.

Was the killer? I rocked on my pumps and tried not to sweat on the bull's-eye.

Suddenly there was a commotion under the west arch. I tensed. Had Herman spotted the killer? The crowd under the arch scattered and a trio of bare-chested teenagers broke free, rowdy, play-fighting. Two cops, walking by, looked back, then said something to each other and moved on. I breathed a relieved sigh.

12:01.

He was late. Maybe he wouldn't come at all, maybe he wouldn't fall for it. The bluff was that I'd kept the real murder weapon, had it tested privately, and turned up some telltale DNA. I said I'd trade the weapon, and my silence, for my father's life. It wasn't a bad bluff. How could the killer be sure the knife, apparently old and well-used, was absolutely clean? It would be too big a risk to take, even for a risk-taker.

12:06. I checked the entrances again. East, south, west, north. Everything looked normal. Herman gave me a discreet nod over his tabloid, knowing I must have been rattled by the teenagers.

I waited. 12:08.

Maybe it wasn't a good bluff after all. Maybe the killer had cleaned the knife completely, or borrowed it. Maybe I'd lost my touch. Then something caught my eye behind an older couple ahead of me. The quick flutter of a Phillies cap. It was Cam, signaling. The couple looked normal enough, tourists with a street map, pointing at the mirrored ball. But over the man's shoulder was a figure I recognized.

Paul. Oh God. I felt my stomach turn over. Not him.

He barreled toward me. His face was anxious, his features strained. His clothes were disheveled and his eyes looked bloodshot as he elbowed the tourists aside.

I told myself to stay calm. "Paul?" I still couldn't believe it was him all along.

"Rita, we have to talk," he said, his voice angry. He grabbed me roughly by the arm.

"What about?" I said, but I could see Cam coming on fast, over Paul's shoulder. He wasn't supposed to take Paul yet, I didn't have anything incriminating on the dictaphone in my breast pocket. Wait, Cam, I prayed silently. Give me one more minute. "Why are you here, Paul? Did you come for—"

"No!" Paul said. "We're not talking here. This is ridiculous!" He grabbed me hard and shoved me off toward the east exit.

Cam looked stricken, then determined. Suddenly he lurched forward and yanked Paul backward. I caught one glimpse of Paul's shocked expression and heard his bewildered shout as Cam threw him to the ground, red-faced, in a fury. "Don't you dare hurt her!" he shouted. "Don't you dare!"

"Cam, wait!" I screamed, but he couldn't or wouldn't hear. The tourists reached for each other, aghast. Passersby stared in horror. Paul's

263

head cracked against the brick. It looked like Cam was going to kill him. "Cam, no!" I screamed. "Help!"

Sal ran over and scrambled on top of Cam, trying to pry him off. A group of teenagers sprinted over. Two cops hustled from the south arch, one drawing a billy club as he ran. I watched, horrified at how it had all gone wrong, when I heard a voice whisper right behind my ear. "Walk, now," commanded the voice.

"What?" Who was behind me? I twisted around, but a strong arm squeezed mine.

"No. Straight ahead. *Now.*"

I felt a hard object press into my lower back. I looked wildly at the mirrored ball, but it was spinning, blurring the crowd. I couldn't find Herman. There was confusion everywhere. "Help!" I shouted, but anyone who could hear thought I was talking about the fight.

"Go! *Now!*" ordered the voice. The gun dug into my upper backbone. I was being pushed away from the melee, toward the east arch.

Christ. He wouldn't shoot me, not before he got the knife. I took a deep breath and broke free of his grasp, running as fast as I could through the courtyard. "Help!" I screamed, but onlookers hurried past me into the courtyard, misunderstanding. I could hear his heels as he ran behind me. A heavy tread. He was almost upon me.

Where to run? Inside. There'd be more cops there and I knew City Hall like the back of my hand, I'd tried hundreds of cases there. I fought the crowd pressing into the courtyard and ran through the east arch toward the stairs. I shoved by a souvenir vendor and hit the stone stairs up to the second floor two by two. I twisted around when I got to the top to see who was chasing me.

At the bottom of the stair was Stan Julicher.

He was the killer? Holy Christ.

I turned around and banged through the wooden doors to the second floor. I scrambled to lock them behind me but the polished brass lock was keyed. I could see Julicher through the glass in the door, his face mottled with rage.

Run.

I skidded on the waxed floor and ran to the left, remembering a second too late that the mayor's office was to the right. I sprinted for the end of the hallway, screaming for help, but the shouts went unheeded. The place had emptied out for lunch and whoever was left must've gone outside to the courtyard. I heard sirens, then Julicher's footsteps right behind me.

"Help! Help!" I screamed.

"Help! Help!" Julicher shouted, louder. "In the courtyard!"

Dick. I hit the doors at the end of the hall and flew up the grand, cantilevered staircase, running for my life. My chest was heaving, my heart pounding. Julicher had killed his own client. Why? The granite steps spiraled up and up in dizzying hexagons. It was dark, the only light came from tiny windows on the landing. I grabbed the mahogany rail not to fall.

Run, run. Faster. Harder. There were six more floors to the top and no one on the stairs but a homeless man, slumped on the third-floor landing. Christ. Run.

"We can talk, Rita!" Julicher said, hardly puffing. "You have it with you?"

Of course. The knife. I fumbled in my pocket but the Polaroids flew out and scattered on the stairs. I kept running. Julicher, gun in hand, picked up a photo and threw it down as he ran up the stairs. "Stop, Rita! We can talk!"

Sure. Right. I climbed higher and higher, sweating through my blouse, gasping for breath. There was an alarm box on the eighth floor in front of the elevator, I remembered it from my trial last week. The case I won on my last bluff, dressed in mourning. Only this time it could be my funeral.

"Do you have it with you?" Julicher shouted, gaining on me.

Get the knife. I let go of the handrail and jammed my hand into my pocket, then stumbled and fell. My chin slammed into the gritty granite step and I let out a cry of pain. I scrambled to my feet. Blood spurted down the front of my suit, but the Baggie was in my other hand, with the knife inside.

"Let's make a deal, Rita!"

I tore through the Baggie with my teeth and ran up the stairs. Sixth floor. My chest was heaving. I shook the Baggie off the knife and took it in hand, feeling its heft like an old friend. Me and knives go way back. I ran up the stairs, running the knife along the banister. Two floors to go.

Running. Like my mother. It filled me with anger, fueling me. I tore up to the seventh floor and fell against the cold marble wall, dizzy from the circular climb. Julicher was gaining on me, starting the seventh.

I stumbled up the staircase to the eighth floor. Right inside the hall, next to the elevator, was the box. PYROTRONICS FIREFIGHTER'S TELE-PHONE. USE KEY OR BREAK GLASS. I took the butt of the knife and slammed it through the glass window. It splintered and I reached through and popped the receiver off the hook. If there was any justice in this courthouse, help would be here in minutes. I was about to hit the elevator button, then I stopped. These elevators were too slow, it would never come in time.

No more running. I had a knife, I knew how to use it. I thought of LeVonne, then my father. No more games. I would take honestly and justly. Face-to-face. Or I would die trying and get the whole thing on tape.

I pulled the knife and went back to the landing to meet him. I felt crazed, hopped-up. "Stay right the fuck where you are, Julicher!"

He stopped at midstairs and laughed. "What did you come back for? I have a gun, you have a knife."

"We had a deal. The murder weapon for my father's life."

"Oh yeah? You got a confirmation letter on that?"

Keep him talking, for the tape. "Why'd you do it? Why did you kill Patricia?"

"She wanted to drop the case. Said she didn't want to go through with it, after what happened at the dep. I told her no, not when I had everything all lined up. Everybody in the loop, talking book deals. Even a TV movie, based on a true story. She told me I had the case of my career, then she tried to fuck with me."

"So you killed her?"

He grew angry. "What was I supposed to do? Let the bitch make a fool of me in front of the goddamned country?"

Sirens sounded outside. "You framed the judge."

"It was perfect. When life hands you a lemon, you know?" He took a step toward me and aimed the gun at my chest. I tried not to look at its lethal black barrel.

"Why'd you hurt my father? Why'd you kill LeVonne?"

"I wanted you out of commission. The nigger was just a fuckup."

Bile rose in my throat. "Why'd you plant the knife, you shit?"

He arched an eyebrow and smiled. "To stir the pot, keep the case in the headlines. Something new's gotta happen every day. Nothing's worse than old news."

"And you got the Jag—"

"What is this, twenty questions? My cousin has one." He laughed and cocked the gun.

Terrific. I swallowed hard at the mechanical sound.

"The way it worked out, it was better PR than winning the harassment case." He laughed, then took a step nearer, so close I could almost grab the gun. "Tell me, Rita. What did these lab tests show? No fingerprints, I know. That knife was whistle clean."

You gotta believe. "A general-purpose knife, used for hunting—"

"Fishing."

Shit. I flashed on the weekend sunburn, the boat he mentioned at the deposition. My father, saying the knife could be used for fish. The sirens sounded louder, but nowhere near loud enough.

"Hey!" came a shout from below. The homeless man was waking up in a stupor. Julicher looked back to see what it was and in that split second I seized the only opening I'd get. I stabbed the hand with the gun, forcing the sharp knife-point right between the bones, using the first grip my father ever taught me. The gun fell from his hand and clattered to the floor.

"You cut me, you bitch!" Julicher screamed in pain.

You're goddamn right I did. Before he could react, I brought the knife down again, slicing clean at the first hunk of flesh I could find. His cheek split like a new pig.

"Aaah!" he screamed, and staggered back

against the railing. Blood poured out onto his shirt and tie.

"Hey, baby!" shouted the homeless man, stoned out of his mind. "You callin' me, sweet stuff?"

Shouting came from the first floor. Not the fire department, but cops. Three of them, with guns drawn, but too far away to do any good. I prayed some of them had taken the elevator. "Help, police! Eighth floor!" I yelled.

Julicher, his hand and face bloodied, reached for my neck. I stepped away, but he was quicker. Stronger. He squeezed me by the throat and slammed my head back into the glass door. Pain exploded in my skull. I couldn't breathe. I slashed futilely with the knife. The staircase grew darker and darker.

Suddenly there was a terrific blast and the glass door behind me shattered. A round red bullet hole burst onto the middle of Julicher's forehead. He fell backward, his face frozen in agony. Another gunshot came from behind. Julicher's chest exploded into crimson and the force of the blast spun him around. Before I could reach him, he fell against the railing like a scarecrow and pitched over the side.

I whirled around to see who had saved my life.

It was Herman, standing behind a Luger, with a faraway look in his eye.

29

Sunlight streamed through the open window and fell in a large oblong on the hospital coverlet. My father was propped against some pillows. He looked drawn but was smiling. "So I guess you think I owe you," he said to Herman, who stood at the foot of his bed.

Herman shook his head. "Did I say that? Did I say anything like that?"

I sat on the side of the bed. "No, *I* said it. You owe him, Dad. So do I. What kinda car you want, Herman?"

"Anything but a Jaguar," Cam said, from the other side of the bed.

I laughed. "Come on, Herman, what do you want? Antique poker chips? I need a hundred pounds of kosher chicken. You don't even have to split the breasts."

He waved me off with a smile. "You already paid me back, Rita. You talked that district attorney out of charging me with murder."

"It didn't take much talking. It was a justifiable homicide and they knew it. Now what do I owe you?"

"You don't owe me nuthin'. Nobody does."

"Then send me a ton of Mindy's business cards, will you do that at least? I'll get one to

271

every member of the Philadelphia bar. I'll make her court reporter to the stars."

"I'm just glad I was there, is all," Herman said. "It was good I was there."

What an understatement. I'd never forget seeing Herman behind the gun. I didn't know he was going to bring one, but I was glad he did.

"Maybe you made a mistake, Herm," Cam said. "Maybe you shoulda thought it over before you saved her. What's one less lawyer? A public service?"

I took a swipe at him. "Listen to you. Big man. Kicking the shit out of a defenseless architect." Not that I was entirely unhappy about Paul's thrashing. It evened us up, almost.

Herman chuckled. "The poor *zhlub*. He was just tryin' to protect you."

"It's not my fault," Cam said. "How long was I supposed to wait, until he killed her? Whose money would I take on Tuesday nights?"

Now I really tried to hit him. "Bullshit! Next week I take your Social Security, Camille. You won't have two hearing aids to rub together."

"Nice talk, from my own goddaughter." Cam waved at Herman. "Go for it, Herm. Ask her for a case of ivory chips. Ask her for two, they're small."

Herman shook his head. "It was just good I was there. It helped me, too."

An odd thing to say. I looked at Herman, puzzled. "What do you mean?"

"Nuthin'."

"It's not nuthin'. Saving a life is not nuthin', especially when it's mine. What?"

Herman shoved his hands into his madras shorts. "Maybe that's why, is all."

"Why what?"

"Why I got out alive. Nobody else did in my company, except two of us. Maybe it was supposed to happen this way. I kept the gun all these years, maybe that's why." He shook his head in a way that said he didn't want to talk about it anymore.

Suddenly the door opened and Uncle Sal came in. I took one look at him and my mouth dropped open. "Uncle Sal?"

"Sal?" Cam said. "You okay?"

Herman laughed. "Can you believe this guy?"

My father was in shock. "What the fuck are you supposed to be, Sallie?"

"What, you don't like the way I look?" Uncle Sal asked. His thin gray hair was slicked back and he was wearing the black leather jacket and boots I'd bought for Herman. He looked like a septuagenarian Fonz. "Betty says I look real good. Handsome, like."

"Betty?" I said.

"The tomato?" Cam said.

"The little one?" Herman said.

"With the red hair?" my father said.

Sal nodded. "You said fun is good, Ree. So I'm having fun. Look out the window."

Cam and I got up and hustled to the window. Sucking on a cigarette in front of the hospital entrance was somebody's grandmother, improbably red-headed, dressed like a nurse. Despite her age, she had a body to die for and eyeliner you could see from three floors up. *"Betty?"* I asked, incredulous.

"Isn't she somethin'?" Sal said, jumping up to see over my shoulder. "I'm takin' her for a ride."

Cam laughed. "A ride? In what?"

"What?" my father said. "What? You don't have no car."

Sal pointed. "In that."

Parked in front of the hospital was a Harley-Davidson, brand new, in midnight black. It had sleek onyx curves, gleaming chrome pipes, and a leather seat that reclined like a Castro convertible. It was parked illegally, but the red-jacketed valets gaping at it didn't seem to mind. I blinked, and blinked again.

"A motorcycle?" Cam said in disbelief. "Can you drive it?"

Sal nodded proudly. "Herm taught me how."

Herman pushed aside the curtain. "I knew from the service."

"A motorcycle?!" my father said. "Did you say a motorcycle?"

I just kept blinking. I had been through a lot. My boyfriend's infidelity, sex with a ponytail I hardly knew, a man shot dead before my eyes, and now this. I was out of words. "Betty?" was all I could say.

"A motorcycle?" my father said. "You bought a motorcycle? Are you fuckin' nuts, Sal?"

Sal turned on his stack heel. "I do what I want, Vito. You're not my boss."

Cam and Herman exchanged looks.

I blinked and blinked.

"Sal?" my father croaked, thunderstruck. He clutched his incision, at least I thought it was his incision and not his heart.

"And I didn't buy it," Sal added.

"The motorcycle? Then how'd you get it?" Cam asked.

I had a guess, but I didn't want to say. I blinked at Sal, who smiled broadly.

"They gave it to me for the whole afternoon, Ree. And they even went for the accent."

"*Betty?*" I blurted out.

At the end of the day, I was left alone with my father. I didn't have any reason to rush away, and didn't want to. The floor grew quiet after visiting hours were over and people with more respect for rules had said their good-byes. My father's eyes closed as I tucked his coverlet under the thick mattress.

"You shouldn'ta done it, you know," he said.

"I know."

"I wouldn'ta let you do somethin' that crazy."

"I know that, too."

"You coulda been killed, Rita."

"So could you, Dad."

"Is that why? You think my bein' here is your fault?"

Of course. "Nah. You needed the vacation. I'm glad you got shot."

He closed his eyes. "Miss Fresh."

Thank you, God. "Did you have fun with David and his boyfriend?"

He smiled drowsily. "They were tellin' me how to bake bread. They said put carrots in, but I'm gonna leave out the carrots. Carrots don't belong in bread."

"No."

"They think I should sell the store. I think so, too."

Hallelujah. "Good idea, Dad."

"I was gonna give it to LeVonne," he said, but his sentence trailed off and his head dipped to the side. He was falling asleep. I pulled the coverlet down over his feet and he roused slightly. "So what are you gonna do, Rita?"

"Go to sleep, Dad. You're half-asleep."

"You got a choice to make."

He meant Paul or Tobin. I had told him the whole story when we were alone. He had insisted on it, and truth to tell, it felt good to tell somebody.

"I bet you go back to that jerk."

I felt a twinge. "It would help if you kept an open mind about Paul, Dad."

"Either way, I love you. So bet me."

"On who I end up with?"

"Yeah." He smiled in a muzzy way, heavy-lidded as an aged cat. "I'm retiring, I need the cash. Fifty bucks says you marry Paul in a year."

276

"You can't bet about stuff like that, Dad."

"Why not? I raised you better."

I laughed. "Fifty dollars?"

"You heard me."

"I hate to take your money, old man."

"Hah. You're just chicken."

"Say *what?* I went after an armed man with a fish knife!"

"He was a lawyer."

"So what?"

"Like I said," he said, but dropped off to sleep before I could demand an explanation.

30

Sunlight struggled through the leaded-glass windows of Fiske's library. Classical violins screeched away on the CD player. Central air-conditioning forced frigid gusts onto my sandaled feet. And just when I thought it couldn't get any worse, my client wanted to play chess. Who says lawyers have it easy?

I made my first move, pushing a white wooden Pawn up two squares. "Ta-da."

"No," Fiske said.

"No?"

"No." He reached across the chessboard, picked up the little Pawn, and put it back down in front of my Horse.

"Don't I get to move my own pieces?"

"That's not the opening you want, dear. Remember what I said about dominating the center of the board?"

No. "Yes."

"It's like playing squash. One dominates the T."

"Italians don't play squash, they eat it. With a little bit of oregano, in olive oil."

He smiled, relaxed today in a polo shirt and white cotton cardigan. "You play tennis, don't you?"

"No, I work. A lot."

He smiled. "But you've seen people play tennis. Paul, for example. Paul is a first-rate tennis player."

Hmmm. Suddenly I suspected where this was heading, why Fiske had asked me here. And it wasn't to move Pawns around. Or maybe it was.

"Unlike some players, Paul knows instinctively when to stay at the baseline and when to charge the net. He has a natural advantage in his height and he exploits it. When he does take the net, he becomes a real threat. Do you know why?"

Because he's God's gift? "No, why?"

"Because he understands the power of the position. He dominates the court. He's quick and sure in his reactions and nothing gets past him, not even down the alley. In effect, he takes the center of the board, every time. Like this." Fiske reached over the chessboard, picked up the Pawn in front of my King, and placed it two spaces in front of its former home. "Do you see what I'm doing?"

Duh. "Yes."

"Now you've taken a power position vis-à-vis the rest of the board. You're asserting dominion. You've taken your advantage, being white, and exploited it. In effect, you've charged the net."

"Ooh, I feel tingly all over."

Fiske eased back into his tall leather chair. "Do you know why I didn't move the Queen's Pawn?"

"What if I told you I didn't give a shit?"

"I'd tell you anyway."

"I figured." I laughed. Fiske wasn't really a bad guy, it was just his upbringing. He'd had a stable family, a stone mansion, and a trust fund, when what he really needed was a butcher and a vinyl stool.

"I didn't move the Queen's Pawn because that would have exposed your King and made him vulnerable to attack. Too much risk without good reason."

I booed.

"Exactly." He smiled, then it faded. "You know, Rita, you took a risk—too much risk—in that gambit of yours at City Hall. I should never have agreed to it."

But you did. "You didn't have a choice," I said, and let it go at that.

"I am grateful to you. Thank you, if I haven't said so already."

"You have, and you're welcome, but I didn't do it for you. I did it for me. I had a good reason."

He paused. "That's just what Paul said, you know, when I took him to task for going to City Hall after you. He said he couldn't just sit back and see you harmed. That's the kind of man my son is, Rita."

I felt a guilty twinge. "I do appreciate what he did."

"I know you do. But I also know he's moved out. He told me you two were having problems. The stress of the trial, the demands of your two careers."

I guessed Paul hadn't told him about Patricia. Wise move. "Is that what he said?"

He nodded. "He wants to come home, Rita."

"I understand that." Paul left messages on the machine every day, but I didn't call back.

"He loves you very much."

"I understand that, too."

"You have a lot invested in this relationship, a lot of time. You own a house together, you've made a life together."

Hadn't I heard this somewhere before? "Like you and Kate."

"Yes. Like Kate and me. Although I feel terrible for what happened with Patricia, I'm lucky to have Kate. We're happy together."

I thought of Kate's French plates, the figures facing each other on the kitchen walls. "And you want me to take Paul back."

"I do. Whatever he has done, whatever is your point of disagreement, there is one fact that cannot be denied and certainly shouldn't be overlooked. He risked his life for you, Rita. He put himself in jeopardy, for you."

Ouch. "So I should take him back, out of guilt?"

"Of course not. But the point is, how many men would do something like that?"

I thought of Tobin, wondering. "Did Paul put you up to this?"

"No. In fact, it would be more accurate to say that I put *him* up to this."

"What do you mean?"

"It's your move, Rita," Fiske said, and looked beyond me, over my shoulder. I twisted around.

There, in the open doorway, with a look of surprise on his bruised face, stood Paul.

31

My secretary Janine shivered with excitement as she closed the door behind her. "Are you ready?" she asked, mascaraed eyes agleam.

"Ready." I nodded and sipped a steaming mug of coffee. It felt good to be in the office again. My gray couch was covered with case files, large trial exhibits were stuffed between the cabinet and chair, and correspondence wafted on my desk in white drifts, like newfallen snow. Everything in disorder. I wiggled my toes happily.

"Are you sure you're ready?"

"Show me, child."

"Okay, here goes." She strode to the front of my desk and yanked up her black blouse to the edge of an orange bra. Sure enough, pierced through the tender pink fold of her navel was a golden ring. It glinted cruelly in the morning sunshine. "Cool, huh?" she bubbled.

Not what immediately came to mind. I leaned closer and caught a whiff of baby powder and the Body Shop's vanilla oil. "You did this over the weekend?"

"Yeah? It's my sixth hole?"

"You sound like a golf course." I stared at her belly button. The new hole looked puffy and red.

"I have three in one ear, two in the other, and this one makes six?"

Not counting the one in your head. "Did you put anything on it to clean it, like a salve or antibiotic?"

"The man put some stuff on it, like goop?"

Goop. I was guessing motor oil. "What about this morning, did you put anything on it?"

"Just spit?"

Jesus. I'd stop by Thrift Drug for her at lunch. "Did it hurt when he pierced it?"

"Not hardly?"

"You mean it hardly hurt?"

"Right?"

"You're brave, child," I said, meaning it, and Janine beamed down at me over her perforated midriff.

"Not as brave as you? I mean, I used to think you were kind of, like, boring? Only into work?"

Oh.

"But now I think you're kind of, like, cool. And brave. You totally inspired me."

I was more surprised by the form than the substance. "Janine, did you hear that?"

"What?"

"The way you just said what you said."

She nodded. "A sentence goes down at the end. Like you told me."

I was about to congratulate her, but just then the door burst open and slammed back against the wall. Janine gasped and dropped her blouse. My managing partner, Mack, was standing in the doorway, puffing like an aging gunslinger in a tight double-breasted suit. I'd expected to hear from him, but not until my second cup of coffee.

"Knocking is always appreciated," I offered.

"We have to talk, Rita," Mack said sternly, then his gaze shifted to Janine. "Privately."

"Oh, let her stay. She's tougher than the both of us, trust me on this."

"Privately," he repeated, but a jittery Janine was already squeezing past him and out the door, closing it behind her.

"That wasn't very nice," I said, when we were alone.

"I'm not feeling very nice."

"You're never feeling very nice, Mack."

"Wrong. I feel nice when I win."

"Me, too."

He folded his thick arms over his chest and stepped closer. Mack's morning smells weren't as pleasant as Janine's; he reeked of high finance and double-dealing. "I understand you're not giving interviews over the Hamilton matter. You canceled the *Good Morning America* appearance and the Court-TV. What's the idea?"

I set down my coffee. "I'm busy. I have my own cases to work and clients to call back, some of whom have been waiting two weeks. And I have to pick up Neosporin for Janine."

"None of that is as important as those interviews."

"To who? Whom?"

"To me."

"I see. Well, my clients are more important to me. In fact, my secretary's belly button is more important to me."

"This isn't funny, Rita."

"I don't think so either. By the way, did you know that there was no raise in my distribution this month? I opened the envelope this morning and it was exactly the same as before the midcourse correction. Wasn't I corrected, Mack?"

"No."

"We had a deal, as I remember."

"We did not."

Dick. "Say *what*?"

"You didn't accept my offer that morning. The Committee made the distributions as they saw fit."

"I had my secretary call and tell you the same day!"

"I didn't get a message from you or your secretary about that."

"But you reassigned my cases."

"She didn't mention anything about the increase."

Terrific. Her navel she remembered, my raise she forgot. "So what? You saw I kept the representation, didn't you? You had me in the papers every day, you got the mileage you wanted. Don't play games with me, Mack. I deserve that raise."

His eyes narrowed. "I understand. No raise, no interviews?"

"I'm flexing. You impressed?" Turnabout was fair play, wasn't it? "The whole thing is in your control, Mack."

"This is ridiculous."

"It's your choice, boss."

He leaned over the cloth chair in front of my desk. "Christ! What's the point, Rita? You don't care about the money. You don't need the money."

"It's the principle of the thing. General principles. They're in the United States Code. You got the index?"

"I don't understand a word you're saying."

"You don't understand general principles, Mack? The first one is 'Keep your word'—you said you were going to give me a raise, do it. Another general principle is 'Don't quit.' The third is 'Don't fink on your friends.' And there's

285

always my personal favorite, 'Get up and get it yourself.' Shall I go on?"

He rolled his eyes. "If I get you the raise, then will you do the interviews?"

"In a word?"

He laughed abruptly. "All right."

"Then we understand each other."

"Hold your horses. I have to clear it with the Committee. That'll take time."

"My Court-TV interview was at three o'clock today. I can reschedule it if you get right back to me. Otherwise who knows when my schedule will allow—"

"Enough already." He scowled. "Then we have a deal?"

"If the number's right. Why don't you call me back with an offer? I don't want to put you on the spot now."

Mack turned toward the door, shaking his head. "I should've known you'd pull a stunt like this."

"Funny, I thought the same thing when I saw my paycheck."

"You're learning, kid," he said as he opened the door.

"Is that a good thing?"

"In a word?" He smirked, and I smirked back. The word I was thinking of was: Not on your life.

"And Mack?" I called after him. "I want a laptop, too."

"Why?"

"For show. I want to put in on my desk and not use it, like the big boys."

"No," he said flatly.

I took it as a maybe.

32

A lot happened in the next year. My father recovered from his injuries, although his eyesight worsened and he had to have an operation on his Cadillacs. His emotional state rebounded slowly, and he hated to see the shop finally sold. We spent Sunday mornings visiting LeVonne's grave, but that wound would never heal. My father couldn't bring himself to accept LeVonne's death, and I didn't fault him for this. The murder of a young man should never pass without notice, though it does, every day.

Uncle Sal and Betty got married and bought his-and-her Harleys. Cam sold the equipment from Lawns 'R Us, took the proceeds to the track, and made a bundle on the Trifecta. Herman amassed a respectable chip collection, and his daughter Mindy became my best friend and maid of honor. By the morning of my wedding day so much had happened I had forgotten about any alleged bet.

"You're out of your mind," I told my father. "What bet?"

"We made a bet, Rita," he said. "You and me." He squinted at the mirror through his new glasses and straightened his rented bow tie. We were getting ready to go into the private anteroom at the Horticultural Center in Fairmount Park.

"I didn't make any bet with you." I stood next to him, appraising myself in the mirror. An ivory sheath that fit only when I inhaled, more crow's-feet than last year, and a horrified expression. I was ready to be married. "I wouldn't bet about a thing like that."

"*My* daughter?"

"All right, maybe I would." And even though I was getting married, I hadn't quit poker. With a great deal of prodding, my future husband decided he would at least try the game and join us on Tuesday nights. "But I still don't remember any bet."

"Fifty dollars sound familiar?"

"Fifty?" I was too jittery to think. Everyone was out there waiting. Fiske and Kate. Mack and half my firm, including Janine. Cam, Herman and Essie, Sal and Betty. David Moscow and his bread-baking lover. Only the press was excluded; I didn't care if I never saw another reporter in my life. Just last week I had declined another offer for a TV movie. Based on a true story, my ass.

"We made the bet when I was in the hospital," he said. "On who you'd marry, remember?"

The first strains of Purcell's "Trumpet Voluntary" floated through the door, and my mouth went dry. "Dad, we have to go." I grabbed his arm, tottering on stiff ivory pumps, and we hustled together out of the anteroom.

"We made it when I was sick, in the hospital. Not the eye operation, the time before."

We stood arm in arm at the entrance to the main room, waiting for our cue. The room was actually a huge greenhouse, with white wooden chairs set in rows amid exotic hibiscus and fragrant gardenia. Rubber and palm trees grew all around, and tiny white lights twinkled from the tropical foliage. It was pretty, but hotter than I'd ever expected. Only Italians would rent humidity in a Philadelphia summer.

"Rita, remember? I bet you fifty dollars that you'd marry Paul."

The music swelled, our cue came, and we stumbled forward onto the white paper runner. Guests turned around, craning their necks. I moistened my lips in an attempt to look virginal. "You put fifty on Paul?" I said, out of the side of my mouth.

"Yeah. Remember now?"

I looked at Paul, who smiled back at me nervously. My heart actually fluttered, he always looked so handsome in a tux. Tall and strong, with nice, long sideburns. "You actually bet I'd marry Paul, Dad?"

My father nodded as we passed the last row of guests. Heads turned when we walked by. Everyone I knew, everyone I loved, grinning. My heart felt light, giddy. I knew I'd made the right decision. I looked down the aisle at the best pony-tail that ever happened to me, and Tobin smiled back. I squeezed my father's arm.

"Sucker," I said.

And he laughed.

About the Author

Lisa Scottoline is the author of two legal thrillers: *Final Appeal,* which won the Edgar Allan Poe Award, and her first, *Everywhere That Mary Went,* which was nominated for the same honor. She was a trial lawyer at a prestigious Philadelphia firm and clerked for appellate judges at the federal and state levels. She is a native Philadelphian and lives in the Philadelphia area.

IF YOU HAVE ENJOYED READING THIS
LARGE PRINT BOOK AND YOU
WOULD LIKE MORE INFORMATION
ON HOW TO ORDER A WHEELER
LARGE PRINT BOOK, PLEASE WRITE
TO:

WHEELER PUBLISHING, INC.
P.O. BOX 531
ACCORD, MA 02018-0531

X